The Dragon's Fire, Reign of Shadow, Book Three

Copyright © 2025 by Rayna L. Stiner

Printed in the United States of America

ISBN—13: 978-0-9967959-9-9

Get exclusive content such as creature art and maps
when you sign up for the author's newsletter at
raynalstiner.com.

THE DRAGON'S FIRE

REIGN OF SHADOW, BOOK THREE
BY RAYNA L. STINER

TAGORBI PUBLISHING, LLC

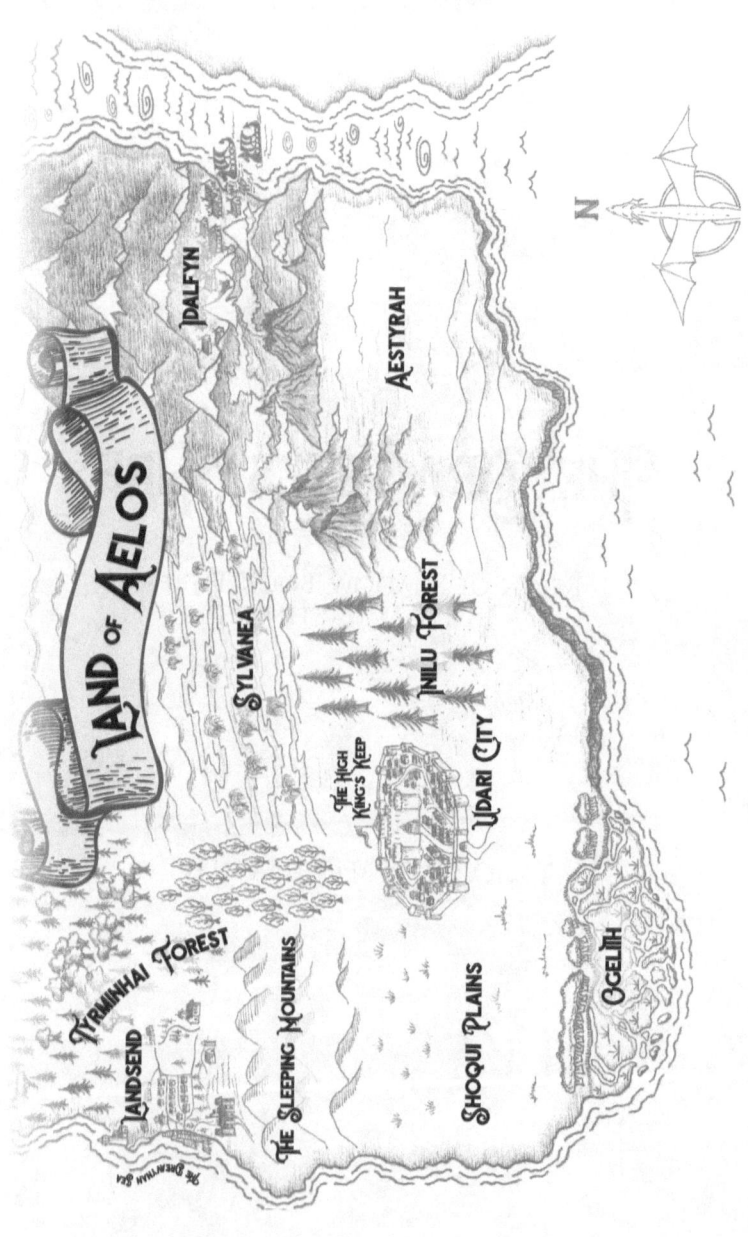

CHAPTER ONE

Darkness held dawn at bay.

Mylah crept within the soft tent walls she and her aunt shared, dressing in silence. The woman on the opposite end of the small space stirred. Mylah slipped a white linen sheath over her head. When the sheath settled over her shoulders, her view unobstructed, a dark face glared at her.

Mylah's stomach squeezed.

"Why must you wake me?" her aunt said, her brows furrowed over dark eyes.

"I'm sorry, Aunt Lein," Mylah intoned, and pulled her sandals on over her feet. "I'm leaving. You can go back to sleep now."

Lein huffed. "That will not be possible, thanks to you."

Mylah ground her jaw. She reached for her bag of tools and water skin. She threw them over her head and onto one shoulder, adjusting a large stone pendant at her throat. She turned, aiming for the exit.

"You know what today is," Lein said from behind her.

Mylah paused, a hand automatically reaching for the pendant that had been her cousin's, touching the grooves that formed the Tijhi's symbol - the fire dragon that had claimed the Aestyrah Desert as their home - and had cursed her people.

Mylah knew what today was. Goddess knew, she knew.

She heard her aunt rise, heard her quiet steps as she made

her way to the center of the tent where she could stand straight. "Look at me, niece," she said.

Mylah obeyed, wishing for escape.

"Come here to me."

Mylah fought the roiling anger gnawing at the fear drumming away in her temple.

"I said, come here to me." Lein's voice scratched with poisonous nails in Mylah's ears.

Mylah forced herself to move closer. She settled into the space in front of her, noting the height difference that had sprung up between them in the last year. Mylah schooled her features, locking away the hurt and disgust she felt. Lein's hair cascaded down her back, pulled into one long dark braid at the nape of her neck, gray streaking the strands. Her dark eyes fixed Mylah, round face drooping with the onset of her middle years, and the constant frown she bore.

Mylah counted her own shallow breaths. She reached seven before her aunt struck.

"Today is the day you remember you live instead of your cousin," Lein said.

Despite all the years she'd been hearing these things, her heart still cracked, while fire licked up her spine and down her arms.

"Today is the day you remember -," her aunt started. Heat flashed through Mylah's core and before she could stop herself, she spoke.

"- a great Tyrmini died, and I lived. I caused my parents' deaths and I ruined the one chance our village had to fulfill the Tijhi's curse." The same words her aunt had said, year after year.

Aunt Lein's dark eyes went wild, mouth trembling in rage.

Mylah went on. "And my aunt," she said, pausing before she finished, "has forfeited her responsibility entirely." Her aunt, after all, was supposed to have been watching the village stranger.

"How dare you!" Lein said. Mylah turned away, stalked toward the door, and was gone before she could say more. Could use those dagger-like words to cut her. She walked away from the tent, temper burning hot inside her. She made her way past the villagers' tents and faced the black mountain looming over them – the Tijhi's mountain, formed here upon their curse on Mylah's people over five-hundred years ago. At least, that's how the story went. Mylah questioned its authenticity.

As Mylah moved, her steps soothed her, the space growing between she and her aunt softening the sharp edges of her mood. She adjusted the water skin and tool bag slung over her body. Other villagers joined her, making a line that led out of town and into the mines.

Sunlight touched the eastern horizon, lightening the azure of night to the cerulean of oncoming morning. Mylah checked the sky for any tell-tale darkness, the first sign of a storm, and saw none. She breathed a sigh of relief. The air chilled Mylah's skin. She wrapped her arms around herself and shivered. By afternoon, it would be comfortably warm.

The group made its way through the north end of camp, gathering more and more workers as they went. Caught up in her raging thoughts, Mylah moved along without thinking of her fellow miners. An abrupt nudge knocked her out of line.

She hopped on one foot until she regained balance, shooting her assailant an annoyed look. The young man named Beeba hurried on, not looking in her direction or giving her any attention at all. Mylah stowed her frustration and continued her march toward the cave entrance.

Kas, a fellow youth, trotted past Mylah toward Beeba as they passed through the outskirts of her people's tent village. Mylah looked at the two friends, her heart whispering of loss. They'd all three been friends once. Before everything had gone wrong.

Mylah listened in to Beeba and Kas, yearning to be a part of their conversation.

"How goes it?" Beeba asked Kas.

She shrugged. "Early," Kas said, brushing through her short strands of dark hair.

Beeba bounced around. "Are we ready for this day?"

Mylah tilted her head, hurried her steps to hear more.

"Today is a triple new moon. Something big is going to happen," he said, raising his hands high into the sky, his smile bright against his dark skin. He turned to Kas, eyebrows raised. "Don't you feel it?"

"I do not," Kas said. "I feel nothing but my desire to go back to bed until the Goddess wakes me, followed by a full meal."

Mylah agreed, but her reason for hiding in the covers had nothing to do with laziness. She wanted to hide from the world today.

"Today is different. Look! I have the shivers." He raised the sleeve of his white linen shirt and showed his skinny goose-flesh-covered arm.

Kas gasped and covered her mouth in surprise while Mylah rolled her eyes.

"I am telling you!" Beeba began, wagging a long, slender finger at Kas. "The Goddess has granted me with foresight. It was passed down from my mother, and from my mother's mother, and from her mother, and -,"

"We get it," Mylah said loudly, hurrying to pass the two, "all your mommies have the gift."

Kas and Beeba glared at her as she passed. "No one was speaking to you, Forsaken," Kas said, her voice sharp.

Mylah held her head high and walked on, eager for the mountain to wrap her in its darkness.

The black mountains loomed ahead, jutting up from the land in sudden stark contrast to the surrounding flat expanses of golden sand. Mylah approached the opening to the cavern with growing unease.

She made it to the entrance as the sky blushed with the Goddess's approach, before the rest of the villagers. Before she entered, she turned to the rising sun, held her hands to the sky, one palm pressed to the back of her other hand, fingers splayed out, in a gesture of respect and gratitude to the Goddess.

She prayed today she would find Tsheyduni stone, and that it would find its way to a Tyrmini and guard them from a fate like that of her cousin's. Mylah possessed no unique gifts, except for her uncanny ability to locate and mine Tsheyduni stone. She hoped she'd find enough to honor him.

Mylah ducked into the cave's entrance, cool darkness washing over her. She retrieved a lamp from the collection gathered near the entrance, all waiting for the other miners. She leaned toward a lit torch mounted in the stone wall, pulling the glass cover from the lamp. Before the wick met the flame, it caught fire, as if of its own accord. Mylah paused, puzzling as the fire shifted and swayed around the oil-soaked wick.

Perhaps she'd been closer to the torch than she'd thought. Shrugging the incident away, she turned to face the path, replacing the glass chimney over the oil lamp. She started when she found herself facing Elder Maka, standing in the path before her. Mylah calmed her racing heart and lowered her head in respect. His presence on this particular day sent a shiver of shame through her.

The Elder returned the gesture, his keen brown eyes boring into her, as if he could see the dark guilt filling her. As if he sensed the inescapable truth so especially clear today: she carried the responsibility of her cousin's death. He had been the Tyrmini her people had waited for for centuries, and Mylah had stripped that chance of redemption from them.

"Our best miner enters before all others," Maka said, smiling, before his features shifted. He tilted his head back and looked at Mylah down the length of his prominent nose. "You are troubled today."

Mylah wanted to retort she was troubled every day. Instead she cast her eyes away, peering into the dark tunnel ahead, aching to escape the elder's piercing gaze, and surround herself with Tyrinth, and stone.

"It is the anniversary of your cousin's passing into the next realm," he stated. Mylah stood still, breathing and maintaining her silence.

Maka laid a bony hand on Mylah's shoulder, and she fought the urge to pull away. She glanced at his face before looking away again, but in that quick moment, she saw something in his face like compassion.

She looked up again. Maka's eyes shone in the lamplight. "You take on guilt that is not yours. I hope one day you can let it go," he said.

Mylah stared, unsure what to say, her belly jumping at Maka's uncanny ability to read her thoughts. Maka dropped his hand and moved aside from where he blocked the path. "May the Goddess guide your search today, Mylah," he said.

Mylah ground her teeth, nodded, and moved down the path.

Dark tunnels consumed her as she moved swiftly down long-mined paths, tunnels dark and swirling with silver and copper. The smell of stone, dry and cool washed over her. The deeper she traveled into the mine, the more her anxiety eased. Away from the people who resented her existence, Mylah came alive.

Mylah scrambled over the rock and rubble, each obstacle a familiar landmark on her path, years of practice and habit giving her confidence. As she sped along, she heaved in lung-burning inhales and exhales. She lost herself to the rhythm, to the exertion, and to the darkness, her lamp casting a globe of light around her, skirted by shadow.

At last, she reached the extensive bridge crossing a deep chasm and stopped. She let her lungs and heartbeat slow, knowing crossing the bridge would ramp it back up again, not due to exertion but that involuntary fear that gripped her as she stepped onto slender planks that were the only thing between her and a long fall to a certain death.

She inhaled deeply through her nose, blew it out loudly, growling as she exhaled. She steadied herself, gripped the rope handle, and stepped onto the bridge. The immediate pull in her lower belly had her standing straight as a rod. Her first step set the planks groaning and she gripped the handrail tighter. Her vision narrowed, her heart slammed into double-time, and a rush of energy shot through her. She focused on the bridge's other side and walked as quickly as she could. Each plank protested her weight, and the bridge swayed.

She flew over the bridge even as it creaked and jostled, her body working against the jittery energy pumping through her to stay upright and steady, until at last her feet touched solid Tyrinth.

Mylah slumped and gripped her knees, clanking the oil lamp onto the ground - light bobbing and swaying around her feet. She closed her eyes against the dancing flame, sweat sliding down her neck even as the cool cave air kissed her skin, hair prickling in response. She inhaled and exhaled, calming her heart and swallowed her stomach back into place.

From here the mine corridor split. On the left, a smaller, barely explored entrance beckoned to Mylah. Ahead of her and to the right worn tunnels stretched away. Most villagers turned right at this point. Mylah squared her shoulders, crouched and entered the smaller cave tube.

She squeezed through the familiar tightness of stone, adjusting her frame to avoid the sharp rocks. The stone seemed to give at her touch, to make way for her. She knew it was her imagination, but she often felt the element was a kindred spirit, a friend of sorts, and they worked together - Mylah moving through the element, searching and finding stone.

Mylah adjusted her pouch of tools to ensure they didn't catch on the jagged stone. The oil lamp cast a cheery gold glow into the lava tube's tight corners. The tunnel narrowed and shortened. Mylah crouched, prostrating herself to crawl through the cramped hard spaces. The lamp jangled and hissed. A steady drip of water echoed off stone. Mylah worked herself through the descending tunnel until it opened up once more, allowing her to stand and walk again.

Mylah assumed no one had been this way before or she would have heard about it. This place would have conjured conversation.

Mylah surveyed the open cathedral room with awe. Massive pillars of minerals jutted from the floor and dangled from the cavernous ceiling. In a far corner light spilled in from a rare opening. Fresh air wafted toward her, warmth filling the space, and green life erupted from the cave's mute browns and grays.

A tree stood in the shaft of sunlight, growing obstinately from a boulder. Its new green leaves shone emerald in a singular pillar of sunlight, shimmering in a light breeze. In tribute to the Goddess, Mylah covered her heart with her left hand, then raised it, pressing the back of it to her forehead before letting it fall again.

Mylah set off across the little stone path crossing a wide and shallow pool of water. Fish and crustaceans skittered beneath the pool's surface, opalescent shells and scales reflecting the rare cave light emanating from the surface opening.

She'd discovered this place sometime before and had saved the location for future exploration. Today was the day.

Once across the pool, she scrambled up a steep mound covered in a fine layer of dirt and small rocks. Her footsteps sent a cascade of loose stones into the water below her, the sound echoing off the cavern room's far corners. Bats fluttered within cloaking shadows nearby. A large spider that would send her aunt screaming crept up a rocky wall, its spindly legs carrying it quietly away from a slash of sunlight.

The cave teemed with life, all moving quietly around the central pool of light and water, the tree a proud matriarch overseeing her kingdom. Mylah had never seen so many critters in one place, neither in the sands, nor in the caves. She considered if she could fish here, whether she would be able to haul the equipment down, and if she could then haul the fish back. At the very least there ought to be some cave crickets she could gather, she thought.

She hunted today, but not for food. Mylah peered around for the Tsheyduni's tell-tale signs. The stone could generally be found embedded in black as night lava rock.

The cavern around her swelled in height and distance, so much larger than the twisting narrow tunnels she was used to. As Mylah peered around, formulating a plan for a systematic search, something glittered in her periphery. She whirled and found nothing. She turned back to the tree, peering past it to the cave room's far wall. She moved forward, but something about the tree and its housing boulder caught her eye.

Beneath the twining roots, under a light covering of soft green moss, faint red light pulsed. Curious, she drew closer. She reached a hand out, tentative, then withdrew it.

She inched forward, drawn not only by curiosity, but something else, some need she couldn't name. She flattened her palm, reached toward the carving, and quickly pulled away as warmth brushed her open hand.

She leaned back, observing the rock, its face buried in twining roots and centuries of dirt and moss. She steeled herself, and poked at the rock, scrubbing a bit of debris away to reveal a groove in the stone. She traced it, halting when her finger bumped into the tree's gnarled roots.

Mylah reached into the bag slung over her shoulder, fishing through her mining tools for the hatchet she kept. Once she held it in callused hands, she went to work on the roots, hacking insistently.

Sweat slipped from her forehead and crawled down her neck, tracking the length of her spine in cooling tickling drips. She swung the hatchet in a steady rhythm, reveling in the labor as the roots fell to the ground.

Her heart sped as she brushed debris away from the rock, that strange warmth seeping into her fingers and palm, sending tingles up her arm. Portions of the carving were very familiar. She held her breath as she guessed the depiction she would find under the vegetation.

Dusting her hands, Mylah backed away from the boulder. Her fingers found the leather string around her neck and pulled the pendant tucked beneath her sheath. The symbol's meaning had been burned into her brain, as it had with all Aestyrians.

Mylah knelt before the rock, bowed her head in respect, closed her eyes and began to whisper a simple prayer. After a few words, a resounding crack interrupted her. Mylah's eyes flew open, head snapping up. A jagged line crossed through the pulsing, red symbol.

Mylah scuttled back, fear shoving her pounding heart into her throat. The tree atop the boulder groaned and popped. Mylah lurched away, covering her ears as the tree split up the middle from its base. More growling protests echoed through the room as the tree splintered away from the growing crack in the trunk. It shivered, showering splinters and precious green leaves from its branches. With one final crack, the tree fell away from the boulder, crashing to the cave floor. A plume of bark, leaves, and dust erupted into the cascading light.

Free from the encasing roots, blue flame erupted from

the crack in the boulder, a blaze of heat washing over Mylah. The boulder splintered again, pieces of stone tumbled away, that ancient symbol crumbling to reveal a pit of flame. Colors shifted, blue, purple, gold, orange. Fiery wings spread up and over the broken boulder, the size of which boggled Mylah's mind. They filled the cavernous space, stretching from one side to the other.

Mylah fell to her knees, this time not in supplication, but because they had gone weak from the power surging from the boulder. Beneath her, the cave floor shook. Real fear gripped her as the room bucked beneath her.

The stone walls and floor went liquid. Mylah clung to the ground as it rolled. The mountain groaned around her as if it meant to pull itself up from its ancient roots and move. A loud crack resounded from overhead. Mylah pulled herself up against the rocking ground and dove as a stalactite crashed down beside her. Heat seared her face and arms as fire blasted up and away from the boulder, reaching toward the sky, toward the Goddess, and her life-giving light.

Mylah lay flat on the ground, gripping the rolling floor. A rock smashed into the back of her leg slicing it open. She screamed. Bats erupted from the darkness, and the cave opening above her darkened by a solid cloud of escaping creatures, their screeching cries echoing around the chamber.

The flames in the boulder turned into a molten rainbow, beautiful even as destruction rained down on Mylah. She ducked and rolled but didn't move fast enough. Rock landed with a sickening crunch on her arm. Tears welled in her eyes.

"Please," she cried, not knowing to whom she spoke. "Please, calm yourself. You're killing us."

As if whatever force had shaken the caves heard her plea, the ground slowly stilled. The world stopped thrashing, and the cave grew quiet.

Mylah panted, her gaze locked onto the crumbled boulder

ahead of her. She sensed it before she saw it. Awareness brushed against her mind.

Grunting, Mylah pulled herself up with her uninjured arm. She hobbled back up the hill, calf screaming, arm aching, shoulder pulsing in steady rhythm of pain. She cradled her broken arm as she approached the rubble that had moments before been a solid boulder. She held her breath as she stepped into the circle of light, onto that maze of carvings under her feet.

There amidst the pile of broken stone shards sat a spherical object as large as Mylah's torso. It absorbed light and color, giving nothing back but black as true as dead coal. Mylah creeped closer, dragged by that awareness still tingling inside her mind. The egg shuddered, paused, and quivered again.

Mylah reached out, her injured arm pressed tightly into her torso. Whispered in silence, a promise lay between her and what lay in the egg, one of connection and belonging, love and acceptance.

She brushed the rough, porous black rock, fingers trembling. The stone sphere cracked, shattered and fell away. A small chirp issued from the rock. Mylah leaned forward and peered in. The creature within locked eyes with her - a perfect mirrored golden stare, save for the elliptical pupils.

Mylah lowered herself painfully to her knees as the Tijhi rose from their centuries-long slumber.

CHAPTER TWO

Mylah scooped the gold and black creature into her uninjured arm, their eyes still locked. The Tijhi's gold face boasted dark markings running from the inside of its eyes and down along its slender snout, down to the tip of its small black nose. Mylah stroked a finger along the Tijhi's nose and the creature chirped, eyes drifting lower at the touch.

Mylah cradled Tijhi, the elemental dragon deity of fire, in their phoenix fox form. The creature had foxish features but also wings. Mylah caressed the creature's down feathers, laid against their sides like two golden clouds. Tijhi's back legs were bird-like as well, with thick black scales and sharp talons. The Tijhi's tail floated behind them in a long mass of gold and black fur. The creature evoked magic, but a dragon? Mylah had her doubts in the ancient folklore.

Dragon, fox phoenix, or fox, it didn't matter; Mylah's heart seemed permanently and instantaneously gripped in the creature's paws. The Tijhi chirped again, and Mylah replied, "Of course I'll take care of you." Tijhi purred and Mylah said, "And you'll take care of me too?" Tijhi rasped a bark. "Very well. We shall take care of each other."

Mylah looked up, surveying the damage around her and for the first time, worry and fear sunk in about her fellow miners. If the whole cave system had trembled like this room had, it could have been catastrophic to them. Mylah looked toward the entrance, unsure if the passage out remained intact. The Tijhi wiggled and whistled, a rhythmic birdlike noise issuing from its mouth. Mylah set the creature down on the ground, wincing at the pain in her broken arm.

Follow me, they seemed to say. They because in the Aestyrian lore, the elemental dragons had no sex or gender.

Mylah cocked her head to one side, unsure of what she'd just experienced. Surely she imagined it, but it had felt as though the little fox phoenix had spoken into her mind. Tijhi trotted away, past the crumbled rock that had cradled them for what Mylah could only assume centuries, if the stories were to be believed. They made their way over the fallen tree, Mylah closely behind them, body protesting from her injuries. At the far end of the cavernous room, a dusty corner barely touched by the sunlight, rose a staircase, seemingly carved many centuries past.

Tijhi approached the stairs, which marched up the cave wall to the opening above them. They turned back to Mylah, a trilling insistent noise urging Mylah to follow. Mylah tried not to think about what would happen if she were to fall from the stairs, which were narrow and had no handrail. She approached the steps, heart fluttering as the Tijhi took the first steps upward.

Mylah clung to the cave wall, injured arm aching, carefully placing each step on the next stair, her dark hair snagging on jagged rocks. The wound on her leg stung with each step. Her world tilted, breath shallow in her constricted throat. She stopped, pressing her face fully into the wall, her uninjured hand pressed into the rock. Her heart drummed in her jaw and ear, sight tunneling, her body shaking so hard her fear of falling only increased. Terror stole through her.

Softness wrapped around her ankles, twining between them before a warm purr echoed up her body. Feeling spread through her. Panic eased. She inhaled deeply, gulping at the air. The cool touch of stone against her face permeated her as

Tijhi wound their way through her legs. Mylah had a sense of reconnection, as if she had gone somewhere outside of her body as it shook and panicked and now returned. Her sandals pressed against her feet, the softness of Tijhi's fur brushing against her legs, the ray of sunlight warming her back all grounded her back in the present.

She breathed, letting the panic die down. As feeling returned to her body, she realized her wounds no longer hurt. She bent her leg experimentally, the place where stone had smashed her muscles flexed without pain. She pulled her arm a fraction away from her body, waiting for the jolt of agony, but none came. She wiggled her fingers, reached her arm up and away from her to find it completely healed. Mylah gaped, eyes going to the creature freed from the stone egg.

The fox phoenix trilled and bounded up the next several steps, staring down at Mylah those golden eyes so alike her own. They cocked a head at Mylah and Mylah nodded. "Yes, I'm ready now," she told the creature, stunned at her healed body. She reveled in her strength and wholeness, her scalp tingling at the power Tijhi had used to heal her, Mylah, the Forsaken. She bit back tears of gratitude, swallowed down her usual guilt and shame, and continued up the steps.

The Goddess's first rays touched her dark hair and filled her with relief. She hurried away from the ledge, each step giving her greater confidence. Mylah traversed the rocky side of the mountain with joy. She paused to gauge her location and the distance from where she'd entered the cave. Mylah set off at a steady rhythm, following an animal trail. Tijhi followed along, tail floating behind them as if on an unseen breeze, their wings tucked tightly into their gold and black body.

The Goddess sunk toward the western horizon by the time Mylah and Tijhi rounded one final corner, flat sandy Tyrinth stretching away from the mountain's feet. At the cave entrance, miners gathered. Some lie in the sand, wounds marring their dark skin. Mylah ran the remaining distance. Several healers tended the wounded, cleaning and wrapping injuries, administering herbs, setting bones.

Mylah skidded up to Maka, still awe-struck at her healed body. A man exited the cave, running toward the elder. "It's no use. We can't reach them." Maka bowed his head gravely.

"Who?" Mylah asked.

Maka turned to her, his eyes shining. "Beeba and Kas."

Mylah's heart plummeted. She'd been so rude to them earlier. "What happened?" she asked.

Maka peered down at her with that same stern, unreadable gaze. "You are uninjured."

"Yes," she said, "I'm fine. Where are they?" Mylah insisted.

Maka stared at her for a moment longer before he turned to the miner next to him, a middle-aged man with fine salt-and-pepper hair and a collection of wrinkles around his golden-brown eyes. He was taller than Mylah, and probably outweighed her by at least half.

"Show the girl where they are," he said, as if in resignation. The man nodded, jaw grinding to one side, casting a distrustful stare in Mylah's direction. Mylah ducked her head, shame coating her insides. The man turned away and headed toward the cave entrance without a word. Mylah quickly gestured her respect for the Goddess before following.

The elder's voice made her turn back once again. "What is this?" he said.

He was staring at Tijhi, except Tijhi was no longer in their fox phoenix form, but appeared as nothing more special than a fox kit with fine golden and black fur, their large ears swiveling up and around as they turned toward the elder, a dark tail tucked between their legs as they skittered past the man to Mylah.

Mylah scooped the kit up into her arms. "It was in the cave.

Alone," she said.

"You cannot have a fox, Mylah,"

"I have sworn to the Goddess to protect them," she stated.

"Them?"

Mylah nodded.

Maka stared open-mouthed before finally asking, "Where exactly did you find this creature?"

Tijhi growled, yipping, then growled again, leaning into Mylah as if to show their claim on her.

"I ventured deep today and found a cave with a pool, a boulder, and a tree. I found the kit there."

Maka looked down his nose at her, his eyes seeming to accuse her of not telling him the full truth.

"I have sworn to the Goddess," she said again, and before Maka could say more, Mylah turned and followed the miner back into the caves. Maka's eyes bore into her back as she hurried away, and she wondered how long she could keep her secret from the wise man.

Mylah set the Tijhi down just inside the cave entrance. The miner leading the way turned right down a wide corridor. Moments later he halted in front of a cave-in, rock and rubble spilled into the tunnel from somewhere above them.

Guilt flooded Mylah. If she had not been exploring the undiscovered, perhaps this would not have happened. She looked over her shoulder at the Tijhi. The little fox looked up at her and chirped, as if to express their apologies. The little fox sneezed then sat, looking up at Mylah expectantly.

Mylah puzzled over the creature's behavior, curious. She turned away and faced the cave-in. "Beeba? Kas?" she called.

"Help!" Beeba's voice called, muffled and distant. "Can you help us?"

Mylah didn't know. There was so much rock. She turned to the other miner. "Did you try shifting the rock?" she asked.

"Of course we did," the man said, crossing his arms. "I don't know what you're going to do that we haven't already tried." His eyebrows were pulled down over his eyes, his features shadowed from a lamp that sat on the floor at his feet. Mylah could feel her temper rising, her heart picking up tempo, fire flooding her belly.

"You're right," Mylah said, and turned, as if she would leave. "Guess we better just leave them there, since you've already tried everything." She walked a few steps away, Tijhi on her heels.

"Wait," the man said. Mylah stopped and looked at him over her shoulder. His arms hung at his side. He clenched and unclenched his fists, jaw working one way then the other. "The Elder has spoken. Let it be so."

Mylah lowered her chin once and turned back to the heap. Tijhi resumed their sit-and-wait position.

The man eyed the fox warily.

Mylah approached the wall right of the cave-in, placing a hand on smooth, cool stone. Following some instinct, she traced their steps back up the tunnel. The man called out, "Where are you going?" he asked, panic tinging his voice.

"I have a feeling," she said, more to herself than the man.

"What?" the man asked.

Mylah ignored him, pacing down the corridor until she found what she sensed. She placed her palm flat against the stone wall, pressing her face close. There. Something hummed against her skin. She closed her eyes as she soaked in the sensation. The stone heated to her touch. Her eyes flung open, and she jerked her hand away, looking at it.

Tijhi sneezed. Mylah looked at the kit. They shuffled then sat on their haunches. Mylah looked back at the wall, shocked to find a glowing handprint with Tijhi's symbol dying away. Curiosity flooded her. She placed her hand back to the spot and yanked it away when embers lifted off the cave wall. She backed away and the stone glowed where she'd touched it, the symbol bright and burning.

Before the fire could dim, Mylah leaned forward and blew, acting on instinct. The red glow turned black. Mylah reached into her bag, pulled out the hammer and smacked it hard into the spot. It shattered and crumbled away. Cool air rushed in.

Mylah backed away from the wall, looking at the little fox in utter shock. Heart pounding, she turned back to the wall. She set the hammer aside and knelt before the stone, just under the new hole staring back at her. She placed both hands on the rock, carefully searching for that something undefinable that had called her to this spot. She closed her eyes and leaned in, sure this time nothing would happen. Certain the first time had been a fluke.

The rock heated to her touch, not burning her, so she kept her hands there. When the heat spread to form a space wider and taller than herself, she pulled away, marveling at the symbol now burning in the two places her palms had rested. She looked at her hands. There in the center the Tijhi's mark burned like fire.

No, a voice said in her mind. *It is fire.*

Mylah looked at the Tijhi who seemed to smile, as if they were on the verge of laughter. Prickles ran down her spine. She turned back to the wall and blew hard. Air burst out of her, gusting hard against the glowing area of rock. She reached for the hammer and struck once, twice, and on the third time the wall shattered, falling on her in a rain of molten rubble. It sizzled and steamed, heat waves radiating up at her. The hot rock touched her skin but did not burn. She shoved a hand into the rocks and received no injury.

"It can't be," a voice said behind her.

Mylah whirled. The man had approached, and stood against the tunnel's opposite side, eyes wide, mouth hanging open. Then the man shouted and ran. Mylah grinned like a fool, even as she climbed through the hole and raced down the tunnel toward

Beeba and Kas.

Her feet slapped against the stone floor, until she heard that subtle call from the stone. She placed her hands firmly into place. Fire flowed through her, air rushed from her, the rock wall yielded to the rap of her hammer.

On the other side, Beeba inhaled deeply as fresh air rushed in to greet him. He looked up at Mylah from his slumped position against the wall. He gripped Kas's upper body. Mylah was relieved, her heart thrilling with the rescue, her blood surging with Tyrmini power. Her power. She was Tyrmini. She was the Aestyrian Champion. The one they'd been waiting for for centuries.

A jumble of emotions rocked through her. Excitement that the Tijhi's curse would be fulfilled after centuries of suffering, relief that she would be accepted by her people, trepidation at the responsibility of being the champion. But above all that was a growing horror that her cousin had died in her place, for nothing.

Body trembling, Mylah crouched down and entered the cramped space, a solid slab of stone above them that had saved her childhood friends.

"I'm here," she told Beeba. "Let's get you two out of here." A new confidence swelled in her. She smiled to reassure him, despite her swirling thoughts and the guilt threatening to overtake her. She reached out to him, but he didn't move, simply looked down at his friend, cradled in his arms. When a sob wrenched from his mouth and tears tracked down his face, cutting clean marks in the layer of dirt and grime, Mylah finally looked fully at her other friend.

Kas's shoulders and chest rested in Beeba's lap, but everything beginning at her torso and down lie crushed under solid rock.

CHAPTER THREE

It had been weeks.

Mylah had become an instant celebrity in her village, and she hated it. Kas had died, likely due to Mylah awakening the Tijhi, yet everyone greeted her with absolute reverence. She and the Tijhi, who'd shifted back to their fox phoenix form, as if to further prove to the villagers that Mylah was not only a Tyrmini, and creature speaker, but a dragon speaker, and the Champion her people had waited centuries for, had started training with Maka daily. No matter what she tried, Mylah could not reawaken the power she'd used in the mines to free Beeba.

She and Tijhi made their way out of the tent before her aunt could awaken and harass her. Tijhi trotted ahead, occasionally stretching their wings and flapping, as if testing them out. The kit grew fast. Yet, the Tijhi had whispered this was normal, and once they'd matured, they would maintain that form for a long while. Mylah wasn't sure what the dragon considered 'a long while', and when she'd pressed, the Tijhi couldn't express the span of time in a way that made sense to her.

They arrived at the village's edge where they met Maka waiting in an empty space of sand, a rolled parchment in his hands. After the traditional Aestyrian greeting – a quick hand placement over the belly, a fist to the heart, the back of the hand to the forehead, and a sweep of the arm toward the other person – Maka launched into the day's work.

"I have had an idea," the man said. He unrolled the parchment and displayed the drawings for a hut. Mylah swallowed hard. Tijhi ran into the sands, pouncing in the dirt to hunt scorpions.

"You want me to build a hut entirely of sand?" Mylah asked.

Maka had said when she grew her power, she'd be able to turn the sand to glass, to shape it to her will. She trusted this might be the case, but since the rescue, it seemed her power had switched off. So far, she'd successfully set a cactus on fire, made a small dent in ant hill, and hardened a glob of sand in her hand so that it had a slight sheen to its surface. Maka wanted her to build a hut.

"It's not that I'm not ambitious, Maka -," she started.

"No, no, no," he said, waving at her assumption. "We start with just a brick, you see." He flipped the page to a new drawing which illustrated a singular stone, rectangular in nature, with rounded corners.

"Is that to scale?"

Maka looked at her, eyebrows lifted in a question. He looked back to the parchment, brought it close to his eyes, then extended it out, turning the page to a slight angle. "Oh, yes, I believe so," he said, smiling and nodding.

"You know this is not what our houses look like," Mylah pointed out.

"No," he said, "this will be better. You will see. It will hold the night's cool and protect against the heat of the day."

Mylah knew nothing of construction. She shrugged. "If you say so."

"I do."

"So..." Mylah looked from the parchment to her open hands and back again. "What do I do?"

Maka looked at her in sharp surprise. "I do not know," he said incredulously. "I am not a Tyrmini."

Mylah looked down at the old wise man nonplussed. She blinked slowly, thumb and finger stroking the talisman at her neck, as if the mention of her talent might make her suddenly vulnerable to the High King's sight. "Aren't you supposed to be my teacher?"

"Do not argue with my methods, young one. You must build a brick. I have supplied the drawing. Now. Build."

Mylah sighed, moving into the empty desert landscape. She looked back at Maka who held the illustration aloft and gave her a wide encouraging smile.

She turned her back to him and stared at a small mound of sand.

A brick.

She knelt and pulled in a brick-sized amount of sand. Then she stared at it for a while. And prodded it. She gathered the sand into something that resembled the shape Maka had shown her and held it, eyes closed, thinking, *Brick, brick, brick.* She peeked from one eye to see the same pile of sand unchanged.

The small success she'd had in the weeks after the Tijhi incident was in bouts of frustration, and if she was honest, in a flare of temper. How was a brick supposed to provoke her anger, though?

She stared at the brick, furrowing her brow, and pretended it had made some heinous remark to her. "How dare you, brick. Who do you think you are?" She extended her hands, willing the power to course through her. She felt nothing.

She tried a different tack, envisioning that stranger's face, a visage that had lost its details and edges from the passing of years. His wild blue eyes and shock of yellow hair, so different than her peoples' features. The sneer of disgust twisting his mouth as he fixed Tiernan with an angry expression. Mylah's excitement had deflated. The creatures that had gathered around them dispersing. And then he'd done the unthinkable.

"What kind of person attacks a child?" she asked the brick.

"What kind of person could kill someone so young and innocent?" Heat rose within her, blood pounding in her temples. She pushed aside her elation and grasped at the anger inflating her power. She rose to her feet.

"What kind of person turns on the very people who've saved their life?"

The center of her body boiled like lava. It gurgled and splashed and then erupted through her. "What kind of man could lash a child to the striking post, stab his caretaker? What kind of man does that?" she shouted at the brick.

The erupting anger burst from her body, its power finding outlet in the impassive, and impartial sands, which had sat inanely as Mylah raged.

A deafening crack split the Goddess-kissed day. The ground beneath Mylah rumbled. Sand exploded up and around her, a shock wave expanding out in a globe from Mylah's epicenter. She clenched her fists as the anger consumed her. She opened her mouth and screamed with the Tyrinth, flashes of Tiernan's face wide with fear consuming her mind and soul. Fire washed through her, out of her, appearing around her in a seductive blue flame. It shimmered and sparked, wrapping the sands in its ethereal grasp. Mylah's flesh prickled, the hair on her body and head rising with electricity.

The flame consumed the sand, eager, hungry, and fast. The wave of its power exited Mylah's feet, traveling through the Tyrinth and up the globe of sand surrounding her. When it reached the globe's apex it shot into the sky. Mylah tilted her head and screamed as the pillar of blue flame rose higher and higher. Until Mylah ran out of breath, and energy, and all at once that intense power petered out. Her head drooped, she crashed to her knees, catching her body with her hands, and wept.

Her eyes remained dry while racking sobs of grief echoed off glass globe walls.

CHAPTER FOUR

Mylah heaved and hiccupped out the last sob, pulling herself into a folded sitting position. She looked around her. Glass wrapped around her in a perfect half sphere.

"Mylah?" Mylah turned toward the muffled voice. Maka stood outside the dome, looking directly at her, his dark eyes wide.

"Maka, I -"

She didn't know how to finish her sentence. She looked around at the glass, looked at the indentation of sand under her, and then at her hands, her body.

She had done it.

"You are trapped in a ball of glass, child," Maka pointed out.

"Oh," Mylah said, her elation fading. She looked around again to find his assertation accurate. She'd made a prison for herself.

"This does not look anything like the picture I drew," he said.

"What?" Mylah said, rising to her feet. "You're teasing with me, right?"

"No," he said. He jabbed a dark finger in the direction of papers. "And you've burnt up my plans."

Mylah placed her hands on her hips and narrowed her gaze. "Oh, I'm sorry... is this -" she gestured around her at the monstrous perfectly globular structure now standing around her.

"- not good enough for you?"

"I am not saying it is not good. It's just not what you were working toward, was it?"

Mylah stared at him open-mouthed.

"And now you are trapped. Did you lose focus, my child?"

Mylah could spit fire. She had finally turned on her power again, and her efforts went unappreciated.

"Maka, look at what I've created," she said.

"A brick would serve you better. If you had a brick, maybe you could bust your way out of this solid bubble you have made for yourself." He chuckled, the sound muffled through the thick glass.

"Okay, Maka. Go ahead and make fun of me," Mylah said, but she slipped into problem-solving mode for the reality Maka keenly pointed out. "Maybe I made a door without realizing it." She swept along the perimeter, hands exploring the smooth glass, the surface warm to the touch.

Maka chuckled again.

"What is so funny?"

"My child a door requires design and this -," he gestured to the globe, "is spectacular but the product of your rage unleashed and your will untethered. If you are to use your power you must use it with intention, my child. All else will cause you heartache and bring chaos and destruction."

Mylah shook her head. "I know I'm trapped, but it's still impressive, Maka."

He simply stared at her, an ambivalent peace upon his wizened face.

She tried not to be uncomfortable with this gaze. She tried feeling proud and strong. She stood straight, squared her shoulders at him, her head high. "I used my powers, Maka. Be happy for me."

"I will be happy for you when you do not have to summon so much anger to drown out the sorrow which you believe leaves you weak. The opposite of weakness is not anger."

"Are you sure?" She raised both hands and twirled around, gesturing to her making.

"Very well," Maka said, lifting his own head high. "Anger yourself out."

"What?" she said.

"You created this problem through your anger. If you are so sure your anger is your power, then," he waved one hand at the glass, "you have the power to get out."

He turned away from her, hands clasped behind his back and strode away.

"Wait," Mylah cried out. "Don't leave me here."

He waved at her without looking back.

She watched him go, exasperation leaving her inert. The sun pierced the glass and with no exit for the heat, and no breeze, the temperature climbed at an alarming rate. Mylah fanned herself with the bit of parchment not burned from her rage.

A raspy high-pitched yowl reverberated through the glass. Mylah whipped around to find Tijhi sitting outside the globe. The little phoenix-fox kit tilted their head to one side.

Mylah shrugged. "I guess I really got myself into a mess," she admitted.

The kit's head tilted the other way. They sniffed at the barrier between herself and her companion – a word Mylah had embraced as the best description for their relationship. Tijhi licked the glass several times, then sat on their haunches and whimpered.

"I have no idea," Mylah said. "It looks like there's no entrance or exit."

Tijhi growled long and low and then yipped.

"I was trying to make a brick," she said and held the half-burned paper aloft. "But I don't even know how to... how do I say this?... turn on my power. So, I tried the one thing that seemed to have set it off before: anger. And then this happened." She gestured to the globe.

Tijhi sneezed with purpose.

"What do you mean that's not the source of my power?"

Tijhi stared, lowered themselves to the ground and exhaled. A sense of quiet calm emanated from the creature. Mylah's awareness thrummed with a deep sense of knowing, centuries of wisdom, and elemental strength.

Tijhi fluttered their wings, which were less downy. The more they fluttered them, the larger they grew. Golden and red energy tracings of Tijhi's wings expanded out. They lifted into the air, their head high, tail swirling out behind them in ribbons of gold, sunshine yellow, deep fiery red, electric blue and touches of royal purple.

Your teacher is right. Your anger is not your power, it is its destruction.

Mylah's stubbornness broke. The elemental dragon of fire had just spoken clearly into her mind. The touch of their words filled Mylah with shame. Her throat burned, her belly hardened, her shoulders ached. She crumpled, bowed, and wept until tears soaked her face, chin, and chest.

Stand, my friend.

Mylah obeyed, rising to her feet even as the tears continued to pour from her golden eyes.

Lesson one: power is. When you use power, you do not harness it or force it, you allow it. This fundamental truth will set you apart from our enemies.

"Enemies?" Mylah asked, sniffling.

That is not the focus right now. Right now, you must simply understand that your power can no longer be bullied into arriving, or activating, or happening. You must simply let go and allow.

"How?" Mylah said.

Your heart is open, is it not? But you aren't listening to it.

Her heart? Mylah wiped tears from her face and wondered: what did listening to her heart sound like? She would have to find out. She folded herself back to the ground.

The heat grew by the moment. Sweat drenched her body. She inhaled and exhaled, slowing her thoughts and racing mind. She cast her questions and logic aside and pointed her attention to her heart. What was her heart saying?

Air caught in her throat. She wheezed. Sunlight pressed into her closed eyelids. Sweat trickled down her back. Her legs ached. Somewhere with her inside the globe, a scorpion skittered across the sand.

The fox phoenix's presence loomed near her consciousness. She dropped into herself. The outside world softened. Color and light filled her senses. Something warm beckoned her and she followed, allowing the sensation to pull her along.

Tijhi appeared in her mind's eye as a small orb of light and warmth that grew little by little to fill her inner landscape. As Mylah calmed and quieted herself, the Tijhi gained clarity, coming into focus through a field of blooming oranges and reds. Mylah allowed these visions to fill her even as she untethered herself from physical reality.

The flames who were Tijhi shifted and swayed, form coming into focus. With a jolt, the dragon masquerading as a small fox phoenix sprang into Mylah's mind. The elemental dragon snarled and clawed, giant curved fangs extending past the lower jaw, a crown of horns jutting wickedly out of their leathery hide, eyes the color of burning embers wide and fierce. The dragon lost to legend for the past five centuries unfurled its wings, inhaled with rattling intention, threw its massive head back and blasted the air with a column of blue flame.

Mylah's lungs burned, her head swam. The place of meditation she'd carefully built to house her companion's presence swayed, shimmered, and shattered.

Mylah gasped for air and found none. Her eyes sprang open. All of her physical sensations she'd set aside during meditation surged to her awareness, sinking sharp teeth into her senses. Her shoulders and neck ached while her chest burned like the dragon's fire. White blobs filled her vision as she gulped for air over and over.

Across the sweltering globe Mylah locked eyes with the Tijhi in their fox phoenix form. With a final attempt to fill her lungs with air that simply wasn't available under the suffocating globe, she slumped forward and let darkness consume her.

Outside the globe, wind swept over the Aestyrian sands, ruffling Tijhi's feathers and fluff. The fox phoenix shook nose to tail, sneezed, and walked toward the barrier between themself and their charge. Without a stutter, the Tijhi's feathers and fur shifted to white hot flames. They reached the glass and touched it with their nose. Flames danced around the small spot of contact, burning bright red and orange.

Tijhi backed away from the dome, then sat on their haunches, and curled their long tail around their feet. The flame ate at the glass, duplicating itself and expanding across the structure Mylah made.

The elemental deity waited patiently. They had never slept for so long. The Aestyrians had certainly taken far longer than they anticipated to complete the task the Tijhi had set them. Ten-thousand lives had taken them five centuries. And what state would the rest of Tyrinth be in by now, under the oppression that long-ago king started. Tijhi snarled at the thought of the twisted monarch who had slaughtered Magyskind, imprisoned the Light dragon, and consequently obliterated the gentle balance of power in the world.

Tijhi reached out into the etyric consciousness. Only the smallest tug of Light magic answered back. It appeared Magloryn was still imprisoned, magic wielders still suffering from the volatility of an imbalanced source.

Their other cousins and sisters were also faint. Tijhi's connection with them hung tentatively, brittle and quiet, as if they slept. And in their sleep their connection to power grew mute.

White-blue flame engulfed the glass globe. Tijhi turned their head slightly, aware it had reached the stage of heat that would...

Like a bubble being popped, Mylah's glass prison exploded. Tijhi sprang into action, leaping to their feet, expanding their young wings. They flapped with all the energy their juvenile physical form could muster. It was nothing compared to their full potential, but it would save their charge from her recklessness and ignorance.

Tijhi snagged the billowing glass, halting it with their intention, an explosion paused mid-expansion. They moved the shards away from Mylah and released them to the Tyrinth's natural pull. Glass thumped and clattered as they fell to the sand.

Tijhi trotted forward, mind heavy with the reality of their home and people. So much work lie ahead of them, and the Tijhi and Aestyrians needed this girl with her volatile powers.

The sun burned warm and bright, exquisite against the fox phoenix's fur and feathers. Tijhi called their sibling, the air dragon, for a gift of wind and received a mumble. Lazy and weak, but it came nonetheless. Tijhi thanked their sibling, then knelt to wake their charge.

CHAPTER FIVE

"Try again," Maka said.

Mylah restrained a huff, but barely. Sweat beaded on her brow, dripped down her body, and soaked into the Aestyrah desert sand. The Goddess should be sated with Mylah's sacrifice alone for the day.

Her arms shook from hours holding them outstretched. Her legs trembled from standing in a horse stance. Muscles in her back and buttocks screamed in protest, and yet the blasted sand she'd formed into a square remained stubbornly unchanged.

Mylah's frustration rose again, and with it the nagging doubt she'd ever make anything of her power. But she had to. She was their Champion. She cast her eyes toward the Goddess.

Surely, you've made a mistake, she thought.

Tijhi sauntered into the circle Maka had made in the sand. There was no telling where the little dragon had been, and what they'd been up to. Tijhi looked up at Mylah as they passed her by, slowing to smile at her. Mylah remained focused on the pile of sand.

Two weeks had passed since the glass globe debacle, from which Tijhi had saved her. Maka had insisted on her training the very next day, despite her fatigue and shame. She had sucked up her pride and followed Maka into the desert day after day.

She had little confidence in her power. Any instance of its arrival seemed more fluke than proof. She went along with these sessions, moving through the motions, following the elder's instructions to keep Maka happy, to appease her people, until she could find a way to let them down easy.

She was not the champion they'd waited for.

Her thoughts wove around a made-up conversation, in her head crafting what she would say, how Maka might respond, and how she would counter. She didn't see Tijhi until the kit stood directly in front of the rectangle of sand she half focused on.

"Move, little one, you are a distraction from the child's training," Maka said, and brandished his walking stick at the fox phoenix. The creature side-stepped the attack, chirping angrily at Mylah's teacher, before they resumed their place in front of the brick. They looked pointedly at Maka, then proceeded cleaning their paws.

Maka growled. "Small menace. You must move and allow Mylah her focus." He made to poke at Tijhi again with his walking stick. The fox phoenix's ears swiveled back, lying flat against their head. They opened their mouth, revealing sharp teeth and hissed.

When the stick got close enough to touch the Tijhi, the creature burst into flames and swatted at the object. Fire raced up the stick and with a shriek, Maka dropped it to the sand. A black line of coals smoldered in the sand before Mylah could rise out of her horse stance.

Tijhi growled at Maka, taking two steps toward him.

"I will not be derailed," he told the creature. He pointed at the lump of sand trying its best to become a brick. "That piece of desert will be a brick before we retire for the night."

Tijhi looked in the direction the elder pointed, then looked back to Maka. The fiery creature swished its tail, maintaining its ember gaze with Maka, and the lump of sand transformed. Not into a brick, but a shining rectangle of glass. They swished their tail again and the glass brick shattered. Their tail passed over the pieces a third time, and the glittering shards were transformed back to sand. Only then did the dragon sit proudly on their haunches, extinguish their flame, and resume their bath.

Mylah didn't speak, and bit down on her inner cheek to control a laugh.

"Do you think pandering to your companion will make things better?" Maka said to the little fox phoenix.

The Tijhi continued cleaning themselves.

"Don't you understand?" Maka went on, his voice rising. "Can't you see? Mylah must be our champion."

Mylah cringed at the responsibility looming before her. Their champion? She couldn't save anyone. In fact, she now counted two deaths as her responsibility.

Maka went on, "The stone is gone. The reserves have run out. The last piece of it hangs around our champion's neck. It is time."

Mylah blinked, grasping for the pendant hanging at her chest. "The last? But, I just found stone last week," she said.

Maka shook his head, his gaze falling to the sands beneath his feet.

A breath of wind stirred, sighing through Mylah's hair, capturing the dark strands and tangling them together. The Goddess shone down on them with impartiality.

"Already issued to another young Tyrmini," Maka said. "There are simply not enough for those who know our secret. And the High King's rampage continues. Recruit or kill.

"Until the High King can be overthrown, the Tyrmini of Aelos will be discovered with ease by the Dragon's Eye. We cannot waste time."

She didn't know the stone had run out. No, she'd certainly been finding her fair share; she hadn't known the other miners weren't uncovering the same amount of stone. Her heart raced. The heaviness of her role in all this settled into her chest, breeding anxiety.

It's too late for all that, old man. Tijhi's voice echoed in

Mylah's mind while the Tijhi continued cleaning. Mylah tilted her head.

"What do you mean?" she asked the creature. Maka's angry gaze snapped to Mylah, but seeing her gaze resting on Tijhi, he simply stared.

Look at the stone around your neck.

Mylah grasped at the flat slab of stone hung on a thin piece of leather. Her fingers caressed the carved surface, a gesture she'd repeated countless times since her cousin's death. But this time her fingertip caught on a jagged edge. Her heart plummeted.

She yanked the stone from her neck and held it up to the Goddess, high in the sky. There, just at the silver setting's edge, sunlight leaked through what should have been a solid mass. Mylah looked at her teacher, tears forming in her eyes.

Maka's jaw dropped. "No," he whispered.

There are troops approaching the village as we speak, Tijhi confirmed their worst fear.

"But," Mylah said, her gaze warped in the flood of tears. "I'm not ready. Are you sure?"

Tijhi leveled her with an intense gaze. *I have seen their coming for days now. You will have to face them, but you will not win. And this is the plan.*

"What plan?" Mylah asked, her voice shrill, her heart raging in her chest, a ringing picking up volume in her ears.

Please speak what I say next to the old man.

Mylah looked from Tijhi to Maka. True fear etched the lines of his wizened face. "I'm supposed to translate," she told the elder.

Maka stood straight, composing his features into the semblance of calm. It reflected a lie, that semblance. A storm of emotions brewed beneath the surface. Her own raged inside her; a tempest of panic for her people.

Tijhi turned their face to the elder and spoke into Mylah's mind. Mylah translated as the words tumbled into her.

"They say you shouldn't fight them. That I'm to be taken to the High King," Mylah quaked at the thought, but continued on.

"They say they'll threaten the people and if I go along with them, they'll spare everyone. This is the way it must be. The time for hiding is over. The reign of shadow can't be tolerated or feared any longer. It's time to act. But how we act is perhaps not as it's been imagined. Trust that they'll keep me safe, or as safe as they can, and know whatever happens next is to end the imbalance of power and make Aelos and its people whole again."

Maka stood stock still for three breaths before he responded. "Are you certain?"

"They say that you have fulfilled the contract's first portion, signed by Empress Tama. The rest is up to me," Mylah translated. She looked to the elder with eyes wide, fear thrilling through her, stomach hardened around a pit of panic. There had to have been some cosmic mistake. She could not be the one her people needed.

"No," Maka said, and shook his head. "You misunderstand me."

"What?" Mylah asked.

Maka took a slow, deep breath, his gaze on the sand. Wind rose and fell, as if in answer. Mylah wanted to shake the elder to get him to speak, but years taught her to simply breathe in and out.

"Are *you* sure? You, Mylah. Not the Tijhi and not your old fool of a teacher. You."

Mylah's breath caught somewhere on her inhale. Was she sure? She didn't know.

"If the Tijhi's wisdom can be trusted, is true -," Maka started. Tijhi hissed at the teacher, ears flipping back, fire catching to its belly and wrapping around its back. " - then you still have a choice, Mylah." Tijhi stopped hissing.

This is true. You have a number of choices in front of you right now, Tijhi stated.

Mylah looked at the little fox phoenix then looked at her

teacher. She felt crushed between two walls of information. To her teacher, she said, "The stone is running out?" Maka bowed his head.

To the dragon deity she said, "If we surrender to the High King, they'll take us and they won't harm our people?" The Tijhi nodded once. "And you'll be with me?" They nodded once again.

"What will happen to my people if we leave?" Mylah asked the Tijhi.

Honestly, what choice did she really have? She couldn't fight anyone, much less a whole troop of the High King's Tyrmini guards.

Your people will be safe. At least for some time.

"For now?" she asked.

For now. I cannot see infinitely into the future. I only know the High King is only interested in you - intensely. Because there are no other Tyrmini amongst your people, he is willing to bargain with you.

"Why is he so interested in me?" Mylah asked.

Because, Mylah, you are a powerful Tyrmini.

Mylah barked out a laugh. "You're joking, right?" She gestured to the lump of sand behind the Tijhi. "You've been witness to my lack of power. There's barely a spark."

Are you not the one who woke me, after my centuries of slumber? Did you not rescue Beeba with your power?

"Rescue?" she asked, her voice climbing. "Had I not stumbled into your cave, Beeba and Kas would not have been in the cave-in," she spat.

Tijhi hung their head. *The mountain's quake was a symptom of my waking. I wish I could have prevented that harm.*

Mylah propped a hand on her hip, ran the other through her dark locks. "I'll cause more damage. My track record isn't great," she said.

Your cousin's death was not your fault.

If she had not called out to her parents, had not been so excited to share the appearance of elementals, to celebrate her cousin being Tyrmini, Tiernan might still be alive.

You cannot know such things. What happened to your cousin should not have happened, but you were just a child, and his death does not sit on your shoulders.

And yet it still did.

Like it or not, despite your history, you are powerful, Mylah. Only by embracing it can you honor your cousin's life.

CHAPTER SIX

Mylah's chest burned as if full of hot rocks, searing heart and lungs, muscle and bone. She marched toward the village, weighing the Tijhi's words in her mind, hoping beyond hope the funny creature was wrong. Better, that she'd imagined their shared mental chatter and when they arrived in the village, no threat arrived.

Everything hinged on whether the Tijhi could be trusted.

And Mylah.

The Aestyrah shimmered in heat waves, the deep blue sky stretching overhead, the black volcanic mountain behind her to the north looming, and golden sand stretching south in front of her. The Goddess dominated the sky's apex, casting her gaze over her land and people with detached warmth. Mylah wondered if it was selfish to ask her to intercede. She prayed, hoping she didn't offend the Goddess, for a way out of her predicament.

It all hung squarely on her shoulders, and it always had, even if she hadn't known, had assumed it had been her cousin's burden. Any battle waged against her would be lost if her Tyrmini abilities were to be counted on. The power within her lurked, strange and foreign, having its own will to spring or sulk.

Mylah flexed her fingers at her sides, wondering just how she could ever harness the chaos and unpredictability of such a power. She hung her head, and tears slipped down her face. She moved toward the village as if pulled.

Just outside of town, the Tijhi halted. Mylah looked down at the creature, curious. Tijhi stretched, first pushing back on its back feet, front legs lengthened out in front of it. Their clawed feet shifted slowly from scaly hide to soft fur, its claws spreading and softening until there were only paws. It then pushed itself forward, back legs stretching behind, wings vanishing with the movement. Finally, the Tijhi shook itself, nose to tail until the creature appeared to be nothing more than a small desert fox.

They drew close to the village, tents springing up in the desert sands, canopies pitched to provide shade to working and resting villagers. Mylah, Tijhi and Maka walked down the center thoroughfare. Maka waved at some, nodding his head to others, smiling at the children running from shady spot to shady spot. Mylah stared straight ahead, hope rising at the empty horizon.

As they reached the village's southern end, she breathed a sigh of relief. Her aunt appeared from under the flap of their tent, her usual tense face tinged with curiosity. The woman had been marginally kinder in the weeks since her power had manifested.

Lein held a clay plate in her hand and approached Mylah. Bright silver streaked her dark hair. She had it pulled back today in a long braid, her round face wrinkled around the mouth.

Mylah reached toward her aunt, sorrow bubbling up inside her, fear threatening to eat her whole. Lein grasped her hand, its warmth the last gift she'd ever receive from her.

Lein extended the plate to Mylah, opening her mouth to ask - Mylah would never know what she was going to ask. She saw the slight tilt of her head, the raise of her eyebrows, the openness of her expression. She inhaled. A strand of hair slipping over her forehead. Mylah reached for a roasted locust. Her aunt had likely been out all morning gathering and roasting them in batches and then distributing them to her neighbors.

Guilt, Mylah's constant companion these last nine years, rose to greet her. She chanted her silent and internal apology to her family, for causing her cousin's death, for her parents' death, for failing them all.

Her aunt's eyes widened, smile faltering, head jerking so that one stray strand of hair jolted, falling across her left eye. The clay plate fell with a hushing thud to the desert floor, locusts scattering across the sand. Mylah grabbed her as she collapsed. Mylah's arms wrapped around her aunt's shoulders.

Lein gasped, eyes still wide as she slowly looked down her own body. Mylah's gaze followed. A black and gold-fletched arrow protruded from her aunt's chest. Red smeared and spread from the shaft. It took Mylah a breath to make sense of it. That bright red staining her aunt's linen was blood. Shock held emotion at bay.

"Auntie," she said, and she heard how small and scared her voice sounded. She was a child again, as a stranger strapped her cousin to the striking pole, and her parents rushed forward to save him. Blood had stained their clothes like this as a knife had plunged in and out of their bodies in the most unreal way.

The very last of her kin reached a hand to her niece's face, stroking her thumb through tear tracks.

Lein's hand dropped to her chest. Mylah's heart cracked. Lein's gaze lost focus, life's light wisping away. Tears streamed, blurring her vision. Her sorrow consumed her. She rocked her aunt and screamed, sobs ripping from her soul and into the hot desert day. She gulped down air as another sobbing scream rent the air. Her body trembled, core clenched. And as the cry expended her breath a horrible rage stampeded right over sorrow.

Mylah lowered her aunt's body to the ground, sobbing as she kissed her on the forehead, brushing her eyelids closed. She pressed a hand over Lein's now still heart, a fresh wave of sorrow breaking through, fighting the rage for space. Mylah placed her other hand over her own heart. A steady ringing intensified in her ears, her vision blurring and clearing as tears poured from her eyes.

Something whizzed past her, a streak of brown and black

tracing a line in front of her. She snapped to attention, a solid door slamming shut on her sorrow. She followed the incoming arrow's direction. There at the next dune's crest a man stood, bow gripped in front of him. He reached behind him, arrow fletching brushing against his fingers.

Mylah tracked the man's aim, eyes falling on Maka. She moved, rising to her feet without thought. She rushed toward Maka, scooping her mentor into her arms and knocking him to the ground as another arrow flew overhead.

"Go!" she shouted to the old man. Trembling, he rolled to his arms and legs and crawled toward the nearest tent, ducking behind it for cover.

Don't fight, Tijhi said, but the words drowned in the war drums thrumming in Mylah's ears. She scrambled to her feet, eyes fixed on the archer, and launched toward him. The sand hardened beneath her feet, heat swelled around her. That lurking foreign power springing to life.

Mylah drew on the heat shimmering around her, calling on the Goddess's own power, and as she approached the soldier, she slammed that power into him with a fiery fist. The soldier was lifted into the air, flame exploding around him. He fell to the ground in a smoking, blackened mass.

Mylah searched the rising and falling sands around her and wasn't disappointed when more soldiers appeared. Grinning, she summoned the power now pouring through her, so willing and eager to answer her demand for revenge. She drew on sand and fire, not asking any longer, but commanding they bend to her will. She reached toward the desert sands, scooping them up and shaping them into crude deadly spears. Fire leaped from her hands as she aimed for her next target. The soldier closest to her paused, knelt, and raised a circular shield. Bolts of molten glass clanged against it, but one found its mark, skewering the soldier's lower leg. Blood sprayed outward. Bone cracked. The man dropped, a shriek of pain ripping from his mouth.

Mylah relished the man's pain, triumphant in his falling at the will of her power. The elemental energy coiling inside wanted more. It sang in her veins, pumping her muscles and bones with vibrant, insistent need.

She jogged into the valley between dunes and began her next ascent when another soldier appeared. Mylah reached deep into the Tyrinth, calling on the sands of her home. She gathered its attention, whispered her command, and caressed it with fire.

"Halt!" a commanding female voice echoed over the dry, hot air. The woman's head piece was larger than the other soldiers, with more black plumage. Mylah steadied the flow of energy pulsing through her, even as it raged for release. The woman paused halfway down the hill. Fear diminished in the giant presence of her anger.

"I am Leviatha, and I am Captain of the High King's Guard. If you come with us peacefully, we will not harm any others."

"You killed my family," Mylah growled through gritted teeth. She would never be able to repair their relationship. She would never know if being the Aestyrian Champion would restore her aunt's love for her.

Leviatha's face opened wide with shock, then clamped down. "That was not part of the plan. An accident. I promise no more will die today if you surrender." The woman shifted, pulling stuck boots to stay steady in the sands. Mylah's own footing stayed firm, the desert answering her call for support. Thrumming energy pushed against her restraint, unwilling to relent. The sand in front of her heated.

"And I promise I will kill you," Mylah said. She unleashed the waiting power, giving into its roaring need, its greed and hatred. The sands beneath the High King's Guard buckled in unison as a deep pop resounded from the Tyrinth beneath her. They looked around, under their feet. One soldier darted, but too late.

"Luther, now!" Leviatha shouted.

Sand erupted around the soldier, red hot and searing. The lava-like Tyrinth dropped beneath her as it wrapped around her in a clamshell-like trap. Leviatha leaped, her face a mask of calm concentration. She shimmered in a way Mylah couldn't identify, almost as if she were surrounded by water. Leviatha pushed through the molten sand wall. Steam rose in a gaseous cloud around her, blurring her figure and visage.

Mylah readied herself for the oncoming water Tyrmini, rotating her feet into the sand for greater purchase, stoking the fire already consuming her. Flames danced around her, the valley boiling with lava.

Leviatha charged Mylah, that encompassing bubble of water steaming away with each touch of lava.

"Come on," Mylah shouted, arms outstretched as she called the lava and shaped her intention to consume the woman. She raised her hands to the Goddess, aiming her power. Leviatha sprinted forward, a sword raised, a name on her lips.

Pain exploded across Mylah's skull. She had the briefest moment of shock before the world went black.

CHAPTER SEVEN

Mylah woke with her hands bound behind her back. Her head sang in a steady throb of pain, left ear ringing in one even high-pitched note. She hissed, slowly blinking to rid her vision of sleep. The Goddess folded down into the crease the Tyrinth made in the sky, tucking into night. Mylah stared at the horizon, unable to take in this night she would go to sleep with no living relatives to speak of.

"You're lucky the High King is so interested in you," a man's voice, judging from its deepness, drawled. Mylah swiveled her head to find the voice's source, which caused the world to spin. Nausea swept over her, chilled sweat broke over her body. She slumped forward and vomited noisily, narrowly missing her legs.

"I do apologize, sweetheart," the man said. Mylah's head tipped up, her mouth scrubbed with rough fabric. Something pressed against her lips. She fought it. "Just water. Drink. You'll feel better."

Mylah obeyed, cool water passing over her tongue, down her throat and splashing into her empty stomach. The water spread through her, washing away some of the awfulness. She slowly opened her eyes again and this time, very carefully looked toward the face of her captor. The world jostled a little less.

The man's skin glistened in a beautiful shade of deep ebony, his eyes rich brown. He squatted in front of her, the weight of his body perched on his toes, his arms draped casually on his knees.

The armor he wore exposed muscled arms and legs while it covered the vital organs in the center of his body. Indented above his heart a circle divided into quarters glinted with gold plating, four gems along the perimeter winking in the daylight – the symbol of the Tyrmini Guard.

Mylah peered past the man, taking in her surroundings. The desert here had hard ground, sparse cactus forests, scrubby short trees, green bushes, and rising mesas interrupted the flat horizon. Mylah had traveled these landscapes many times. The company headed west and south, away from Mylah's village which abutted the dark volcanic mountains they mined. Before the sands became great rolling hills and valleys of dunes, which ultimately led to the sea, they would cut west through a gap in the mesas. They would then turn sharply south on the road, traveling in a narrow gap between the Inilu Forest and the Aestyrah's mesas.

"So, you're new to your power? And yet, you're so much older than our normal query," the man said. He tilted his head to Mylah. Mylah focused on the looming mesas. Beyond them the Inilu Forest squatted between the desert and Udari City, the edge of which she'd only ever glimpsed from the main road that skirted its borders.

Mylah shifted, and the world whipped around her again. She squeezed her eyes shut, panting against the nausea and swimming sensation.

"I do apologize, so I do," the man's warm voice slid through Mylah, and she found its comforting tone annoying. "I knocked you on the head pretty good. But, I couldn't very well have you take out the whole guard, could I? Plus, the High King is eager to meet you. 'Specially now you gone and wiped out half a dozen guards in a matter of minutes. You are powerful!" He paused, then, "What's your name, sweetheart?"

"My people," Mylah asked.

"Oh, fine, fine... long as you promise to come quiet with us.

But that's a conversation for you and Captain Leviatha. She's gone off to find us some water." He rose from his crouched position and took up a seat on a nearby rock. "I'm Luther, if you wanted my name."

"You killed my aunt," Mylah said, ignoring his introduction.

"I most certainly did not," Luther said. "That was Matthers, whom you killed in like. Favor returned. Score even." He flourished his hands as he spoke. Overhead, a hawk cried, the high-pitched whistle echoing across the vast and darkening sky. The man watched the hawk intently.

"Why should I not do the same to you?" Mylah asked. "How do I trust you that my people are safe?"

He laughed. "I s'pose you could try, darlin'," he said. "Could be a fun fight... for about two seconds."

"You think I'm not a match to you."

"No, I know you're no match for me," he said, and his face turned hard, eyes flat and filled with an emptiness that set Mylah's nerves on edge. He let the silence stretch between them with nothing but that unsettling gaze upon her. She shifted. "Now, you listen up good," he said, and pointed a finger at her. "You're lucky to be alive right now. Who me and Leviatha are is the High King's highly trained Tyrmini retinue. We're the only ones on Aelos allowed to even live with Tyrmini powers. Do you know our purpose?" He leaned in toward Mylah. Mylah flinched back.

"You're Tyrmini hunters," she said, lip curling.

"No, sweetheart," he said, and shook his head. "You've gone and missed the whole point of this little arrangement you find yourself in. You're alive because the High King wants you." He jabbed his fingers at her. "He wants you with your power intact, and he's willing to sacrifice two good Tyrmini for just one of you. Just one. So, what do you think that makes you?"

Mylah stared and stared, chin jutted high, wrists barking at the pain from the rope, heart aching.

"I did knock your head pretty good. Let me save your scrambled brains a little work and explain it to you." He perched an elbow on a knee and pointed first to her and then to himself. "You and I are the same. And you're damn lucky for it. All that raw power is shit without somebody to train you. So, you and I, we're now locked up together for a while, darlin'." He stretched out the word, 'while', the h strong, the vowel long. "Because it's not just Leviatha and I who are Tyrmini hunters. No, friend. We all -," here he traced a large circle with his hand and arm as if to encompass himself and Mylah, "are Tyrmini hunters."

Mylah swallowed against a growing lump in her throat. Everything she and her people stood for, to aid Tyrmini with Tsheyduni stone, carefully connecting with young Tyrmini across Aelos to ensure their survival, stood in opposition to the High King's Tyrmini Guard. Now, Mylah was one of them.

"No," she said, shaking her head. "I will not."

Luther pushed himself up, hands now grasping both knees. "You will. You'll join our ranks, and you'll train with me, and you'll report to Leviatha and the High King. Because if you don't, the rest of your people will become extinct." He snapped his fingers in front of his face. "Like that. That's how fast the High King will eliminate your people if you refuse him. I've seen it before. Don't tempt him. The High King would relish wiping them out."

He walked away from Mylah before he turned to face her again. "Don't think we don't know what y'all have been up to. Nah, we figured it out, and the only reason the High King is staying his hand is for you." He jabbed his pointer finger at her again, suddenly more intense than Mylah could handle. Her heart sped up and her breathing increased. "So, if you care at all... at all," he made another gesture with his hands palms down and passing over an invisible plane in front of him, "you best straighten yourself up, and get onboard with the plan."

Leviatha, the woman whom Mylah had seen clear her sand

and fire trap in a protecting bubble of water, approached, several water skins bulging from where they were slung over her shoulder. She passed one to Luther. Luther took it, still looking at Mylah.

"So, welcome to the club," he said. He paused, uncorked the skin, dragged a long swig, then re-corked it. "Now. What was your name again?"

Leviatha extended a water skin to Mylah. Mylah glared up at her and didn't move to take the skin, because her hands were still tied behind her back. "Oh, yes. Of course." Leviatha threw the water skin back over her shoulder. She looked to Luther. "Is she up to speed?"

Luther tore his gaze from Mylah and looked up at his Captain. "Hard to say," he said, and snapped his eyes back to Mylah. "Well?" he asked.

Mylah sneered at him. Leviatha dropped to a knee in front of Mylah, cutting her gaze with Luther. "Do as you're told, train with us, and you get to keep your life and the lives of your people. Step one foot out of line, they're dead. This seems like a simple choice, girl. What will it be?" As she finished speaking, she pulled a long dagger from her belt and held it in front of Mylah.

Surrender, Tijhi's voice echoed in her head.

You want me to become a Tyrmini hunter? You want me to seek and slaughter innocent children? Or recruit them to this unholy cause? Mylah's fury and disgust couldn't be heavier. *Wouldn't it be better to die?*

If only your life hung in the balance, yes. Yes, it would be better to sacrifice yourself and your power rather than allow it to be used to cause harm to the innocent. But, there is more at stake. It's not just about you. If we navigate this carefully, we will be saving so many more than the lives of those you may impact as a hunter. For now, you must surrender.

What if I don't trust you? Mylah said, her anger and fear roaring in her ears. *What if what you say turns out like this turned out, with all these bad things that happened and are happening because I put my faith in your words.* Her aunt was dead. The Tijhi had said if she were to surrender, her people wouldn't come to harm.

Your aunt's death was unfortunate and unforeseeable. I am so sorry for your loss. The rest of your people might be spared still. If you don't trust me, then don't listen to me. Don't heed my wisdom. But listen to your own wisdom, Mylah, and trust the power and instinct you have inside of you.

Mylah's emotions swirled, tears spilling over her cheeks as she closed the conversation with the Tijhi and watched the knife in front of her glint with hard truth. She didn't know if she could trust the Tijhi. And she didn't know what wisdom she had available, what her internal power had to do with making this decision. She only knew saying yes meant becoming the very opposite of what her people wanted her to be. But saying no risked the safety of her remaining people.

She closed her eyes, breathed deeply, and stilled herself. The pain in her head, her wrists, her aching muscles grounded her. She let go of all the questions, all the anger, and hurt. She slipped down into meditation within several heart beats, following her teacher's instructions as she had practiced the last several weeks. The road in her soul spiraled away, and she let loose of her tight hold on reality and followed the path.

In the solitude, she breathed deeply, allowing her breath to be the only thing she heard.

Everything cleared. Her mind, her heart, her emotions. When she simply allowed herself to be herself, her own truth shone brightly as a singular source to make this decision. If there was anything she could do to save Tyrmini, she would. And this position she now found herself in could possibly allow her to do more than she'd ever thought possible.

This could be an opportunity.

She simply had to make it so. Her eyes flashed open. She couldn't be sure how long she'd sat there, but the woman named Leviatha still crouched in front of her, still held the knife between them.

Mylah inhaled deeply, then exhaled before she stated, "Mylah."

The woman, her eyes big, round, and deepest blue, blinked. "What?"

"My name. The man asked for my name. It is Mylah," she said.

"Good," the woman drawled. "Mylah, do you accept your new position with the High King's Tyrmini Guard, or do you forfeit your life and those of your people?" Leviatha's stern face gave nothing away, those sea-blue eyes reflecting as coldly as the ocean's depths.

Mylah allowed the calm center of herself to radiate through her, swallowed against fear and loathing and said, "I accept this."

Leviatha nodded once. "That makes my job a lot easier," she said, moving past Mylah, knife still in hand. Mylah jerked away, thinking the bargain wasn't good enough, or that Leviatha had suspected some lie in her acceptance. The woman reached behind Mylah and sawed the bonds at her hands.

The final threads broke and Mylah's hands came free. She rubbed at her wrists, twisting her hands to bring feeling back into them. As she did, a sensation tickled in her mind and Tijhi appeared. The fox chirped, pointedly looking in turns at Luther and Leviatha.

Mylah cocked her head, listening to the creature masquerading as a simple fox kit. Luther and Leviatha pulled weapons faster than Mylah could track.

"Stop!" she said to them. "This creature is my companion. Do not harm them."

Luther immediately stowed his weapon, as if this were routine. Leviatha gave Tijhi a piercing gaze before she moved to sheath her dagger. "Is it an elemental?" she asked, seeming wary.

You must move from this spot. Quickly, Tijhi stated. The fox barked, a high pitch signal that could only be interpreted as an alarm, and turned south.

Why? What's wrong? Mylah asked the creature. But, even as she posed the question a distant rumble reverberated under their feet.

"What did that creature just say to you?" Luther asked, looking down at the ground, then out at the seemingly calm horizon. The hawk overhead cried again, causing Luther to jerk his gaze skyward. "Uh oh," Luther said.

"What the fuck is happening, Lieutenant?" Leviatha asked, eyes wide as she whipped her head around, searching for danger.

"Something's coming," Luther said. Mylah turned and followed a now-bounding Tijhi southward.

"Run!" she screamed over her shoulder to the other two. The ground rumbled, rattling Mylah's teeth and shattering her sensitive head. Her vision sparked in white splotches of nothingness as she pushed herself away from the coming creature.

The three Tyrmini had barely cleared the spot they occupied when the dry, even ground burst open, chunks of rock and clumped sand spraying over them. Mylah covered her head with her arms as she lunged forward, debris pelting her back.

The ground beneath her bucked. Her footing buckled and ground leaped up to meet her, shins and knees banging hard. She scrambled to her hands and knees, flipping over to crab crawl away and get a glimpse of their attacker. A creature of myth and legend, only spoken of in whispers by her people, used as a story to keep children in their tents at night. Mylah had dismissed it as fiction long ago, having never seen any sign of its existence.

The giant black creature, shiny scales muted in the near-evening light, opened its mouth wide, revealing a blood-red interior and four curved fangs, two on top and two on the bottom jaw. It hissed, and the noise it emitted made Mylah's guts shiver.

54

THE DRAGON'S FIRE

The creature stared at Mylah, locking her with a red gaze. The creature hissed once more, then turned toward Luther, who'd fallen several yards from Mylah.

It flew over the flat Tyrinth its many-segmented body hushing through the hard sand. Luther rolled to his back in time to see the creature's pronged tail strike with lightning speed. He rolled again, screeching, and narrowly avoiding the piercing blow. The creature reared back, hood flaring wide.

"Don't look at it!" Mylah screamed. "Don't look into its eyes. None of them!"

"Fuck!" Luther said, hiding his face from the onslaught of eyes now on display in front of him. "How'm I s'pose to see if it's about to strike again?"

Mylah scrambled to her feet, a wave of nausea threatening to overtake her. Her head wobbled and throbbed like one giant mass of hellfire. "There's a trick," she said, gritting her teeth against the pain. She dredged up the stories her mother had told her by the fire at night. She'd dismissed them so well in her youth, she wasn't sure she could recall the details. Except her mother had repeated the same rhyme so often, she hoped it'd made a lasting dent in her memory.

What was it she'd said?

If the Watcher watches, you must hide your eyes
When the Watcher watches, it knows your lies
And hisses twice to tell you so
Before its stinger seeks you out
It closes its eyes to swing about
When the Watcher strikes, it cannot see
Yes, when the Watcher stings, its tail you cleave
And take down the Watcher if you dare
But careful, careful, its blood won't spare
It burns, and singes, and rips through skin
It won't spare you, be you thick or thin

It's your bones it wants, and your bones it will get

Unless you are cleverer than it

But best to bed at sunset

When the Watcher prowls the Aestyrah

You'll be safe tucked in tight

And let the Watcher have its night

"Wait until it hisses twice!" Mylah shouted to Luther. "Then chop its tail. But be careful of the blood."

Leviatha was creeping up behind the creature. She crouched behind a cactus, a large sword in her hand. The Watcher hissed twice, closing its hood, lowering its head. Its golden eyes closed. "Now!" Mylah shouted. Leviatha and Luther both charged toward the tail from opposite directions. Their strikes were true. Luther swung his curved sword down on the tail's base where it segmented into the last section barbed with two long stingers.

Leviatha's aim was just above Luther's target. Her blade clanged against shielding scales like metal armor. Luther's cut sliced into the creature's body.

It screeched, thrashing wildly, ruby drops of blood spraying into the evening air. Luther jumped away, but Leviatha was not as quick. The watcher's body writhed, swung, and hit Leviatha squarely in the stomach. She lifted into the air and launched away from the Watcher. Her body sailed a yard before she collided with a cactus. She yelped, body flailing back before she slammed to the ground and toppled to her side.

Luther stood at the ready, watching the creature coil itself and rear back to face him again. "I got a good hit, but I didn't sever the thing," he said.

Tijhi ran for Luther, a streak of gold against the beige sands and muted green vegetation. The sun sank, the Goddess a semicircle of golden glory on the western horizon. Tijhi halted between Luther and the Watcher.

Tell him to hold. There is no need to attack this creature.

56

"Tijhi says don't attack," Mylah yelled at Luther.

"I'm not gonna stand and get skewered by it," Luther said.

"Just wait," she said. The Tijhi's tail swished, its head leaned forward, black nose sniffing the air, eyes locked onto the two eyes in the Watcher's head. Its hood remained closed. The Watcher hissed at the small creature, rearing back. Its hood fluttered on the verge of splaying open. Luther covered his face, bracing to block his view of those many eyes. Leviatha lay on the ground, arm wrapped over her middle.

The air around Tijhi flared, their dragon form shimmering to life in ethereal blue flames. Tijhi barked and a dragonish roar filled the desert night. The Watcher circled back on itself, backing away from the Tijhi. Then it lowered its head, all the while hissing, its red mouth gaping in an angry scream. It turned back again and again, keeping its gaze locked on Tijhi, lowering itself ever closer to the ground, until at last the black creature turned completely and slunk away into the oncoming night.

The fire extinguished around the Tijhi and they trotted back to Mylah. Leviatha at last hauled herself up to her feet and tenderly walked toward Luther. Luther met her, eying the Tijhi all the while. "What on Aelos was that creature so scared of? Little ol' fox?"

Mylah blinked. Had he not seen the giant rendering of a dragon in fire that had loomed around the little elemental?

He and the other cannot see or hear me as you do. You are my companion and can see my true form, as did the elemental. Mostly because I meant for the elemental to see me, as I mean for you to see me.

But, you don't mean for these two to see you? Mylah asked.

Tijhi sat on their haunches, and in answer, sneezed, their head shaking in a solid no gesture.

Leviatha turned her back to Luther. "Help me out, will you?" she said. Luther whistled low and slow before he reached for the first needle embedded in Leviatha's arm. The woman's back was luckily saved by her chest and back armor, but her exposed arm, all the way to her shoulder had been peppered by the cactus needles.

Luther gripped a needle and yanked. Leviatha yowled. Mylah considered not saying anything. Considered keeping to herself that there was a method for removing those particular cactus spines that would be less painful. As Luther extracted the second needle to Leviatha's scream of pain, Mylah decided to have pity.

"Stop," she said, sighing, annoyed at her own compassion. She walked gingerly toward the captain, her head still throbbing with each movement. "Let me show you," she said, resigning herself to help her captors. Luther shuffled out of the way, two needles still pinched in his fingers.

Mylah rubbed her hands together to warm them. "Let me see one of those," she said and held out her hand. Luther placed a needle into her waiting palm. Leviatha turned, hissing at the movement. Mylah held the spine up to the dying daylight. "These have a small barb in them. Look here," she said and pointed to the hooked flexible thorn at the end of needle.

Luther whistled.

"Those are in me?" Leviatha asked.

"That is why they hurt so much when you pull them out. Especially if you just yank them with all your might," she pointed an accusing glance at Luther.

Luther wrapped a hand over the back of his neck and cast an apologetic look through his eyebrows at Leviatha. "Apologies, Captain," he said.

Mylah turned the needle from one side to the other, pointing at each side as she said, "See how one side is slightly more brown than the other black side? That indicates which side the barb is tipped." She handed the needle back to Luther. "If you'll turn please," she asked Leviatha.

Leviatha obeyed, grunting at the pain.

"Watch," Mylah said to Luther. She chose a needle more

isolated from the others. "If you gently -," Mylah pressed in on the needle's base on the brown side and pulled, " - press and pull, it comes out with less pain." Leviatha hissed as the needle came free. "It's still not painless," Mylah noted.

"That was better than the first one, though," Leviatha grumbled. "Okay," she inhaled and exhaled, preparing herself for the continued extraction process. "Let's get to work on the others."

"Yes, Captain," Luther said. He tossed the two needles he held aside and raised his hands toward the collection peppering the captain's arms.

Luther looked back to Mylah, pausing. His eyes lingered in a way that sparked discomfort – a sort of bubbling intensity in her gut. She scowled and turned her attention back to the work in front of them. She flicked Luther another glance and he hadn't moved. She squared herself to him. "Help," she directed, her tone on edge, annoyance rubbing against raw nerves, and her head still a pounding mass of pain. Luther shook himself and turned to the captain's arm.

"Yes, ma'am," he said. He reached for a spine, then pulled his hand away. "You better show me one more time."

Mylah's annoyance grew. She extracted the spine she was working on first, then turned to Luther. "Find a needle," she instructed.

Luther pointed to a needle on Leviatha's shoulder, carefully not touching it. "That one," he said.

"Which side is lighter than the other?" Mylah asked.

Luther looked from her to the needle, surveyed first one side, then the other. "I -," he said. He moved his head back and forth, his body following as he examined the needle. "Maybe this side?" he asked, pointing. Mylah confirmed that was indeed the lighter side.

"Place your pointer finger gently on that side, close to the base." Luther followed her instruction. "Now press lightly toward me, put your thumb on the opposite side, and pull." She talked to him as if he were a bothersome child. Luther obeyed, and when the needle came out smoothly and Leviatha merely grunted, he looked at Mylah and grinned lopsidedly.

Mylah couldn't help the smile tugging at one corner of her mouth. That grin eased her annoyance. She straightened, dropped the smile and said, "Good. Now, help." She turned back to Leviatha's arm and they continued removing the spines until minutes later they'd all been removed.

It was dark when they finished. Tijhi lie curled next to a boulder, tail wrapped around them, concealing their face, large ears protruding above their body. Luther collected rocks and built a small fire pit. Mylah gathered scrubby dry brush and tumbleweeds. Once she'd piled them into the pit, Luther stood in front of it in a wide stance. He inhaled deeply, eyes fluttering closed, exhaled, and a flame sprang to life within the dead foliage's heart.

Mylah marveled. It was a small gesture, a small stroke of power. She'd never been able to exert so much control. Her power was big and destructive. To accomplish a focused task with a singular element of her Tyrmini magic seemed a huge feat.

"How did you -," she started. She shifted her gaze from the small flame dancing and cracking in the pit to find Luther grinning at her. She snapped her mouth closed, embarrassment washing over her. She looked back at the fire, closing herself off from the question she'd wanted to ask him.

"I'll show you," Luther told her. Mylah looked back up at him, and his grin had turned to an honest smile of encouragement. "After you've gotten a good night's rest and your head is healed up, I'll share what I've learned. All of it. I promise," he said.

Mylah wasn't sure why the man seemed so fervent in his commitment to her. It unnerved her and set her stomach churning with deep shame. She and Luther had to be close to the same age. Maybe he had a few years more on her. And yet, she could not summon a small flame. She could only call on the elements in her deepest rage and use it as a weapon against her enemies.

Mylah wrapped her arms around her stomach and stared into the fire, sitting with all that emotion that coated her soul in grime. Her actions from the day, the loss of an aunt who had hated her, welled up in front of her, threatening to overtake her. She rocked from her heels to her toes and wished she could undo what she'd done.

CHAPTER EIGHT

A dark smudge stained the horizon. The Goddess rose, but deep gray clouds marred her appearance. Even as Mylah watched, the storm ate away at the blue sky, and with it her composure. A cool wind swept over the sand, sending tumbleweeds rolling.

Lightning flashed, tracing blue lines across the storm clouds gathering on the distant horizon. Mylah counted to ten before the thunder cracked.

The noise flipped a switch in Mylah. In an instant, her heart galloped, chest aching, throat sore, head pulsing with the pressure from the frantic pounding of blood. Her cousin's visage sparked and faded across her mind's eye. Tiernan's determined face loomed in her memory, his eyebrows pinched as he stood between the strange, injured man and her.

Mylah closed her eyes, but the scene played out anyway. The stranger's fear and violent-streaked eyes fixed on her, her cousin stepping between them, arguing that it was he who'd drawn the elementals, that it only made sense because of his age. He'd been thirteen summers, that volatile time her people knew well as when Tyrmini came into their power.

Her cousin had argued with the stranger, warning him not to harm either of them. That they would turn him out into the desert sands and let the Goddess take her revenge.

It had all been true, and it wasn't enough to stop the man from gripping Tiernan by the upper arm and dragging him to the striking pole.

A hand touched Mylah's shoulder, and she whirled, yelping and jumping at the contact. Luther pulled his hands back into a surrender gesture. "I mean no harm, darlin'," he said.

"We have to get out of here. Low ground. We need a ravine or a ditch. And one deep enough so we won't drown from the rising rainwater," Mylah said, and pointed to a distant dark line crookedly marring the western horizon – a ravine she knew well.

Luther looked at the eastern horizon and the swell of black clouds that even in the few moments since she'd spotted them, had grown exponentially and boiled toward them.

Luther seemed to realize the shift in the morning energy, brought on by the sigh of wind. Everything stilled, a quiet settling into the desert morning with the held breath of anticipation. The sudden lack of skittering critters, birds flying overhead, and far-off animal cries pricked at Mylah's trained awareness. But this man who hailed from a city, what would he know?

"Doesn't look like much," Luther said, peering back to the gathering storm.

"It may not look like much now, but if you wait and see, you'll be left out in this wide-open space," Mylah opened her arms and gestured around to the expanse flat ground surrounding them, "as the highest point in a lightning storm."

As if called upon, lightning danced across the growing gray clouds. Mylah waited, counting, and steeled herself for the resounding crack and boom of thunder. She still jumped. The remaining blue sky overhead seemed to mock her fear.

"Hey," Luther said. He slowly reached for her and placed his palms gently on her shoulders. Her body quaked in a constant vibration of fear.

"You don't understand," she said. A more-insistent wind sprang up, whisking her words away from them. The sky grew darker, the smudge on the eastern horizon expanding. "We could die if we do not make ourselves smaller. The lightning is deadly."

Luther took a step closer. And then another, until he was so close Mylah thought she would drown in his proximity. She needed to run. She needed to get away from the storm. She pulled back and he gripped her tighter.

"Look, doll," he said. "I'm going to need you to take a nice, long, slow breath."

Mylah hadn't realized how rapidly she was breathing. She tried to obey but couldn't make her lungs slow down. "We have to go!" she shouted at him and struggled against his grip.

"We will. We will," he assured her. "We will. But, to make it fast and safe, we must control ourselves, okay, darlin'? Otherwise, we might trip and fall or miss an opportunity for shelter because we're seeing, not thinking clearly. Does that make sense?"

Mylah shivered as she looked overhead, blue chinks rapidly shrinking as darkness consumed the sky.

"What's your favorite color, Mylah?" Luther asked.

"What? Why does that matter right now?" Mylah's nerves raged in need of escape.

"Answer the question, sweetheart. I promise you're gonna be safe."

Mylah still quivered but thought. "Red, gold, orange, the colors fire," she said quickly.

"Good, good," Luther encouraged. "That's good. Now, what's the name of your people?"

She fought the rising panic, but the intensity lessened. "We are the Goddess's people, we are Aestyrians."

"What's so great about this Goddess of yours?" he asked, in a soothing, soft tone.

Mylah inhaled deeply, a big rattling breath. She exhaled it. "The Goddess blesses us with warmth and light."

"Good," he said. "What else?"

"She provides for us, shines light on food sources and shelter."

Luther nodded, releasing his grip on Mylah enough that the touch warmed and assured her, rather than gripped her.

"Now, look at your feet," he said. "What do you see about them?"

Mylah looked down at her feet. They were brown, coated in sand, a silver ring around one of her toes glinted dully in the weak, gray light. She inhaled again, exhaling deeply.

"Good. How about your legs?"

She looked at her legs, both wrapped in white linen strips to reflect the Goddess's intense gaze. Noting the linen, she could feel the fabric against her skin, dry, a little scratchy, loose since she hadn't re-wrapped them yet for the day.

"Now, look at me, doll," Luther said. "What color are my eyes?"

"They're brown, with bits of red and gold," she said. She breathed evenly, her heart slowed, the pain in her jaw and neck subsided. She watched his eyes, clear, beautifully big, framed in black curled lashes.

"Feeling better?" he asked, and stepped back from her, opening the space between them.

She inhaled deeply again and nodded. A soft prick on her face caused her to look up. All blue was gone. Another gentle drop of rain splashed innocently on her exposed arm. Luther shook her arm, just enough to draw her attention. She swiveled her gaze back to him.

"Now, we're going to head in the direction you've pointed out, because you are the native to this land, and we are not."

Mylah blinked, seeing Leviatha standing nearby, watching the sky with a grim sea-blue stare, her golden plait coiled around her neck like a kerchief. It was only then Mylah realized both Luther and Leviatha wore metal armor. Luther's voice snapped in her ear.

"What do we need to do to get out of this storm? Start from the first thing we should do," he instructed.

"First," Mylah said, and dragged a breath in through her nose and let it escape from her mouth. "First, you need to remove the metal." She took a hand and gently knocked against Luther's breast plate. "This is an invitation to the Goddess's wrath."

Luther nodded grimly, turned to Leviatha who also nodded. Their helmets were already off, having slept without them on. Leviatha and Luther gathered. Leviatha turned to her side and Luther began untying thick leather strands.

The occasional drops turned into an insistent patter. Mylah hurried over to Luther and began copying his movements. At first, he glanced over his shoulder, seemingly startled, but let Mylah proceed. She matched his pace without trouble, and as Leviatha rotated to allow Luther to untie the other side, Mylah made her way around Luther, untying the opposite side. As her fingers moved, she looked toward the eastern horizon, gaging how close the storm's speed. They did not have long.

Before she looked back the ties were loosened. Leviatha bent, proffering the top of the armor. Luther grabbed at the metal encasing and pulled. Leviatha wiggled out of the armor. Luther dropped the armor with a solid thunk as Leviatha emerged, her muscled body clad in a sheer linen sheathe. Leviatha reached for Luther's armor. He mirrored her movements and grunted against protective gear, wriggling awkwardly.

Mylah joined Leviatha and pulled at one shoulder pad. She moved both hands to the opposite side and they yanked. Luther yowled. "Try to keep me in one piece, will ya?" his voice was a muffled, but alarmed growl. Mylah couldn't help a manic bubble of laughter that burst from her mouth, even as she eased her pull on the man's armor. In the distance, a low rumble echoed across the Aestyrah.

"Exhale and slide, man!" Leviatha ordered.

"My muscles are bigger than yours! This isn't easy," he groused.

"Don't be a baby," Leviatha countered.

Mylah's giggle made her eyes stream.

"Now you're laughing? This is serious! Help me out!" His arms stuck half out of the arm holes, his head nearly all the way inside the armor. Mylah stopped heaving and stepped back. Overhead the sky had fully darkened.

"Take the front end, I'll get the back end," she said to Leviatha, who only nodded and took both shoulder pads in her strong hands. Mylah rounded Luther and gripped his hips. She looked at Leviatha. "Ready?"

"Hey, wait. What're y'all -," Luther started, but didn't finish.

Mylah shouted, "Pull!" They yanked in opposite directions, Leviatha pulling at the metal encasing Luther's upper half, and Mylah pulling at Luther's hips. He squealed, his arms popping through the armor. His feet shuffled back, scrambling to maintain purchase. Mylah tried staying upright, but there were too many feet in too small of a space. Momentum shoved her and Luther backward. Mylah still had a hold of his hips. She landed hard on the ground, breath exploding out of her as Luther's backside punched squarely in Mylah's stomach.

Luther rolled off her as she fought to make her abdomen release its tight grip. He groaned but immediately rose to his feet. He held out a hand for Mylah, who gripped it and was hauled up. Seeing stars, her muscles relaxed and she took a mighty breath in, using the air to shout, "Run!" and pointed to the ravine dropping away on the western horizon.

They pelted across the hardened sand, past cactuses and low shrubby bushes. Her hair rose on her arms and legs. "Oh, no," she said. Mylah's heart raced, panic stole through her, fueling her legs to move her faster toward safety. Memories cascaded through her vision, replacing the current landscape with the vista of that long-distant past.

In her mind's eye, the stranger strapped her cousin to the tall, metal pole. Rain cascaded around them, drumming in their ears, drowning out her words. Mylah shouted, screaming at the man to let her cousin go. The small elemental creatures they'd played with surrounded the clearing's edge, little more than mounds rising above the desert floor, dark eyes fixed on Mylah and her cousin. The stranger's eyes – Belfys had been his name – reflected storms of their own, enraged, in fear.

Mylah grabbed at Belfys's arm, yanked with all her might, but he remained immovable. She scratched his arms, lines of red appearing beneath her fingers, and when that did nothing, she opened her mouth wide and chomped down, hard enough blood spilled into her mouth, its coppery tang startling her. She growled like an animal, fighting for her cousin's life.

Belfys screamed and flung her. She stayed latched to him. She bit down harder. He raised a fist. Her father's face appeared, and hope had swelled in her. He grabbed the man's raised arm and yanked. The glint of a knife flashed from seemingly nowhere, and then her father had stumbled back as blood blossomed on his linen shirt.

Her mother's shriek was drowned by the crack of thunder. She rushed toward her husband who motioned toward Tiernan. "Hurry," he said, breath heaving.

Belfys followed. "No, you don't," he yelled, but her mother was faster. She skidded up to the pole, nimble fingers working at the knot. Belfys fell upon her, shouting in a rage, twisting her arms behind her as she screamed

A solid blue pillar erupted around the striking pole, encompassing her cousin, Belfys and her mother. The impact threw Mylah backward in a spray of sand and rocks.

The rest she could not remember. She'd woken in her bed, her aunt knelt nearby, wailing. She'd never heard such a cry before, and try as she might, that scream of loss and agony would forever ring in her mind. It was what she heard every time her aunt had looked at her, spoke to her, and now that would be what she heard whenever she remembered her family.

The ravine drew near, and Mylah's anxiety eased a fraction; safety was within sight. Rain poured down on them in thick, heavy drops. A resounding crack filled the air, blue light illuminating the space behind them. Leviatha screamed, but it was cut short by the immediate boom of thunder. The ground shook beneath them, jolting Mylah's steps out of rhythm. She cast a look behind her. Luther ran, seemingly unperturbed by the sudden lightning strike. Leviatha caught up to Luther within a few strides. Mylah led the pack, and as another bolt of lightning found purchase, they flung themselves forward, pushing their bodies with everything they had.

Mylah cleared the ravine's edge first, jumping into the open space and sliding down the gently sloping wall of dirt and rocks. She clawed into the ground to slow her descent. Luther and Leviatha jumped past Mylah. They clung to the ravine wall, its bottom far below already filling with rainwater. Wind thrashed over them, spraying sand into their faces. Rain poured down, giant thick gray clouds roiling overhead. Mylah covered her head and prayed to the Goddess that they would survive.

Lightning sizzled across the sky, splitting the clouds, illuminating the deep steely gray with wicked blue light. Thunder cracked around them in staccato percussions. Mylah clapped her hands over her ears, swearing she could hear her aunt's wailing cries of mourning echoing in the storm around them.

Warmth slipped around her shoulders, and it was only then she realized she'd been shivering. She opened her eyes to find Luther closed in around her, arm gripped around her upper body. Startled, she froze, looking up at him. His gaze was fixed to the sky, determination hardening his features. She wanted to wriggle away, but the warmth of his body slowed her shivering. She stayed put.

Rainwater rose in the ravine below as sheets of water washed over the desert terrain. Mylah's muscles shivered, her calves, thighs, and core burning from the effort to hold herself in place against the sloping ravine wall. She monitored the sky then the ravine, as the precipitation gathered, swelled, and sluiced in growing stream below them. The water rose at an alarming speed and when it had reached a mere feet away, new panic gripped her.

The thunderstorm rolled on, and they watched from the perch in the ravine as lightning found a mesa, striking it over and over. Water lapped against Mylah's feet, hardened sand becoming mud and disintegrating under her hold. She dug in deeper, struggling with wet fingers and sandled toes to maintain her tentative safety amidst the storm. Her foot slipped, and Luther gripped her tighter.

"Rain's lightening up," he said. "You think it's safe now?"

Mylah peered into the sky. The dark clouds marched westward, the storm smaller and smaller as it emptied its watery contents.

The clouds lightened, the wind slowed, and the thunder receded into the (missing a word) like a lost memory.

Luther pulled away, scrambling up the ravine. Mylah followed suit, hauling her body over the muddy ledge and standing.

Leviatha heaved herself over the ledge. Mylah extended a hand, which Leviatha took with mumbled gratitude. Mylah pulled the woman over the bank, steadying herself against the now-slippery desert ground.

Every stitch of Mylah's linen clung to her body, her sandals squishy and slippery. She squeezed the hem of her light sheath skirting her thighs, ringing the worst of the water from the garment.

She and Leviatha reached simultaneously for their hair, pulling at the strands now drenched in rainwater. Mylah's panic evaporated with the retreating storm, and as her emotions balanced back to normal, embarrassment flooded her.

Luther stalked toward the spot where they'd dumped their armor, seeming to ignore her intense reaction to the storm.

Mylah clenched and unclenched her hands, restrained the urge to twist them into her linen skirt and followed Luther, Leviatha on her heels. They passed over the wet Tyrinth in silence.

Mylah breathed in a long, slow, deep breath, inhaling the rain-soaked desert fragrance. The vegetation gleamed with new color, having been washed clean with the rain's drenching. The sage greens were greener, the browns deeper, the reds brighter. Weak golden rays cast light through evaporating clouds. Mylah knew the cover would burn off before the sun had passed another hand's width.

Luther and Leviatha donned their armor, helping each other with the bindings and they began their sodden journey. The terrain passed swiftly, Mylah's heart an aching thing in her chest.

They would travel across the Aestyrah for two more days before they reached the road. She had been to the road many times, trading goods, discreetly passing Tsheyduni stone to teenagers with budding Tyrmini gifts. The path they followed was well-worn. The wrongness of traveling with these people instead of her own community filled her with twisting unease.

Each passing step drew her closer to her enemy. And yet those steps and the growing distance away from her people guaranteed their safety. So she plodded forward, further into exodus, and into the service of the High King.

CHAPTER NINE

Mylah woke early. She sat with her legs curled into her body, arms wrapped around them, chin resting on her knees. She faced south and rocked herself as the sky blushed with the Goddess's arrival, comforted by the saw and huff of Luther's snoring.

To her right, the Inilu tree line rose above the tops of mesas, a collection of black, scrubby spears against the sky. The Inilu. A forest of giant trees Mylah had never ventured into, and for good reason.

Mylah hummed. Tijhi appeared at her side, the golden fox peering into the horizon with Mylah. Mylah turned her head, facing Tijhi and the forest looming to the west. Tijhi shifted from foot to foot, their golden gaze flicked from the Inilu to Mylah.

How I would love to see the Inilu once more, Tijhi said.

When was the last time you were there? Mylah asked.

The Inilu and I were fast friends before my slumber.

You speak of it as though it's a person.

Indeed. I do miss them. Tijhi sighed as they gazed at the dark tree line.

Mylah puzzled over the words, the stories of her people welling up within her. The Inilu was a place of great peril, with many elementals and a race of people so intrinsically enmeshed in the Magys magic system that when the High King captured and enslaved the Light dragon, the race of people hadn't survived. Something had survived, though. What exactly that something was remained a mystery, however It (Mylah always capitalized the word mentally) had protected the Inilu with a vengeance so intense, the Aestyrians dared not venture there.

Today will be the day, she told the fox. *We travel west and south.*

Perhaps I will stop in and say, hello, the dragon said.

Mylah watched the tree line and imagined It swelled and deflated, as if taking a breath. She rocked, leaning her chin on her knees as she continued to hum. Tijhi picked up the melody to match her harmony. A song of mourning.

Mylah's heart ached. Today, she would leave her homeland behind. And with it, any ability to properly mourn her aunt, once and for all.

Not for her death. No, she'd lost her years ago when her parents and cousin died. Because she was still living then, she'd never been able to mourn her. Mylah's aunt had been cruel, she realized. She didn't blame her. Mylah had been the cause of her cousin's death. The Goddess rose and set thousands of times and still her heart ached for his loss, the guilt solidly amassed within her core. Try as she might, there never seemed to be action enough to erase that mistake.

She hummed as the Goddess crept higher, brightening the eastern horizon. Mylah sensed Luther's presence before she heard him. The mourning song dried up in her throat. She unwound herself, straightening her spine, changing her position to cross-legged. Luther dropped down by her side, copying her position.

"Don't stop, on account of me, doll," Luther said, his voice gravelly with sleep. He yawned and stretched his arms over his head before letting them rest on his knees.

Mylah maintained her silence.

Luther pointed. "We'll pick up the road this morning and follow it south, then 'round the Inilu's southern border. Should be there in a couple more days."

Mylah inhaled and exhaled quietly. "So, you do not enter the forest either?" she asked.

"Oh no," he said, shaking his head. "Too dangerous. Been like that as long as people can recall."

"What poses such great danger to mighty Tyrmini guards?" Mylah asked, sarcasm lacing her words.

"Not sure, to be honest," he said, not noticing the tone. He rubbed at his nose, yawning again before continuing. "Some say it's the forest itself, others say it's a giant elemental." He cast a glance conspiratorially her way, waving a hand toward the monstrous trees ahead. "And there's some that believe it's a magic wielder."

"You have never been into the forest?"

"Nah," he said, drawing out the word. "No reason. The High King says, 'stay out of the forest', so that's what we do."

"And you do all the things the High King orders you to do?" she asked, the undertone of her words cutting through to the heart of the issue: you kill children.

Luther's body shifted the barest amount, straightening, his head twitching, blinking before his face settled into something hard and flat. "I do. And you best too," he said. He rose to his feet and extended a hand to Mylah. She stared up at him. "C'mon. We've got a ways to go still."

Mylah pushed herself to stand without his aid. He dropped his hand to his side, staring intently before turning away, that same flat, hard expression sealed on his handsome face.

Mylah turned to watch him go and found Leviatha watching from her bedroll. There was impassive observation on her face and Mylah couldn't assess what it meant. If she were the captain, she could only guess how many Tyrmini - how many youth - she'd executed to reach that position. Mylah fought the disgust rising within her and turned back to the horizon, then to Tijhi. The little fox peered up at her with their golden eyes, black marks running like tear tracks down their snout.

Be strong, Mylah, Tijhi said. Mylah ground her teeth as her unease swelled. Be strong. But, for what?

The company packed up camp and set off at a clipped pace. Mylah fell in line to the rhythmic clanking of the Tyrmini Guards' armor. By noon they turned south on the road, the giant trees of the Inilu towering over them. Tijhi disappeared into the tree line, a glimmer of white and gold wings stretching to either side of their gold body. Mylah hoped the dragon had the opportunity to say hello to whatever friend in the forest they'd been missing.

The day's travel ended after turning west around the skirting southern border of the Inilu. As they made camp, Mylah peered into the forest, imagining flitting light zooming through the tree trunks, and a distant sound like laughter. She turned to Leviatha, since Luther seemed to be avoiding her after their morning conversation. "You sure it's safe to camp here?"

"No," the woman said resolutely. "So, stay out of the forest and try not to piss off whatever ancient curse haunts this place."

"And how does one do that?" Mylah said.

Leviatha dropped the bedroll she'd been unwinding and stomped past the firepit Luther constructed. She gripped Mylah under the arm, over the linen wrappings soiled with rain, sand, and sweat, and hauled her over the width of the road. Mylah dug in her heels, but Leviatha's hold won out and Mylah yanked forward despite her obstinance.

When they'd walked off the opposite side of the road, rocky shoulder sloping down toward mossy Tyrinth, Leviatha pointed to the ground. "Do you see that?"

One foot's length from where they stood a subtle but perceivable dusty red line marched in both directions, hugging the forest's edge.

"What is it?" Mylah asked.

"It's some sort of trip wire."

Mylah yanked her arm hard out of Leviatha's grip and backed

away from the irregular line. Leviatha stared at her, chin jutting up, eyes sharp, as if she considered how much offense to take. "And what does this line trigger?" Mylah asked, crossing her arms over her torso.

"If you step over this line, if you trespass, a demon of foliage and plant material will appear and it will have no mercy as it slowly kills you," Leviatha said.

Mylah laughed. "Right," she said.

Leviatha cocked her head. "You're quite valuable to the High King, and I will suffer if I don't bring you back." She lunged forward, her knife appearing in a flash of polished steel. "But, if you put one sandal close to this line, I'll cut your ankle tendons so your calf muscles roll up behind your knees. Then I'll have Luther cauterize the wounds so they won't heal properly. And I'll drag your ass to the High King and say I did my best but you were insubordinate to my commands. Punishing you is completely within my right."

Leviatha turned the knife so it glinted in the day's dying light. She stared into Mylah's eyes, craze shimmering in the sea-blue gaze. "Do not threaten what I've earned."

The Tyrinth beneath them trembled, heat rising within Mylah. Everything in her wanted to rebel, to run into the forest and leave her chances to whatever lie within. To hell with this woman and her threats. Goddess blaze the High King and his hold over her people. Flame licked up the center of her body, stoking her anger. Her hands dropped to her sides, fisting, readying for a fight.

A warm nimbus expanded around her, but Leviatha didn't budge.

"Get back to the camp," she ordered, "and get your temper in check."

Mylah wanted to do no such thing. She shifted back. She'd never thrown a punch before, but she imagined how good it would feel for her knuckles to slam into this woman's face.

"Whoa, whoa, whoa, now," Luther's voice precursed his arms wrapping her shoulders as she bared her teeth at Leviatha, a growl slipping through her clenched jaws.

"Take her back and calm her down," Leviatha said. "Before I kick her ass."

Luther lifted and dragged Mylah from the spot, even as she fought against his hold.

"Pickin' a fight with the wrong person, sweetheart. You're not nearly where you'd need to be to go toe-to-toe with Leviatha," Luther stated. He grunted as he hauled her back over the road and to the fire pit he'd built. He slammed her to the ground. She yelped in fury and pain as his iron-strong legs wrapped around her lower half in a grip she had no hope of breaking.

"Calm down," he shouted, to which she screamed and growled like a caught animal.

"Get off of me!" she yelled.

"Not 'til you get settled. You can't go after her, you fool. Are you crazy? Are you stupid?" his voice in her ear.

Mylah thrashed against his hold, thrusting an elbow into his ribs.

"That all you got?" he said. "And you wanna pick a fight with the captain of the Tyrmini Guard? You still haven't recovered from that knock on the head I gave you. She would obliterate you, or did you not see how easy it was for her to combat your fire power with her water? Hm?"

"I don't care!" Mylah shouted. "Let her kill me. Let her end me."

"Oh so you're feelin' self-destructive," Luther said. "Tell me, doll, do you think the High King will spare your people if you're dead?"

Mylah's thrashing slowed.

"Give him any reason at all and he'll go after them. Ask me how I know," he said.

"Why?" Mylah asked, not following Luther's command. She wriggled but it was half-hearted.

"Because he can," he spat. "It delights him. And your people have proven troublesome. You are the only reason they're still living."

Mylah went limp, her head slowly shaking. Tears sprang and streamed, emotion rocking through her until she sobbed, then screamed into the evening air. Luther still pinned her arms but loosened his grip on her legs. Mylah took it as an invitation and broke free from him, scrambling away. She perched on dusty patch opposite the fire pit from Luther, curling herself around her folded legs, head tucked into her crossed arms, and wept.

The scuff of boots in the dirt, cracking wood, and finally the whoosh of igniting fire filled the air. Mylah turned away from the flames, lay on the ground, curled tightly into herself, and let sleep take her.

The next morning, she woke stiff and sore, her head aching, and her insides hollow, both from lack of food and her emotional outburst. They packed up and set on the road before the Goddess had fully appeared. The forest loomed to their right as they traveled west. Mylah noted the ruddy red line along the border of the forest, marching away as they went, without a gap in sight.

The morning air snapped with chill. Mylah trudged along behind Luther and Leviatha, arms wrapped over herself in an attempt to get warm. Leviatha handed Mylah a water skin, heavy with fullness. Mylah snatched it from her, scowling, but drank deeply when Levitha turned away with a tsk and an eye roll.

They traveled all day and arrived in Udari City as the sun hung high in the sky. Despite the Goddess's face shining openly above them, the day remained cool. Mylah shivered, wishing for another layer of clothing.

Leviatha and Luther marched confidently down a main thoroughfare, past shops and bustling people. Mylah observed different clothing and skin colors, and relief swept over her at her own light attire, made to survive the heat of her homeland.

Mylah followed the Tyrmini Guards closely, noting the barely concealed sneer of some, and the utter fascination of others. Most people gave the two a wide berth, parting the crowd to allow them an unhindered path forward. One man in a plain tunic and trousers, a simple vest hanging open around a generous belly called from the front of a building.

"On the king's business?" the man inquired, his voice a tinny whine. "What's it this time, Captain?"

Mylah closed in tight to Luther and Leviatha, hoping to conceal herself from the curious man.

"New recruit," Leviatha told the man. She turned, and the man's hungry gaze gobbled Mylah's appearance. She wanted to hide, to not exist.

"What's she in for?" the man asked, this time turning to Luther.

"Fire for sure. We'll know more soon," Luther said. Mylah noted the easy way the guards spoke to what she assumed to be a shop owner. Mylah took in the building. The sign on it read, "Tavern," in the common language. Barkeep, she corrected herself mentally.

"Another fire breather? Well, look at that. Got yourself a friend, haven't you?" the man said.

Luther chuckled. "Not sure how friendly she is, this one."

The barkeep turned to Mylah and fixed her with a serious gaze. "Listen here, girl. Our King's a good man, protects us all. He says you're worth savin', that's what you are. You've struck gold gettin' to come serve him. And we're awful grateful for your service. Welcome to Udari City, love."

Mylah ducked her chin in acknowledgment, head spinning with the man's words. They appreciated the king, revered him. She couldn't fathom it, and she didn't have the words handy to say anything intelligent.

"Speaking of his majesty, we're heading there now," Leviatha said. "Forgive us for not staying to chat."

"Off you go," the man said and made a shooing gesture. "Tell his majesty I say hello."

Leviatha and Luther walked on, Mylah scurrying to keep up, Tijhi on her heels. Leviatha waved a hand behind her at the man as they strode away.

"And tell him to stop in soon," the man called after them.

The street teemed with color, noise, and smells. After they passed through a row of buildings that seemed to be city people's dwellings, they turned sharply right and into a sprawling market.

Vendors at individual stalls displayed their wares. Mylah passed a man cooking atop a large circular flat surface, the grill sizzling, heat waves dancing as the man shifted bits of vegetables and meat around. He scooped the food with a large knife into a bowl and handed the dish to a patron. The patron, a young woman in a beautiful full dress, hair capped in a bow-tightened bonnet, took the food and proffered the man a coin with a gloved hand.

A woman on the opposite side stood next to a cart overfilled with blooms and plants in every color Mylah could imagine. The seller cried out, "Flowers! Brighten your home, cheer up your misses, bring a smile to your mum's face! Flowers!"

Another vendor displayed works of leather. One next to that proffered meat pies. Mylah's stomach growled and she leaned into the warm, meaty scent. Luther gently pulled her away. "Not that one," he whispered into her ear. "They use stray cats and dogs." He pointed a glance in Tijhi's direction.

Mylah paused in the walkway, bent, and scooped the creature into her arms, passing the woman at the stall, eyes locked on her. The woman eyed Tijhi, licking her lips, and shuffling forward. Mylah wrapped her arms tighter around the fox. Tijhi leaned toward the woman, growled and barked. The woman merely smiled, taking one more step toward them. Mylah hurried on.

"Don't you worry," Luther said, "Sybille'll make sure you're eating right. To your heart's content."

"Sybille?" Mylah asked.

"You'll see," he said. He and Leviatha smiled at each other. Mylah thought the smile they shared was a warm thing, a cherished secret between them that lit up their features and shone in their eyes. Mylah puzzled on this, but soon they passed through another gate with guards in gold and black looking down from the battlements overhead with distrust and a healthy amount of fear on their faces.

"Nearly there," Luther said.

They passed through one more gate, the stone portcullis raised, metal teeth rimming the upper opening like a mouth ready to bite. Towers rose on both sides, windows facing the town below. Guards stood stationed at the openings behind mounted crossbows pointing into the space below.

Spacious, verdant grounds stretched before them. Mylah sucked in a breath of shock at the abundant plant life rolling up to impressive castle walls in tidy rows. Aromas of herbs and flowers, the buzz of flitting bees, and the flap of bird wings filled her senses.

People in plain tunics and overalls, or dresses covered in aprons, tended the budding plants. Many of them looked their way as Mylah, Luther, and Leviatha marched up the main rock-covered path, faces impassive, before turning back to their work.

The building ahead loomed large, the biggest Mylah had ever seen, which wasn't saying a lot since she was unaccustomed to any sort of permanent building. Her people shifted and swayed with the desert sands. The castle before her was a stone monstrosity, gray walls reaching to the Goddess herself, black and gold pennants snapping in the wind.

The building's front seemed like a slightly different stone, or maybe it was older material, than the wings to the left and right. The lower floors as well appeared newer than this main entrance, which had more cracks and crumbling mortar, the stone's face less polished than the building's other parts.

Mylah placed a foot on the first of a set of shallow stone steps and paused. Before her, the castle entrance towered, oak doors and iron fastenings glaring down. Mylah hugged the Tijhi, soaking in their warmth one more time before she set them on the ground.

"I don't think you'll be welcomed inside," Mylah told the creature. Tijhi cocked their head to one side then the other, yipped and trotted away, into the green castle grounds. *Find me later?* She called after them.

I'll be here, Tijhi said without turning back.

Luther and Leviatha were at the doors, which groaned open under the insistent push of two servants. Mylah cast one more glance at the Goddess, silently praying for whatever grace she could spare. She rolled her shoulders back, straightened her spine, and walked into the High King's castle.

The castle entry's high ceilings boasted a twinkling chandelier, walls lined with portraits, and ornate furniture dotting an open tile floor. Mylah had never seen anything of the sort. Before she could fully take it all in, they whisked down a wide corridor that jogged left then right then left again. They halted at a set of ornately carved white doors, flanked by two guards. The guard on the left, a woman, waved a gloved hand at Leviatha, looking bored as the Captain of the Tyrmini guard pushed the right door open.

Mylah shuffled in behind her two captives, wanting nothing more than to disappear into Luther's shadow.

They stood in a long, rectangular room, white marble pillars stationed evenly along both sides of the room. Situated along the walls were chaises and chairs, some with ornate pillows. Lamps lined the walls as well, and sunlight leaked in through an array of tall windows. Mylah looked beneath her sandaled feet to find the floor covered in an ornate rug, vibrant with a rich array of color. She could get lost in the swirling patterns, the stitching finer than any painter's brush.

"You've arrived at last," a voice drawled, a pleasant smile in the voice. At the room's opposite end, a dais boasted a giant chair, opulently decorated in jewels and inlaid with streams of gold and silver.

Atop the monstrosity sat a young man who couldn't be much older than Mylah. He wore an ebony tailcoat, a swirling pattern of black and gold embroidered over the breasts. Under his coat, he wore a matching vest with shining gold buttons, and a pristinely white dress shirt buttoned nearly to his jawline. One gloved hand propped under his jaw, a silver and black bracelet dangling over the edge of his shirt cuff. He stared down at a book sprawled open across his lap. He turned a page gingerly. It looked ancient, the paper yellow, the sound of its turning brittle.

The High King looked up to peer down at Mylah. Deep sapphire eyes snared her. And yet for all their beauty, there was somehow flatness to the stare. Atop his golden hair sat a gold crown encrusted in black stones.

A warm hand wrapped around Mylah's upper arm. Mylah turned. Luther was looking at her from a bowed position. "Bow," he murmured. She turned back to the king, his blue eyes still on her, a spark sizzling down her spine. She bent at the waist as the hair on the nape of her neck rose. Luther's hand fell from her arm. Mylah took that as a signal to stand straight.

Leviatha moved ahead of them and knelt, her helmet tucked under her arm. "We've returned with her, your Majesty. We lost two guards in the effort."

"You really should have trained them better, Captain," the High King said, his voice echoing casual disappointment. "Luther?"

"Yes, Majesty," Luther intoned, his voice warm and low.

"I want you to take this one on," he said, gesturing to Mylah with a lazy wave of his hand.

Leviatha made a small noise, surprise lighting her features. The king ignored her.

"Get a good night's rest and get to it in the morning." The king paused before turning his sapphire gaze to Mylah. "You now have the burden of making up for the two guards you killed. I do hope you're up to the task. It would be a shame if the scraps of your once-mighty people were completely wiped out."

He stared at her, cold and distant, ire dancing behind the mask of calm beauty. Mylah ground her teeth to one side, fought the welling anger building in the pit of her gut, and rather than open her mouth and potentially say something her people would regret, nodded once.

The High King turned back to the book in his lap and waved them away. Leviatha rose and turned, her features pinched and stern. When she reached Mylah and Luther, they turned and joined her, making for the exit.

"Luther?" the king asked. Luther stopped. Mylah did too, turning back to face the monarch. "Stay a moment, please."

"Yes, Majesty," Luther said, a question on his voice. He recovered quickly and turned to Mylah, "I'll see you in the morning," he whispered. Mylah nodded and followed Leviatha out of the throne room, leaving Luther behind.

CHAPTER TEN

Mylah faced Luther across the training ring. Her heart raced. Last time she'd unleashed her power she'd killed two people. She shuddered at the thought. That she had so much power and so much anger she could wield it without thought of the regret she would have later.

The Goddess shone weakly through a blanket of clouds. A breezy chill swept through the air, so unlike her desert home. The clouds, cold, and moisture soaked into Mylah's bones and made her soft and ineffectual.

Mylah plucked at her clothing as she took in her surroundings. The leathers scratched against her skin, pinched her inner thighs, and bit into her waist. The boots she'd been provided squeezed her feet mercilessly. The only semi-comfortable article of clothing was the tunic which draped lightly over her shoulders. She'd left the top few buttons open, exposing the golden skin at her neck, unwilling to choke herself with the closures.

The training ring had been built outside the castle's walls to keep people safe from the volatility of elemental magic being unleashed. The land had been cultivated to provide differing terrain to train in. A large copse of trees occupied the northeast, a lake on the southwest side, open prairie to the northwest, and here where they trained, an expanse of sand devoid of vegetation. A water-filled ditch circumvented the sandy pitch. A water and Tyrinth Tyrmini - Luther had told her – stood stationed near the ditch, prepared to douse any fires that raged out of control. The Tyrmini on duty, a man in the prime of his years, muscled in a lithe way, eyed Mylah warily. Mylah guessed he'd heard about her capture and how it had ended for many of his colleagues.

Luther closed the space between them. He wore similar clothes to her own, basic leathers skimming his muscled lower half, and a linen shirt, buttoned just to his chest, muscles rippling beneath. On his left breast a pin glistened in the sun, a golden circle divided into four quarters, four different gems winking at her.

As he approached, Mylah caught his scent, warm and spicy like cinnamon and vanilla. During their journey to the High King's castle, there had been no available water for bathing, but more than the accumulated sweat and grime, the armor's odor overwhelmed all other scents.

"Did you rest well last night?" he asked.

Mylah stared at him for a moment, considering what her answer would be. She'd hardly slept. The bed was too soft and the thick walls around her made her claustrophobic. She'd tossed and turned, paced the length of her bedroom, and finally walked through several exercises to try and wear herself out. She shook her head. There was no point in lying. She was sure the evidence hung under her eyes.

"There's an adjustment period," Luther said. "The training should help."

Mylah nodded, although her nerves jangled.

"Today, we're going to focus on grounding," he said. "But, first, I've been instructed to test your elements." Luther pulled something from a belted pouch slung around his hips. The object was sleeved in leather. As he cupped it in both hands, soft whirring and clicks emanated from it. Mylah leaned in.

Luther reverently pulled the object from its wrapping, holding it in one hand while he stowed the leather back into his belted pouch.

THE DRAGON'S FIRE

Mylah had never seen anything so beautiful. The circular device gleamed in a bright opalescent, as if it shone with its own internal light. The surface shimmered, revealing every color of a rainbow in broken, scattered pieces. The object's face overlaid the mysterious base material, crafted of some fine metal which formed an ornate circle, split into four sections. There were two inner circles that met to form an endless overlapping loop. These were an empty silver.

From the middle circle four hands whirred, as if in orbit. Carvings on each hand glowed with unique colors: red, orange, gold, and blue. As Mylah watched, she realized the hands were on their own level of metal, overlapping one another as they raced around the circle.

Luther held the object until the hands slowed, ticking into their final resting place in the center of each quadrant. As the final hand snicked into place, the four quadrants began to fill with color. Bright, life-giving red filled the lower-left quadrant. Rich, warm gold filled two-thirds of the lower-right, while an even smaller amount of orange appeared in the upper-left. The upper-right section remained empty while the corresponding hand pulsed blue. The two silver pools, an upper and a lower, which formed the overlapping loop, remained empty.

Along the outer perimeter, symbols marked each quadrant. Mylah recognized one: the Tijhi's symbol. Mylah had a guess then what the four quadrants symbolized. "These represent the four major elements?" she asked.

"This is an ancient tool they used," he paused, looking around. The Tyrmini standing guard near the water-filled ditch stared off into the distance, eyes glazed over. Seeming comforted by this, Luther continued. "They used these before the the Achylas overthrew the Magyses - history that is now outlawed. This is a tool to identify the amounts of each element that comprise our individual magic. See?" he lifted the device higher to Mylah.

"This red is Tyrinth. My magic's primary source is land-based. That second largest color is gold, which represents fire. Then, I have a little bit of water, represented by the orange, and I have zero - not one stitch - of air element."

"And these two silver parts?" Mylah asked.

"Nobody knows anymore. But, what we do know is this opal-looking part that makes up the base as it were..." He lowered his voice to a barely audible whisper. Mylah leaned in to catch his next quiet words. "That's fashioned from two scales of the light dragon."

Mylah snapped her head up. From his wide-eyed expression Mylah could tell he was both excited and scared to be sharing this huge secret with her. "Magloryn? The imprisoned?"

Luther stepped back a pace. "I didn't think anyone knew she lived, or any of the other dragons for that matter."

Mylah shifted, trying not to look in the small fox's direction, who currently lie curled into a golden and black ball atop the training ring's wall. How much should she say? He had shared with her, seeming to trust her with the information he maybe wasn't supposed to have. "Our people..." she began, trying to sum up their complicated history; the Tijhi's curse for Empress Tama's horrible mistake so long ago, and their centuries' long mission to unravel the curse by saving the lives of ten thousand Tyrmini. She decided only the barest truth could be shared. "They have been protected in a way from the shifting of history."

Luther slowly nodded. "That makes sense. Your people live so remotely, and in an area that is difficult to survive. It stands to reason y'all would have been left alone these last several centuries."

She didn't say that her own companion creature was one of those dragons lost to the erased history. She didn't say her people were ever passing on true history so that they could one day break the curse. And she didn't say that Mylah was meant to be the representation that their goal had been achieved, and that she was also meant to somehow right the imbalance of power in the world.

THE DRAGON'S FIRE

All the implications of having manifested Tyrmini abilities crushed her. It had been meant to be her cousin. And now, it was her. Her people had looked to her in those brief weeks before her capture as the catalyst that would bring them back to their historic greatness. So much for that, she thought. Here she was, in a training pit at the High King's castle just trying to keep them alive. There was no returning them to glory. They would not uncover their hidden city, their buried libraries, and mine the volcanic mountains for jewels and fine metals instead of Tsheyduni.

No, their reality was simply to survive.

Truth shifted over the centuries across the rest of Aelos. Her people had gathered information when they traded on the main road, gaining an understanding on the state of the continent, its rulers, and its changing culture, monitoring the growth and declines of both Tyrmini and elemental creatures. She didn't say they were not only aware of the High King's ancestor's involvement in overthrowing the dragon of light but had been involved in his ability to do so. They had handed the young Achyla the First the knowledge, and that knowledge had plunged the world into shadow so intense it altered the very nature of magic. The Aestyrians had watched as the true history had been altered to paint Achyla the First as a savior who slew a dragon to keep Aelos safe.

The Aestyrah kept its histories, passing it along from one generation to another, quietly saving as many Tyrmini as they could with the Tsheyduni stone, to break the curse and to right the imbalance of power.

Even so, they were so removed they didn't know everything, like where the dragon of light was now. So many centuries had passed, many youth believed the histories to be nothing more than myth and legend. Mylah herself had wondered as much, but her power awakening, and Tijhi's return had all been too much of a coincidence. At least some truth remained to all the stories Maka had recited around the nighttime fires.

Luther held out the object. "Your turn," he said. Mylah held out her hands and noticed they trembled. "Don't worry, doll; there's no trick to it. You just hold it and the device will do the rest." He lowered the device into her hands. Color drained from the quadrants. The levers whirred around the perimeter, clicking softly, until at last they snicked into place, leading with gold.

The quadrant filled from its base to its top, a vivid gold shining out and casting their faces in its vibrant glow. Rich red fell into place next, the meter filling three-quarters. After that, blue illuminated with a menial one-third, while the orange quadrant remained empty.

"You see how we have three elements showing up?" Luther asked. Mylah nodded. "That's rare. Most Tyrmini have just two, and they lean heavily on one. If they have a third, it barely shows up. Heck, even Leviatha only has two."

"What are her elements?" Mylah asked.

"Water and air," Luther said quickly. "But they're massive, which is why she's so powerful. Because she's so heavily weighted on just two, her power can be volatile and difficult to control. Something we all have in common."

"Really?" Mylah asked, somehow feeling relieved others also had a difficult time controlling their power.

Luther nodded slowly, a grimace painting his face in what Mylah interpreted as deep pain. "We all have at least one story like what we saw with you in the desert. Though, you're probably one of - if not the - most powerful Tyrminis we've ever seen. Which means, it's all the more volatile."

Mylah looked back at the device, still wondering at the two empty silvery pools and what they represented. Luther pulled the bag from his belted pouch and carefully took the device from Mylah's hands, placing it back into the bag, and stowing it to the pouch once again.

"Okay, then," Luther said, backing away from Mylah, rubbing his hands together. "Day one. Grounding exercises. Let's get to work and see if we can't get you wiped out and sleeping good tonight."

Luther walked Mylah through what she considered general calisthenics. They did push-ups and squats, lunged their way across the shifting sand and back again more times than she could count, they did crunches until her abdominal muscles seized from overexertion. She vomited halfway through a run that circumvented the training area, at which point Luther finally let her take a rest and drink water.

At the end of the day, Mylah's muscles protested even the small task of bathing before she fell into bed. Sleep stole over. A sharp knock at the door woke her. "Dinner!" a voice said. The voice was small and high and it pulled Mylah from her sleep more efficiently than the knock.

"Could you hurry?" the voice said. "The tray is quite heavy."

Mylah jumped from the bed, grunting as every muscle in her overworked body rebelled against the activity. She hissed as she hobbled to the door and pulled it open. A young bespectacled woman, close to Mylah's age she guessed, stood in the frame, carrying a tray laden with dishes. Her mousy brown hair wisped and frayed at the edges. Her wide brown eyes pinched in concern. She stood a few inches shorter than Mylah. Her dusty blue dress fitted her in what could only be due to custom tailoring, with loose sleeves and neckline that covered her throat. Over the front of her dress hung an apron which boasted a healthy spattering of unidentifiable foods. The petticoats made the ankle-length skirts fluff out and away from her legs, her feet adorned with stylish leather boots. Mylah took the tray from the young woman.

"Thank you. Bless the Father and the Mother, that was heavy," the girl said, as she entered the room without invitation, dusting her hands over her apron.

Mylah set the dome-laden tray on the table situated under a large window. The room filled with warm aromas. Mylah's mouth watered. The oil lamp on the table offered little light, and the darkening sky meant the window remained dim. Mylah frowned, postponing food revelation until she could get her other room's lamps going.

Mylah took matches from a dresser on the far wall and set about lighting the lamps hanging from chains mounted to the walls. Once the hiss of oil permeated the air, and gold light chased away the evening's darkness, Mylah turned to the young woman. The stranger had seated herself at the table and pulled one of the many plates scattered across the tray to her. She removed the lid from the plate to reveal a whole roasted chicken, surrounded by fire-blistered vegetables.

Mylah folded herself into the opposite chair, as this new arrival pulled the lid off of a second plate to reveal not one loaf of bread, but three of varying colors of gold and brown, surrounded by hunks of food which Mylah had never seen before. Some were yellow, some white, some veined with blue. Mylah's eyes widened. She leaned in close and sniffed the unidentifiable foods and quickly pulled away, pressing a hand to her nose. It stank, like unwashed feet.

"We've been cooking all day," the young woman said. "For you." She smiled at Mylah, her mouth a crooked line.

"Why for me?" Mylah asked.

"Because you are the mighty Mylah," she said, her voice light, but did Mylah detect nerves or fear?

Mylah frowned. "Mighty?" If this stranger used the term to describe the devastation and death she'd caused, 'Mighty' was not the correct word.

"Leviatha told me you're very powerful," she said.

Mylah hung her head. "I am ashamed of my actions," she said.

The stranger exhaled, as if she'd been holding her breath

since entering the room. "It was a tragedy to lose two Tyrmini soldiers," she agreed.

Mylah peered at the young woman, heart plummeting into her stomach. "Did you... know them?"

She nodded, then shook her head. "Not closely, but I fed them all." She gestured toward the meal. "When they too entered the castle, some of them terrified, some of them elated and relieved."

Mylah placed a palm over her heart in her show of reverence. "What are their names please, that I may honor them."

"Dusty and Gal," she replied, quickly. Mylah was impressed. The young woman had not known them closely, but had paid careful attention to each of their names, had fed them upon their arrival, and mourned their loss.

"And who do I have the pleasure of dining with?" Mylah asked.

"Oh!" she said, seeming to shake off her mourning, and covered her open mouth with a hand. "My apologies. I can be a bit scatter-brained." She pushed herself away from the table and stood next to Mylah, offering a hand. Mylah turned to face her. "I am Princess Sybille, daughter of High King Achyla the Seventh, sister to High King Achyla the Eighth," she said.

Mylah took the girl's arm in her peoples' customary greeting, clasping her forearm with her hand. She placed her other hand over her heart and intoned, "The Goddess smiles upon our meeting."

Sybille's face went slack with awe. "That's a genuine Aestyrian greeting. I've never been greeted under the Goddess's light before." She released her arm and looked at it as if it had just been imbued with power.

Mylah smiled. "How do your people greet each other?" she asked.

"Oh! Well, for *not* royalty, we typically extend our hands -

same as you - but, then we grasp hands and not arms. Like this," she said, and extended her hand. Mylah took the hand she offered and shook it. Sybille's whole body rattled. "Maybe a little softer, Mighty Mylah," she said, grinning. Mylah shook slower. "Perfect."

Sybille sat again and Mylah wriggled against her crimes that lie between them. Sybille didn't seem to notice. "Okay, let's eat. I'm starving, and I bet you are too," she said.

Mylah nodded, rolling her eyes and exhaling dramatically. "Luther is a thorough trainer. I am famished," she agreed.

As Sybille scooched herself into place, Mylah removed a third lid to reveal more vegetables, which were green and vibrant. Sybille removed the lid from the fourth and final plate displayed on a round golden dish, but peeking through a pattern of leaf-shaped holes was a sticky, purple-red substance.

"I am unfamiliar with this," Mylah said and pointed to the last dish.

Sybille blinked slowly at her. "You've never had pie before?"

"Pie?" Mylah felt the word in her mouth but had no reference for it.

"I have so much to teach you, Mighty Mylah. Never fear. You will soon learn the all the ways of pie; sweet, savory, sweet and savory, berry, apple, peach cobbler, meat, cheese, egg, plum, pear... the list is endless." Sybille's eyes went wide, leaning into the table as she counted the various pies on her fingers.

"What is pie?" Mylah asked.

"I think that question is best answered with a bite," Sybille noted seriously, and took a spoon from the tray. She dug into the pie, scooping crust and filling onto a plate before handing it to Mylah. Mylah found a fork and took the tiniest bite.

Rich, warm, flaky textures juxtaposed with tart sweetness filled her senses. Her mouth watered, tears springing to her eyes. She chewed, savoring the flavors, and swallowed before asking, "What kind of pie is this one?"

"Mixed berry," Sybille said. "One of my favorites. It's even better with cream, but I didn't have any whipped up."

Mylah caught the ownership of her words. "Did you cook this pie?" she asked.

"Bake. One bakes a pie. And yes," she said and smiled crookedly. "But before we eat all the pie, we have to eat our dinner first. House rules. Or Bess will have a fit."

"But, you are the princess. Surely no one would reprimand you."

Sybille placed a hunk of bread on her plate, then reached for the roasted chicken, sawing into the breast with ease. She didn't stop cutting as she replied, "Tell that to Bess."

Mylah reached for the chicken and pulled a drumstick, twisting until the joint popped free and the meat came with it, and set it on her plate. She piled on vegetables, helped herself to bread - sweet and glorious yeast bread that she'd only ever tasted a handful of times - and the other unidentified substance, despite it smelling like unwashed feet.

Once she finished filling her plate, Mylah propped her elbows on the table, open hands facing the sky. "We are grateful for this bounty," she intoned.

Sybille paused, fork halfway to her open mouth. She snapped her mouth shut, laid the fork on her plate, and copied Mylah's gesture. "We are grateful for this bounty?" Sybille asked.

Mylah nodded and lowered her hands, reaching for her fork and diving in with gusto. Sybille followed suit.

Mylah sent up another prayer to the Goddess for her people as she refueled her body. After several moments passed, each diner focused on their meal, Mylah interrupted the dinner.

"How many other Tyrmini are here?"

Sybille chewed and swallowed, holding a finger demurely in front of her until she wiped her mouth with a napkin. "We currently house yourself, Luther, Leviatha, Slate, and Rone."

"Who are Slate and Rone? What are their abilities?" Mylah asked, marveling at how few Tyrmini were under the king's rule. Mylah wondered how many were on Aelos, if they were a dwindling population.

"Slate is solely water. You probably saw him at the training pitch?"

Mylah nodded, recalling the man on the raised wall near the ditch.

"Rone is usually out scouting," Sybille waved at the air, as if to gesture toward the distance outside the castle walls.

Mylah bit into the chicken, chewed and swallowed before asking, "What is it Rone scouts?"

Sybille shrugged. "Don't know. He's gone more than not, and that's good for everyone, trust me." She took another bite, nudging her glasses up her nose with the back of her hand.

"Why is that?" Mylah asked.

Sybille peered over her glasses at Mylah, fork loaded with a bite of pie. "That one's... just not right," she said. "And that dog of his? Rumor is it's part shadow wolf. Not a creature you want to run into in a dark alley alone."

"Are a lot of Tyrmini like Rone? Not-," Mylah paused around the saying, a common-tongue phrase she was unfamiliar with, "right?"

Sybille set her fork down and leaned back into her chair, wiping her face with her napkin, nudging up her glasses, and sipping from her water glass, as if to give herself time before she responded. She met Mylah's eyes at last, her face pinched in thought. "It must be difficult." She paused again. "To contain so much power and to feel at its mercy in some ways. At least, that's what some Tyrmini have told me. That the elements coursing through you have their own mind and it can feel like it's wielding you, instead of the other way around."

Sybille cocked her head to one side as she finished speaking.

Mylah set down her own fork as emotion bubbled within her.

"I think some Tyrmini resent that loss of control, and they swing hard the other way to gain it back, then go about wielding it in a way that makes them feel powerful. Unfortunately, sometimes that includes harming others. They're always on the attack. That way they feel like nothing and nobody can take their independence away."

Mylah knew exactly what Sybille meant. Her extreme emotions had translated to extreme use of power and in some ways she'd felt in control, wielding that power in retribution and revenge.

Shame ravaged Mylah and tears slipped from her eyes unbidden. Sybille watched her, giving nothing away with a calm placidity that left her face unreadable.

"I promise," she started. Air rattled in on a jagged inhale. Tears streamed and Sybille's face blurred. She wretched out the next words from the depths of her dirty soul, the shame a tattoo on her heart. "I promise to not be that." Her body trembled with the truth that she could be. That she had been. And it would only be with singular effort to be something other than a slave to the power.

Sybille tilted her head back the barest amount as she observed Mylah. At last, she said, "Then I urge you to train as much as you can with Luther. He's the only Tyrmini here whose heart remains fully intact."

CHAPTER ELEVEN

Mylah struggled through pulling on her clothes, sore muscles protesting against the movement. Before yesterday, Mylah would have considered herself in good shape, owing to the regular physicality needed to traverse mining tunnels and hammer away at rock to free the Tsheyduni stone. As she rose from bed, stomach muscles screaming, she realized how wrong she'd been.

Mylah lowered herself onto a chair, thighs burning, and pushed one foot into a boot she'd been provided. Even her feet hurt. The room's window reflected a gray and rainy day. It was unlike the rare rain she was accustomed to, which came on quickly, poured hard and fast, and went on its way. This rain seemed content to fall soft and steady, and Mylah found it annoyingly calm.

As she shoved the second foot into the constraining boot, a burst of cool wetness splashed against her heel, followed by a burning sting. She pulled the boot off and scowled at the hanging flap of skin and raw tissue beneath it. She stared at it open-mouthed, tears springing to her eyes. Not because it hurt that much, but because her whole body hurt, she was alone in a goddess-forsaken land, being forced to serve the High King whom her people secretly and vehemently opposed.

She set the boot aside and let her tears stream unchecked, sobbing quietly into the foreign enclosure that was her quarters. She lifted her heel to her opposite knee, wondering just what she was going to do about this new hurt.

A knock at the door interrupted her. She straightened, swiping her face. She was being childish. She would gladly serve her people in this way to keep them safe. She huffed out an exhale and straightened her spine. She rose from the chair – cursing stiff leg muscles, the pull in the new tender wound on her heel – and yanked the door open.

Luther leaned against the door frame with one hand, the other propped against his hip. He wore the same style of clothes he'd worn the day before, though these were clean, as hers were. She marveled at the luxury of someone else doing her laundry. Regularly. The fact that it was required by the High King intruded on her independence in a way that even the comfort of clean clothes felt like shackles.

Luther looked her over, his gaze landing on her bootless foot. His eyes shot back to her face, eyebrows pinched. He stood straight. "May I come in?" he asked, brown eyes soft. Mylah showed him in, closing the door behind him.

"Come sit down, lemme look at that heel."

"It is nothing. A small wound," Mylah said, but sat down anyway.

Luther knelt beside her chair and pulled her leathers up to reveal the ravaged heel beneath. "Your feet aren't used to boots," he said. "I apologize, darlin'. So I do." He rose, grunting slightly. Thank Goddess. He also seemed to be sore from their training.

Luther opened the leather pouch strapped to his belt, proffering bandages, then knelt again. He set the bandages on the table and rolled the leg of her pants twice. Pulling the bandage strip out from its roll, he held one end and wrapped it around her heel, then the arch of her foot.

"We are headed to the practice pitch again today?" Mylah asked, watching as Luther continued to wrap. She tried not to think about the warm strong hand pressing the bandage tenderly in place, the calluses scraping against her exposed skin, and how

102

that touch sent a thrill tracing up her body, heating her core.

Luther secured the bandage and looked up at her through curled eyelashes. "You up for it, doll?" He gave her one of those lop-sided grins that threatened to melt her. "Nobody would blame you if you needed a day off. Catch your breath. Recover from our travels. If you need it."

Last night's dinner conversation with the princess swelled within her. Shame accompanied commitment. She would not allow this power to control her. She would heed the princess's advice. She furrowed her brows, squared her shoulders and looked down her nose at him. Despite the detestation of her muscles, she stuck her chin out and said, "Lead the way."

Ten minutes into the training exercises, Mylah regretted it. She was drenched in rain, the constant drizzle having soaked into her clothes, her skin, and her bones.

"Now that we're warm -,"

Mylah made a phlegmy noise of disagreement and rolled her eyes.

Luther continued as if he hadn't heard. "- let's practice opening your magic."

"You're kidding me, right?" Mylah said.

The pitch was completely empty except for her and Luther. No need. The spring rain was guard enough against any fiery catastrophe. The gray sky pressed down on Mylah.

Luther ignored her outburst. "I'm going to teach you a meditation my mother and grandmother and all my older sisters taught me." He stretched out the word 'all'.

"You have many sisters?" Mylah asked.

"So many," Luther confirmed. "Seven. And I am child number eight of eight."

"The baby," Mylah noted.

He sighed.

"You were loved and protected by your family," she said.

"Fiercely," he said, eyebrows rising. "Even when I didn't deserve it." Rain splashed on his short hair, nose, cheeks and shoulders, a frown spreading down his face. "But they sure scolded me good when I needed it," he said and a grin returned. "Now, go on ahead and have a seat." He folded himself right into a puddle in the sand.

"Here? In the rain?"

"No better weather for ya, doll," he said. "If your power opens up there'll be less destruction. Now, sit yourself on down. Embrace the wetness." His mouth quirked into a grin.

Mylah scowled.

Luther cleared his throat, dropped his grin, and mumbled, "Sorry."

She huffed, uncrossed her arms and searched for the highest mound of sand to avoid getting her backside wet. When she found the best option, she lowered herself to the ground and crossed her ankles as Luther had.

"Very good," Luther said, his words muted through the steady patter of rain. "Close your eyes and keep 'em soft, don't press your lids too tightly."

Mylah obeyed, the familiarity of meditation folding around her. "I know how to meditate, Luther."

"Your people have your sort of meditation and mine have our sort of meditation. Now, relax and follow my instruction."

Relax. Relax? Water snaked down her spine from the opening at her shirt collar. She shivered. Gooseflesh covered her entire body.

"Stop thinking about how cold you are," Luther said.

Mylah cracked an eye open and frowned at her instructor.

"Your shoulders are tense, and your face is all squished up."

"I am not accustomed to sitting in the rain. Where I come from, one has the sense to get out of a storm and weather it inside our homes," Mylah said.

"You are a fire Tyrmini and a powerful one. There's no better way to open your power than in the opposite element to dampen the explosivity of your magic," Luther said.

Mylah glared at him, her discomfort a growling beast inside her. "Fine," she said.

"Close your eyes," he said. "And open your awareness to your inner landscape."

Mylah cracked an eye again. "Inner landscape?"

"All the stuff that makes you Mylah," Luther said.

Mylah closed her eyes and peered around. At first, she looked at the back of her eyelids without any connection to her inner self, as Luther called it.

"Focus on the steady rhythm of the rain and let it fill your awareness," Luther instructed.

That wasn't difficult. The rain pattered on, steady... unrelenting. Mylah wriggled to rid herself of negativity and let the rain fill her mind.

"Allow any passing thoughts to flow through you," he said.

Mylah's thoughts came and went, neither clinging nor disappearing, simply flowing.

"We are from the Tyrinth and to the Tyrinth we'll return. Feel the ground beneath you and know you are a part of it as it is a part of you."

The sand beneath her shifted, wrapping up and around her bottom half, as if to embrace her. Its calming sturdy presence filled her with a sense of rootedness.

"Feel the rain on your skin, listen to the steady patter, soak in the water," Luther said.

Soak in the water? She didn't care for such a practice. Her breath sawed in sharply and she exhaled out her displeasure, hoping this would allow her to focus more on the rhythm and sensation without the cold. Luther moved on and Mylah gladly followed.

"The center of your body is your source of fire. Very gently reach down into your belly and say hello to the fire."

Mylah twisted and turned up through what she visualized as a waterfall, its deluge a source of frustration, and when Luther opened the invitation to move into the fire, she leaped from the water and dove into the bubbling lava waiting at her core. Warm flames engulfed her. She sighed in relief as the fire burned away the water, her skin and clothes and hair dried out in an instant, the rain sizzling up into mist around her.

Luther's voice whispered distantly under the fire roaring within her. Her inner self swayed with the shifting flames. Colors danced around her in vibrant blues, oranges, and golds. Warmth enveloped her. For the first time in weeks, joy cascaded through her. As if the fire washed away her stress and grief, burning through her heartache. Or was she fire? Was it separate and distinct from her soul or were they one and the same? The more her soul stood in the flames, the boundaries blurred and the less distinction there was between it and her.

"Mylah!"

The shout reverberated in her ears. Her eyes shot open to find Luther's face inches from her own. He gripped her arms.

"Come back, now," Luther said, and shook her firmly.

Reality reached out, brushing against the flames' warding comfort, threatening to drag her from this found respite. She wanted to be the flames again. To close her eyes and feel that touch sizzling through her. Her lids lowered, but Luther shook her again.

"You can't stay in the fire, doll," Luther said.

The hurting, aching part of her that had been lulled by the flames growled at the distraction. Every hurt she'd suffered in the last several weeks surged through her, reminding her that her family was dead, her people were in danger, and she was enslaved.

Mylah looked down at one of Luther's gripping hands, faced Luther's gaze and bared her teeth. She snarled at him.

THE DRAGON'S FIRE

"I know, darlin'. I know. The flame is soothing to us, but you can't stay there forever. It will consume you. Come back to me. Please."

No! Everything inside her shouted to be left alone with her fire, to live in the cocooning safety of it, to relish its color and light and let the world burn.

Mylah lifted a hand and placed her palm solidly on Luther's chest. His heart beat beneath her touch, muscles firm, body warm. He looked down at it then back to her face. His head minutely turned in a no gesture that Mylah interrupted with a solid, willful shove.

Luther launched away from her, his head snapping forward, arms trailing as his body retreated. A swirling tunnel of absence parted with Luther's trajectory through a wall of flame Mylah had been unaware of. She believed the fire had only been inside her mind, locked under the meditation. Luther's body collided with the opposite wall and crumpled to the ground, slumping over.

The spell broke.

Mylah inhaled sharply as she took in her surroundings. The entire pitch shimmered in flame. Around her, sand boiled, rolling and belching hot, liquid lava. Rain sizzled and spat against a dome of fire with Mylah as the epicenter. And her teacher, the one who could talk her through this, had just been knocked unconscious with her anger and annoyance.

You got yourself into this. Now you must find a way out. Tijhi's voice echoed in her head. Mylah cast about, searching for the little fox. And there, skirting the perimeter the fox pranced through the flame, each brush of fire revealing their shifting nature. First fox, then fox phoenix, then dragon and back again. They approached Luther and nuzzled at the man's cheek.

Stop or he'll burn alive. He can't protect himself if he's unconscious.

How? Mylah asked, frantic now, heart beating at a door that wouldn't open.

If you care for this individual at all, you will find a way.

I don't know what I'm doing! She shouted.

Figure it out, Mylah. Better hurry. Your flame and glass are burning him.

Mylah closed her eyes again, this time dropping back into that inner pool of lava and bobbing to its surface. She floated in a vast sea of her power, its enormity beyond her comprehension. The flames beckoned to her, called her to let loose of her need to control, begged for freedom. Outside of her, she knew their freedom meant destruction, but the idea of slavery, the idea of imprisonment didn't feel right. It didn't feel like the solution for the problem.

She called out to the flames. "You can't do this. You can't explode and run away any longer. If you do, we both die, along with all the other casualties you cause. Calm yourself."

With her words she breathed in and out, picturing the exhale as cooling the flames. With the breath a realization came. "It's okay. I know really awful things happened and that's hurt you. I know you're angry." She paused, sorrow spearing her chest. Tears slipped and dried on her heated cheeks.

Her voice quivered as she said, "I know I'm angry. And sad. Over and over again, we've had our heart broken." She breathed again and spoke to the flames within her.

"You are not evil. You're beautiful. I promise. From now on, I'll take care of you. I love you."

The flames shrank, coalesced into a central pillar. Mylah inhaled and exhaled, sending love into the fire, feeling something she'd never felt before: compassion for her own self. There was an odd sense of separation even as she realized the power was her. The pillar shifted, turning humanoid. Mylah rose and approached the fire.

THE DRAGON'S FIRE

She offered a hand to the flaming feminine figure. It returned the gesture, like the image in a mirror. "I'm sorry you've felt the need to be so strong and then felt so weak. That has been so confusing and painful." She reached the other hand out and was rewarded with the warmth of the figure's hand in her own. "There's no more need to rage. We're together in this."

She pulled the figure close, embracing it and her power.

Mylah opened her heart wide to all of her, even the ugly pieces she despised, and even the parts that hurt and were unworthy. She pulled in her fire and held it close and let the flames wrap searing arms around her.

CHAPTER TWELVE

Mylah's eyes sprang open. Rain pattered down again, soaking into her hair, clothes and skin. Relief washed over her as the gray sky above stretched away, no longer interrupted by swelling flames. She rose, making to dash across the pitch to Luther's still inert body and slipped.

The entire training ring, previously filled with sand, now glinted in the harsh gray afternoon in a solid sheet of glass. Beneath the glass lay dark soil. Mylah's fire had burned all of the sand and left the wet Tyrinth beneath it untouched. The perimeter fence smoked from doused flames. Tijhi still stood next to Luther, gold eyes trained on Mylah.

Mylah reached Luther and knelt. *Is he hurt?* She asked Tijhi.

I believe the male will be okay, Tijhi said. *You have found yourself.*

Mylah blinked at the fox who did not blink back, their huge gold eyes fixed on her. She wrestled with the concept Tijhi so concisely summed up. She had found herself. Her body quivered with the realization, the magnitude shaking her to the core. To that lost aching piece of her soul that needed what she and the rest of her community had never given her: acceptance, love, compassion. She placed a hand on her belly and a hand on her heart. Something had clicked into place today. Something so profound she couldn't even fathom how important it was. So, to the Tijhi, she simply nodded, unable to voice her feelings.

This is good, they said, and turned to leave.

Where are you going? Mylah asked.

You and I both have, in our own ways, been asleep for far too long. I have much to do. Tijhi leaped effortlessly to the top of the steaming wall. Mylah watched the rain around the creature, a nimbus of steam swirling away into the wet afternoon. Their golden fur gleamed against the dreary daylight, completely dry. As Mylah observed the fox, not one drop of rain landed on the Tijhi's fur.

Neat trick, she said to the fox. *The rain isn't even touching you.*

Tijhi puffed out their chest, nose lifted in the air. *It wouldn't dare.*

Mylah chuckled as the Tijhi leaped from the wall and out of sight.

She turned to Luther, his eyes still closed, breath shallow. She laid a hand gently on his shoulder as she looked him over. There were burn marks on his shirt, holes torn wide and singed, revealing the musculature of his arms beneath. No marks marred his skin. He appeared completely intact and unharmed, save for being knocked out by his collision with the wall.

Suspicion growing, Mylah cast a thought to her companion. *Was he actually in any danger?*

Perhaps he was in less danger than I let on, Tijhi replied.

Mylah's mouth fell open. *You tricked me?*

I gave you proper motivation, they said. *And it worked.* Their voice a genderless and wordless sound conveying intention inside her mind, seemed smug in a proud sort of way. Their tone softened. *You've done good work today.*

Mylah didn't respond because emotion had clogged somewhere between where her heart and words connected, but she took the little dragon's words to heart and allowed herself just this moment to celebrate her progress.

"Luther," she said and gently shook him.

"Mmm," he grumbled, eyes peeling open, revealing a dazed stare. A moment later he sat up. He hissed in pain and raised a hand to his head.

"I am very sorry," Mylah said.

Luther squeezed his eyes shut, groaned, and opened them again, heel of his hand still pressed to his temple. "'salright," he said. "Happens to the best of us." He looked down at himself, noting his tattered shirt. "Been a long time since I got my clothes burned." He looked up at her. "You alright, doll?"

Mylah nodded. "I think I figured some things out," she said.

"Good," he said and looked around at the pitch. "Holy Mother," he said, eyes going wide. "That's a neat trick." Mylah smiled at the same words she'd just used with Tijhi.

He gestured to the glass surface. Mylah looked in the direction he pointed. "This means your connection to Tyrinth is real solid. While your fire is what's volatile. How'd you get it to calm down?" he asked, looking back up at her.

She crossed her legs, lowering her backend to the ground, and placed a hand on her heart then her stomach. "I just needed to connect these two."

"You had to show yourself some love and care. That accident was my fault. I apologize, Mylah." The sound of her name shaped by his voice warmed her.

"How so?" Mylah asked.

"Well, we should have started with your heart. I shouldn't have clung to the idea that things had to go in order. I knew your fire was explosive and could have guessed at its cause. I didn't," he said.

"Do not take this burden on all by yourself. I accept my responsibility to navigate my power. Perhaps this was the way I could learn best. All you had to do was survive the fire." She smiled at him.

He tilted his head. "Oh, is that all I had to do?"

"Well, maybe you did a little more than that," she said.

"Hm," he growled, and crossed his arms. "Maybe you need a few more training sessions like yesterday."

Mylah effortlessly rose to a standing position from her cross-legged spot on the ground and offered Luther a hand. "Maybe so," she said, not willing to admit just how much sorer her body was the longer the day wore on.

"If that's the way you feel, doll, we better get a move on." He took her hand and pulled himself upright, rather than leaning into her weight at all. "Allow me to introduce you to the running path."

As she ran, she made peace with the rain, allowing it to dampen the deep well of power simmering inside her, that other piece of herself stowed away, but not forgotten or closed off or separated.

Hours later, Mylah had never been sorer and more drenched in her life. Her fingers had pruned, and her teeth clattered as they made their way to her quarters. She dumped her sodden clothing into the provided basket and set it outside her door where it would be magically whisked away by servants in the night.

Her adjoined bathing room was another thing of extreme luxury, and as she entered the space, scented by soaps and oils, she wondered how easy it would be for some to embrace this lifestyle despite the consequences. She fiddled with the knobs and levers until the tub filled with water. Plunging into the cold bath, she washed herself thoroughly, shaking wildly as she scrubbed her body with soap, finally dunking her head under the water to clear her hair of soap and grime and rainwater.

The clean, what she was told was called a towel, soaked

the moisture from her body and hair, after which she felt like an altogether new creation. She wasn't sure she'd ever been so clean in all her years in the Aestyrah, where water was scarce and prioritized for drinking.

She donned fresh clothes which had also magically appeared during her absence from the room. This set of clothing seemed more casual to the soldier training uniform. The khaki slacks were wide and loose, and she tucked the hem of a long, white blouse into them. She left the string at the throat untied, revealing her golden-brown chest above the cleavage.

There were soft slippers lying on the wardrobe's floor. They were violet velvet and cushioned at the sole. As she slipped her feet into them, she purred in delight. Each of her steps were cushioned like walking on clouds. Clean, dressed, and ravenous, Mylah stepped out into the hall, closing the solid wood door behind her. Luther had promised a trip to the kitchens. On their way back from training, he'd pointed out his own quarters, dropped her at hers and double-backed.

She walked down the hall to Luther's quarters and knocked on the wood and iron door. The door swung open and Luther looked her over in a way that made Mylah squirm.

"What is it?" she asked.

"Well, doll," he said and wrapped a meaty hand over the back of his neck. "That shirt is for sleeping in."

Mylah looked down at the shirt. "I do intend to sleep tonight. Come on," she said, turning away from him. "Show me to the kitchens. I'm starving."

Luther closed the door behind him, his own dirty clothes basket sitting nearby, and caught her up. He pointed the way, one turn after another, until Mylah was hopelessly lost. At last, they turned into a large room.

Mylah's mouth fell open. The space stretched away, large enough to house half her village. On the side of the room they'd entered, eating areas sat in two columns, eight wooden tables with sturdy benches perched in perfect rows. In the kitchen's other half, a mass of workers flitted between sinks, vats, fires, ovens, counters, and shelves. On one long counter facing the eating area a man stood behind a mass of food lining the counter.

Luther approached and took a plate and utensils, all laid out in tidy piles. He handed them to Mylah and then took a set for himself.

"Welcome, welcome," the man behind the counter said, his accent thick. Short black and gray hair lay against his head and gray stubble coated his light face, and grey-blue eyes twinkled above round cheeks. The man smiled revealing a gap between his two front teeth. He stood a head taller than Mylah and a round paunch extended past his belt, covered with a plain beige tunic and dark apron, untied and flowing in front of him. He held a wooden serving spoon aloft and waved it to the food. "What would you like to eat?"

Behind him, amid the kitchen's hustle and bustle, Sybille stood over a row of round dishes, all heaping full with sliced fruit. She carefully covered one with a sheet of crust. Her glasses slipped down her nose. She nudged them with a knuckle, leaving a smudge of white against the lens.

Mylah waved in the girl's direction, trying to catch her attention.

"No use," Luther said to her. "Sybille is in her own little world when she's back here."

"Sybille," Mylah shouted.

Sybille looked up from her pies, face a mask of concentration. When her eyes found Mylah, they lit up, smile spreading across her face. She climbed down from a stool, wiping her hands on her black apron and making her way to them.

"Mighty Mylah," Sybille said. "It's so good to see -," a look of confusion crossed her face. "Are you wearing a night shirt?"

Mylah ignored her. "Come eat dinner with us," she said.

"You want to eat dinner with me?" she asked, her brown eyes suddenly glistening.

"Of course," Mylah said. "Join us."

Sybille looked over her shoulder, then back again. "Just let me finish these pies."

A small stout woman approached from a nearby cooking fire, cheeks flushed. "Nonsense, girl," she said, waving her hand in front of her. "Go. I'll finish the pies."

"But –," Sybille started.

"You're in my realm, Missy, and what I say goes. Get your food and go eat something. You've starved yourself all day back here working harder than my staff. Shoo," she said, dark eyes wide as she gestured for the crowned princess to get moving.

"Mylah," Sybille said, "this is Bess, the Kitchen's Head Mistress."

Bess turned to Mylah. "Well, you're the one she's been talking about all day. I'm sure it's lovely to meet you," she said, but it really didn't seem to be lovely at all to her.

Mylah lifted her hand to offer it in greeting to the woman, but she said, "Now, if you'll excuse me," and turned away. Mylah's hand drifted back to her side, cold and awkward.

"She's just like that. Don't take it personal," Sybille said. Luther nodded in confirmation.

Sybille removed her apron and hung it on one of a dozen pegs where several other aprons hung before rounding the counter and taking a plate and utensils.

The man behind the food smiled genuinely at each of them, deep wrinkles crinkling the skin around his eyes, under which sat a large, bulbous nose. "Now, then, ready for dinner you three?"

Mylah, unable to help herself, smiled back. She gestured to the food she wanted, and the man cheerfully heaped healthy servings onto her waiting plate. She waited as the man served Luther then Sybille and then they made their way to an empty table. Mylah dug in with gusto, purring with contentment at the astounding flavor, texture, and general deliciousness of every bite. Potatoes, meat, carrots, bread with butter, and finally pie. This time with slices of fruit that Luther identified as apple.

"You made this?" Mylah asked Sybille. Sybille had barely touched her other food and was digging into the pie, eyebrows pinched as she chewed. Sybille set her fork down and finished her bite, clearing her mouth with a swig of water.

"Yes, we have a surplus of apples in the cold storage lockers downstairs. Bess is trying to make space for some early spring crops coming in. So, everyone gets pie." Her mouth quirked in a half-smile. "Now," she said growing serious, "both of you must tell me your thoughts."

Mylah looked at Luther, who shoveled the last bite of pie into his mouth, grunting in pleasure. "Delicious," he said around a mouthful. He wiped his mouth with his napkin and slumped back, resting a hand over his flat stomach. "Mama was a damn good cook, but I do believe that's the most amazing pie I've ever eaten."

Mylah took another bite, reveling in the crust's soft chew, the warm gooiness surrounding slices of apple which had just the bare amount of crunch in the middle. There was spice in it as well as sweetness, which hit Mylah's tongue in an exciting sort of way. "This is one of the best things I have ever eaten," she said.

"You two are so sweet. Promise? Anything I can do to make it better?"

"Oh, I don't know," Luther said, one dark brow rising. "Guess I'd have to have another piece before I could say for sure."

Sybille shoved away from the table and was back with another slice before Mylah could finish her next bite. Luther rubbed his hands together, with an "ooh, hoo, hoo!" sound of excitement. He reached for his fork and dug in with joy.

Mylah finished her pie and Sybille asked, "Would you like another piece?" Mylah waved her off, feeling she'd burst if she ate another bite. Contented, she sipped her water, watching other servants and guards enjoying their meal. All were clean, seemingly content, and with the glow of health owing to being fed on a regular healthy diet. But, as her belly filled, her uneasiness grew.

Do not grow comfortable, that inner fire seemed to say. *Your life is not meant to remain in this luxury for long.*

She reminded herself why she was here. To protect her people.

And more, the voice inside her said. *So much more.*

CHAPTER THIRTEEN

Over the last month, Mylah's days fell into a regular rhythm. She rose to the sting of sore abdominal muscles, dressed with the ache of worked arms and legs, and went to bed each night clean, fed, and utterly exhausted.

The cold spring days dampened her power in a way that allowed practice with the elements less extreme. She meditated to the sound of Luther's voice, lifted heavier and heavier weights in their training, ran the training grounds' perimeter with more ease. With each passing day, her body transformed. Her arms became defined, her torso now had distinct bulges of muscle, her thighs grew thick and powerful.

Since opening her power, Luther had tasked her to find a way to transform the pit of glass back into sand. She sat on a portion of the pitch she'd successfully broken back into sand and walked through the seven energy centers to Luther's warm, rich instruction.

She connected to today's section of solid clear mass and used the energy to vibrate it until it crumbled. First in big chunks, then into smaller and smaller bits.

It was a fitting consequence of her actions, and she dove into the work with humility and dedication, grateful it had been the only damage done, and not more deaths added to her conscience

"That's good for today. Let's focus on arrow making with

the finer sand," Luther said, rising from his seat on a glassy region.

Mylah followed suit, brushing herself clean. The jacket she wore was overly warm after her work with the sand, and she removed it, setting it on the perimeter wall to reveal the shirt and wrappings she'd recently commissioned the tailor to create for her.

"Nice threads," Luther noted.

Mylah extended her arms, feeling more comfortable than she'd felt since arriving in Udari City. "I am pleased with the result," she noted, observing the strong linen fabric wrappings, the sleeveless shirt revealing her bare shoulders between where the shirt ended and the wrappings began.

Mylah situated herself in the mound of fine sand, rooting physically and energetically into the Tyrinth. She drew the arrow into her intention, gesturing to the sand with a pulling motion, meaning for the sand to harden into a single line, tipped in a sharp arrow. Her concentration teetered, then collapsed. Lying in the sand a crooked mass of thickened sand crumbled as she watched.

Mylah exhaled, inhaled, and tried again.

CHAPTER FOURTEEN

Mylah crouched behind a guard wall and waited for the telltale sign of igniting flame. That subtle hiss was the only sign that would give him away. She fingered the stopper at the end of a large water pouch slung across her body. In her other hand, she held a bow.

Spring had given way to summer and summer had tripped right into fall. The months of practice had honed her abilities to a level of comfort that felt second-nature.

The sun shone down on the training ring, and cool dry air snapped around them. She breathed in slowly through her nose, paused, and exhaled just as slowly through her mouth. Her boots ground into the sand, and she extended her energy into the solid Tyrinth. Magic sang through her as she opened the series of seven doors inside her, each with its own energetic signature and purpose, all working together.

Over the last two seasons, she'd practiced this until the doors swung open in rapid succession with little thought or concentration. After her initial failure with the meditation, Luther had guided her from the top to the center, then from the bottom to the top and then starting in the heart center and moving through them based on her intuition of what needed to open next. Mylah felt her intuition was more whim or chance, but she humored her teacher in his attempts.

In the end, it had all worked to create a corridor down which her power could be funneled in a steady, controllable stream.

Mylah adjusted her jacket, the high collar chafed against her sensitive neck skin. Sand shifted beneath her boots as she adjusted her crouched position. A soft hiss hushed in the air behind her and to her left. She shot up, body springing into action. The well of power within her surged at her command.

She flicked the stopper on her pouch and let dry sand pour out. Her will was absolute and the sand obeyed as she formed it into a blunted arrow - a task she'd mastered over countless practice sessions. Fire sizzled and crackled as it consumed the sand and transformed the arrow into glass. In one swift motion she nocked the crystalline weapon into place. Her weapon already pointed, she let it fly. The glass arrow sang across the training ring. A yowl filled the air after it.

"Ye god by nose," Luther said.

He was doubled over, both hands clamped to his face, blood dripping in a puddle between his feet. Mylah laughed. "Yes!" she exclaimed.

"Thad's nod funny!" Luther said, turning his head to cast her with a hurt-filled gaze.

"It is, actually. Or do I need to remind you about last week?" she said. Hidden beneath her pants, a bruise still covered her thigh in varying shades of purple and green. It looked better now than it had a few days earlier. "You hit me with a boulder," she said.

"It was nod a boulder," Luther groused. He stood up straight, mopping at his face with a handkerchief. "It was just a really big rock." He nodded at her as he said it, as if to assure her this was the accurate recollection.

Mylah shook her head in return. "Nooo," she said. "Boulder."

"You exaggerate."

"Tijhi?" she asked the little fox, curled up on the wall, snoozing in the afternoon sun, their fur the color of sand. Tijhi turned their head to Mylah, chirped without opening their eyes, then turned back into themself to continue napping.

"See?" Mylah said, "we have it on the Tijhi's authority."

"I'm not takin' the word of a little ol' mischievous fox. Sybille?"

Sybille had taken to watching the two spar when the weather was pleasant. Everyone agreed this was a good break from her obsession with the kitchen. Sybille, having just turned eighteen summers, looked up from a notepad, eyes unfocused as she peered through her round spectacles past Luther. "Hm?" she asked.

He waved a hand at her. "She's not even payin' attention. Probably writing another recipe," Luther said good-naturedly.

Sybille took this as an invitation, shaking from her reverie. "Yes! Oh, just wait until you try this one. It's going to be the most exquisite brownie you've ever tasted. It'll have chunks of chocolate and a glaze of cinnamon and this new sweet cheese Bess recently acquired from a dairy farmer on the city's south side. I'm trying to come up with the perfect combination to complement its smooth creamy texture and slight tang. You can't even imagine how mind-blowingly amazing it is, and I think with the spice of cinnamon it will pair with the chocolate's dark richness. You'll be transported to a place of gourmet pleasure, the likes you've never visited before." She heaved.

Luther and Mylah stared. Sybille's eyes had glazed over, having widened with each word, until she appeared manic in her need to cook this particular dessert. Bake, Mylah corrected herself.

"Well, doll, that sure does sound tasty," Luther said, and quirked a smile in her direction. Sybille blinked and seemed to see Luther for the first time.

"Tasty?" she laughed. "Oh, it'll be more than tasty. You'll see." With that, she jumped down from the wall and walked away, presumably toward the kitchens, muttering to herself as she went. Tijhi popped their head up, watched Sybille's retreat, stood, stretched, yawned, and followed, running to catch her up.

"That little critter of yours sure has taken a likin' to Ms. Princess," Luther said, watching them go, the flood of his nosebleed finally stemmed. He fixed Mylah with a questioning gaze. "Should we test her? She's a little too old, but so were you."

"Does the fox indicate something to you?" Mylah asked, eyebrows raised. They had never discussed Tijhi's nature, had always pretended the fox was nothing more than a fox. In fact, for a long while, Mylah was sure Luther was incapable of seeing their true form.

"You and I both know that ain't no ordinary fox. Every time it comes around while we're practicing, my abilities get -," he held his hands out in front of him, lowering them slowly, "-calmer. Easier to control. Especially the fire abilities." He looked at her accusingly.

Mylah crossed her arms. "I'm sure I don't know what you mean."

Luther sighed, rolled his head to the sky, and dropped his arms to his side. "Very well. We will continue this little charade. But, next time Little Miss Sybille comes around, I'm making her hold the meter."

"Can you do that? What would the High King say?" Mylah asked, real nerves rattling inside her.

"She's not gonna tell her cousin," he said and waved off Mylah's fear. "She's more afraid of him than we are."

"And sometimes that is a motivating reason to spill the truth," Mylah said. "Let's not tempt fate. Let us watch the girl and see if she manifests in another way."

"I suppose that's wise," Luther admitted. "I just thought -,"

But what he thought remained a mystery. A bell peeled, deep and sonorous, the long echo reverberated out, the note going flat as it fell away, before clanging to life again. Mylah looked to Luther, whose face went stony. "Time to go," he said, grinding his teeth. "Follow me."

Mylah's nerves sparked. "Now? But I'm not ready."

"Ready or not, you're comin' with us. By the High King's order," Luther said.

"He ordered it?" Mylah asked.

"Yes, after the last raid." Luther walked past Mylah, crossing the pitch to its entrance. "We better jog. Don't want to keep him waiting."

Mylah gulped and followed Luther, starting out at a trot, then gaining speed to a rolling jog. Her stomach lurched. "We have to see the High King?" she asked.

Luther yelled over his shoulder, "He's the only one who can see exactly where they're at. You're about to see how. Brace yourself."

They met Leviatha at the castle gate and together they pelted across the courtyard. Guards in the royal black and gold moved aside, pulling open doors as they jogged through. "Your first Tyrmini hunt," Leviatha said, breathing hard. Mylah wondered where she'd come from. "How do you feel, young Mylah?"

"Sick," Mylah said.

"Better get it out now, then," she said and pointed to a vase. Mylah obeyed, heaving into the brass receptacle as if it were put there for just this occasion. She puked thoroughly, not holding back, trying to ensure there would be nothing left to wretch when she was standing in the High King's presence.

Once she was finished, she wiped her mouth on her linen wrappings and ran to catch up to Luther and Leviatha.

"Better?" Leviatha asked. Mylah grunted.

They slowed only after their fourth or fifth turn down inner corridors. The walls closed in around Mylah, the scent of oil lamps thick with the lack of fresh air. They moved through alternating pools of sallow, stagnant light and dim shadows. The hiss of the oil lamps accompanied the irregular clip of boots against stone. The ceilings loomed low enough Mylah could reach and touch them. She had never been in this part of the castle. They paused as another door swung open for them by a set of Tyrmini guards Mylah had never met before. One was a beefy middle-aged man cut from solid muscle which made his uniform stretch to the point it looked as though it would break the stitches.

The Tyrmini guards were dressed in the same garb as Mylah, Leviatha, and Luther, which was different than the rest of the royal guards. Their black pants were loose and tucked into high black boots. Black jackets cropped at the waist boasted two dozen or more brass buttons and embroidered weave that traced lines between them. Beneath the jacket was a light linen tunic that Mylah always wished was the only top piece she had to wear. And over their left breast clung the Tymini guard's royal symbol, smudged and mean in the low light. Mylah didn't know what one had to do to earn the badge, and hoped she'd never have one.

Mylah had nursed the two seasons of training, dreading the day she'd be ordered to participate in a mission. The High King seemed content and patient as she trained with Luther. As she and Luther grew ever closer, her mastery of her elemental power somehow intertwined with Luther. It gave her pause in some moments, wondering if she had inexorably linked herself with her captor.

She watched him run ahead of her, his motions smooth and effortless, and felt a familiar calm wash over her. She wondered if his power was not just Tyrinth, water and fire. Because she often felt bewitched by the man, her fierceness ebbed in his presence, her hatred abated, her sorrow smoothed.

They halted inside an antechamber on a beige rug woven in a pattern of rich red and purple. They all panted, catching their breath from their hurried pace over the castle grounds and through its twisting corridors. As she inhaled and exhaled, Mylah could not help her wandering gaze, feasting on the opulent sight like a starved person. Light danced off stone walls cast by ornate oil lamps the size of which she'd never seen before. Overstuffed chairs of rich leather occupied the room's four corners, interspersed with low tables. Covering the walls, tapestries depicted scenes from battle.

A hero was painted in each, pale hair illuminated, sword flashing brightly, armor glinting against a dark wave of people and elements. In one tapestry a wave of fire crashed against the hero's impenetrable sphere of light; in another, a wall of water dashed against an invisible shield surrounding the hero; and yet another, boulders crashed down on the hero, but none hit the man. He stood in varying poses of power and majesty, and Mylah snorted at the idiocy. In the next panel, the hero stood in front of a snarling white beast with wings, teeth and talons. Its maw dripped blood as it stood atop a mountain of dead soldiers, women, and children.

Mylah's stomach rolled at the detail of the faces, the marred bodies, bloodied and ruined as though by the beast. If only Tijhi could see this. What would the little fire dragon say?

In a final panel, the hero stood atop the dragon, its eyes closed as though dead, the hero lifted his sword to the sky triumphantly. Mylah sneered at the portrait of false history. Then checked herself. Had the High King not accomplished something close to this? It was true. Achyla the First had conquered Magloryn, and while she may still be alive, she was as good as dead, wasn't she? But the tale's truth ended there, the details of which remained lost to the ages.

The antechamber's door swung open, a trapezoid of light slashing into the small, cramped space. Leviatha and Luther passed through the door. Mylah paused, nerves alight. Luther's face appeared around the open door, eyebrows lifted in a question. Mylah made her feet move, bracing herself, and entered her enemy's lair.

CHAPTER FIFTEEN

Mylah blinked in the sudden wash of intense light. As her eyes adjusted she took in her surroundings. The room was a perfect circle. Windows lined one half of the room, spilling in the afternoon light, vaulted ceilings domed and painted with a scene of a cloudy, blue sky. Mylah wondered how such a thing was accomplished, given the last room's tightness, and the tiny corridors they'd passed through. Shelves lined the room's circular walls, all burdened with books of varying colors, widths, and heights. In the center, its back against a section of books, its side next to windows, a giant wooden desk squatted on curved legs. Its enormity dwarfed the beautiful man standing behind it.

Aelos's High King wore a plain white linen shirt and black breeches. There was no crown or jewels, save for a single silver and ebony bracelet on his left wrist. While his clothes were so opposite to the first set of finery she'd seen him in - save for the bracelet she'd seen him wearing then as well - he still somehow exuded royalty. He looked up from a map laid out across the desk's surface and fixed them each with a wide sapphire gaze. For a moment, Mylah lost herself in those deep blue eyes. She shook herself, mentally wrenching her concentration, but found her eyes roaming the perfect symmetry of the man's face, his straight nose, high cheekbones, strong jaw, and full pouting lips.

He smiled, and the spell shattered.

There was something about the curve of his lips, how light

didn't quite reach his eyes, that felt cruel to Mylah. He was a predator; a lovely one, but still a predator.

"Mylah," he intoned. His voice was silken and warm, welcoming, soothing. "It's good of you to join the guard today." He looked her over, appraising her. Something about those unsettling blue eyes made her squirm. It was as though he looked into her soul, and she worried whatever he saw would be used against her and her people. She struggled mentally to shield herself in some way, thinking it was foolish even as she scrambled to protect her mind and soul.

"What do we have?" Leviatha asked, her voice all business.

High King Achyla the Eighth turned his blue eyes from Mylah to the Captain and Mylah breathed a sigh of relief. The High King's face pinched in a look Mylah assumed she should take as concern, although there was something about it that felt insincere.

"We received report of a water Tyrmini in Sylvanea. He's constructed some sort of dam for a group of water elementals, which has cut off flow from farming fields further downstream. And unfortunately, I'm concerned there may have been casualties," the High King said.

"How many?" Luther asked.

"It's not clear to me," the king said, his tone flat. "Come around here you three and let me show you where you're going."

Luther, Leviatha, and Mylah heeded the High King's command. Mylah moved woodenly toward the predator. Leviatha and Luther seemed unbothered and walked swiftly to stand behind the desk. Yet, Mylah noticed they gave the High King a wide circle of space around his presence. As Mylah took up a spot near Luther, so that Luther was between herself and the High King, the High King caught her gaze.

"Mylah, come here and get a proper look at this map." He stepped around Luther, a pocket watch clinking from his waistband. He scooped Mylah's arm into a sturdy, but gentle grip.

Mylah went cold at his touch. All the normal heat of animation and life seemed absent from the High King. She wanted nothing more than to yank her arm from his grip and run. She steeled herself as the High King steered her toward the desk, releasing her, then pointing to a spot on the map, in its center.

"Here is Sylvanea," he said, pointing to the center of Aelos, depicting a collection of rivers, lakes, and creeks. "It's maybe a day's ride by normal horse, but luckily we have something faster." Mylah craned her head toward the High King, who smirked at her. "You'll see," he said, and turned back to the map.

He reached past her, brushing against her body and filling her aura with a chill nothingness unlike anything she'd ever experienced. He grasped a spherical object covered by a silken square and propped on a short, three-legged stand. The object was large enough he needed both hands. Once he'd removed it from its stand, Leviatha took the stand and moved it to the map's center.

Mylah wanted to move herself, wanted to get away from this man who felt dead, and get closer to Luther, who was on the king's opposite side. She stepped away from the desk. The High King carefully placed the orb on the stand, and without looking behind him, drew Mylah in again, pushing her lower back with a firm hand.

"I want you close for this part," he said. "Stay put." His tone shifted, the words affording no argument. Mylah squirmed. She looked past the High King to Luther who mouthed, *Brace yourself.* Mylah did. But it couldn't have prepared her for what came next.

The High King grasped the silk cloth from the globe beneath it and pulled it away. Mylah stifled a scream as she came face to face with a giant, glass-encased eye, floating in an ambient liquid. Fleshy cords dangled from the back of the eye, its white expanse tattooed with light red lines. Bits of unidentifiable debris floated in the liquid. Mylah's empty stomach lurched.

The eye fixed on the High King, its vertical pupil narrowing in the wash of light from the expanse of windows. The iris shifted color, at first a deep violet, then fading to the same sapphire blue as the High King's own gaze.

Mylah leaned in and the eye swiveled in her direction. The iris again shifted colors, sapphire to violet, green, hazel, brown, then mirroring Mylah's golden eyes, flecked with shards of green. As Mylah stared deeply into the eye, her power surged within her and a soft whisper echoed in her mind, as though down a long corridor.

Companion of the Tijhi, desert dweller, and Tyrmini. You will change our fate.

"This is a lost relic of the dragon my ancestor slew," the High King intoned. Mylah felt as though her being had been suddenly split into two, one part existing in the physical realm and the other wandering in some etyric plane.

Lies, lies, lies, the voice said into her mind.

"This relic allows us to locate the Tyrmini. Its magic calls out to the Tyrmini -," the High King said.

Because we long to reunite with our children.

" - and then we are able to take proper measures to eliminate the threat," he finished.

A threat that would not be a threat if he had not enslaved us.

Mylah had become accustomed to listening to Tijhi as they inserted thoughts into Mylah's head. She had grown comfortable and even looked forward to the mental conversations she and the dragon had. She'd learned their voice, their personality, their sense of humor since they'd been united. This voice was so different, so powerful, so full of emotion and feeling and depth.

"Watch, Mylah," High King Achyla said to her and pointed at the eye, silver and black bracelet winking in the sunlight. "Show us the Tyrmini in this region."

The eye shuddered and at last broke its gaze with Mylah, the iris shifting colors so that it seemed to reflect a collection of every color imaginable, until it settled on a vivid blue. The glass's surface encasing the eye seemed to cloud and then reflecting back at them, the image of a young man came into focus. He was maybe fourteen or fifteen summers; blond hair and Mylah was unsurprised to see the glint of vivid blue eyes. His skin shone pale in weak gray light, with lips so deeply colored they were nearly purple. The boy perched on a riverbank, twirling a long blade of golden grass in his hands. His nose angled crookedly, as though it had broken and healed. His mouth moved but no sound emerged.

"Who is the boy speaking to?" the High King asked, notes of curiosity shifting his tone. The vision shifted, panning away from the boy and toward the river. A creature came into view, large black eyes filling the glass's expanse prominently. Orange skin glistened in weak sunlight, scaled and sparkling. The creature's limbless, long body seemed to be floating, but then Mylah realized it hovered on an unnatural pillar of water.

The creature undulated in the water, its ceaseless movement seeming to keep it atop its watery pillar. The creature cocked a squarish head to one side, elongated snout tipping, long whiskers bobbing with the movement. Short, feathery appendages sprouted from the creature's head, forming a crown of vivid purple.

"A vepierus," Achyla said, pointing to the water creature. "Foul beasts. Those scales are toxic to the touch."

The vision zoomed out to show both the boy and the creature. The boy spoke again, then paused. The creature tilted its head in the other direction, circled its body atop the pillar of water, and launched into the air, spraying water droplets over the boy. He laughed shortly, wiped his face, and frowned. He spoke, rising to his feet. The creature backed away, its water pillar moving with it, deeper into the river. The boy's face contorted into a scowl, his words seeming harsher, arm flailing out. The creature circled again, tilted its head once more. The boy shouted something, flinging an arm, and the pillar of water and the creature riding it washed away down the river.

The boy's face twisted in anger, his shoulders heaving. He turned from the river and stalked away.

The orb lightened, the image fading until Mylah looked once more at the multicolored gaze of Magloryn. The dragon's voice remained silent as the High King shifted the orb and its stand aside and looked closely at the map. He pointed.

"That looks like Uul River. Go find this Tyrmini and hurry," he said. His face pinched in worry. Mylah reeled. Moments before nothing but apathy emanated from the man. Now, stress and concern painted his face. "He seems agitated. If he finds a fight to pick let it be with you and not with an innocent citizen of Aelos. I won't have my subjects in fear of those with such power."

Mylah stepped away, her eyes fixed on the High King, her intuition not trusting her senses. Warmth enveloped her arm, and when she looked to find the source, she was face to face with Luther. He gently tugged her, bowing to the High King. "We will," he said. Mylah shook herself, following Luther's lead and bowing to the monarch.

"We'll report back once the Tyrmini has been apprehended and dealt with," Leviatha said, also bowing, teal eyes alight with grim purpose. The three of them turned from the High King, and as they exited the room, the dragon of light's voice called out to Mylah.

Eyes wide open, child.

Mylah shivered, skin prickling with gooseflesh. She followed Leviatha and Luther out of the High King's personal study, his gaze drilling into her spine as she went.

CHAPTER SIXTEEN

The trio of Tyrmini crossed the royal grounds at an even clip. They reached the royal stables and entered through open barn doors. Mylah's senses were overwhelmed by the smell of hay and horse poop, and something else she couldn't quite identify. Curious, she made her way down the stables' center aisle, seeing every sort of horse imaginable - horses that seemed best suited for pulling plows, and others that looked sleek and swift, yet others looked docile and sturdy, meant for those new to riding.

Up ahead, a set of stables spilled golden light into the center aisle. Mylah had only ever heard stories of these creatures. She inhaled in surprise and rushed forward. One stall housed a mare and foal. The small golden horse-shaped creature had barely budding wings, fluff-covered with down. The mare circled the foal, standing between Mylah and her offspring, pointedly staring at Mylah in a protective glare. Mylah held her hands up and backed away from the stall.

She moved to another stall, eyes fixed on the creature within, craning her head back to take in its height and stature. "Are these hestias?" she asked, not because she could not see them standing in front of her, but out of shock to see them in person.

"They are indeed the elemental flying horses of legend," Luther said. "And they're a bit of a hand-," he began to say, but Mylah reached toward the giant golden creature in front of her. The horse-shaped elemental flared his wings, approached, sniffed at Mylah's hand and nuzzled it. She reached into her coat pocket where she'd stowed a cookie Sybille had given her the night before. She offered the treat to the horse, who greedily lipped it up, ears pinning back as it chomped. Once the creature was finished, its ears swiveled to the side as it nudged at Mylah.

Mylah stroked the horse's nose, reveling in the soft velvety texture, and whispered, "good horse" over and over. Mylah took the lead and walked the creature away from the other two, falling into the meditative mood needed to lead a horse. She hoped the approach was the same for a hestia. Her years on horseback when she was young clicked into place and she found the creature a companionable presence. She stepped back and observed it, letting - she looked, and confirmed - him soak in the experience, and process their meeting.

The creature backed up, looking deeply into Mylah's eyes. Mylah met the gaze with confidence. After a moment, the golden creature nodded his head twice, bowed, flared his wings and turned to present his flank. Mylah approached the hestia, sensed the ground beneath her feet, called on Tyrinth and allowed it to boost her onto the creature's back, just behind the wing joints. It felt natural, normal, and invigorating.

Thank you, she thought to the hestia. *May I know your name?*

She hadn't spoken to other creatures before, so she didn't know if it would work. The horse flicked an ear in her direction, his head tilted. Mylah let him think about it, wondering if he would choose to speak to her. When the creature turned his head away, tossing his mane in a shake, the meaning echoed through her.

I have no name, the creature said, the quality of that inner voice light-filled and breathy.

Surely the other hestias call you something, Mylah pushed.

I was born here and have never roamed with others of my kind.

Mylah's heart quivered. This creature had been born and bred by the High King and had never experienced a normal existence with other hestias. He'd been robbed of family and community, of his native lands in the Shoqui Plains, and the ability to fly, except when employed to do so.

Mylah stroked the stallion's neck, a leaden sadness settling into her chest. *What if I gave you a name?*

The hestia blew, casting a wide-eyed glance down to Mylah. *You would do such a thing?*

It would be my honor, Mylah said.

The dam in the first stall with her foal stamped and whinnied, throwing her head back in outrage. *A human may not name a hestia,* she proclaimed.

"What's going on?" Luther asked, looking between the dam and Mylah.

I'm not a human, Mylah said, *I am a Tyrmini and a creature speaker. I am a dragon speaker.*

I see no dragons here. The dragons sleep, as they have for centuries. We are left alone and unguarded. The dam's fierceness radiated through her thoughts, her anger and sorrow melding into her meaning.

One dragon has risen from their sleep, Mylah noted, but her confidence wavered. She hadn't known the other dragons slept.

You lie, the hestia asserted, tossing her head.

I do not, but that's neither here nor there. I'm speaking with you now and only a Tyrmini has that gift; therefore, not human. And so I shall name this stallion, as long as he wills it.

Don't you dare, the dam insisted to the stallion.

Why do you care now? We've been imprisoned for tens of season cycles. You have not granted me a name.

And I am the only one who may grant you a name.

Then why do you not give me one?

You are an abomination. Born in a stall instead of in the open plains under the sun with the wind in your mane and tail and wings.

Your child and I are the same, the stallion pointed out. *Will*

139

you not grant your own child a name?

It is my child and I shall grant her a name.

Then I shall take a name. And you will not stop me.

Mylah stroked the stallion's neck as he turned back to her, dark eyes fixing her with an intense gaze. She considered the creature, its light golden hide and white mane, wings, and tail all floating as if on an unseen wind. She rubbed the stallion's cheek, reveling in its deep breaths, and proclaimed, "Aerys. I name you Aerys, in honor of the great dragon of air, Aerylia."

Blasphemy, the dam said.

I invite the dragon to wake and say so herself, Mylah said.

The stallion straightened, lifting his head high, and glowed warm and bright. Aerys stretched his wings wide, flapped them in one mighty stroke and air erupted around the creature. Mylah clung to the creature's leg to keep from being blasted away, hair swirling around her face, air causing her breath to catch and pause.

Because you have named me, I am forever in your debt, Aerys said, lowering his head to Mylah in reverence.

"Well, well, well," Luther said, his mouth hanging open. "Don't know what that was all about but you sure seem to have a way with these creatures."

"Aerys is an amazing creature," she said, and stroked his neck.

Leviatha had mounted her hestia and Luther approached the third warily. "Whoa, horse," he said, hands up in a surrender gesture, head tilted back. The hestia pinned its ears and danced away.

"Wait," Mylah said, sensing disaster. "You've got to be more confident when you approach."

"Confident?" Luther asked. "What are you talking about? I'm confident. Here, horse, let me climb onto you."

Mylah clambered down from her mount as Luther drove into his own, stubbornly moving in despite the horse dancing away, tossing her head, and snorting. Mylah reached Luther just as the horse reared. She pulled Luther out of the creature's path before its hooves slammed into the Tyrinth, thunder reverberating under their feet. Wind sprang up around them, and Mylah looked up to see the hestia's wings batting the air around her.

"Have you never ridden this animal before?" Mylah asked.

"Nah, I did once. She didn't like me much that time either."

"Did she buck you?" Mylah guessed. Luther rubbed the back of his neck and shrugged, looking sheepish. Mylah nodded. "It's scary, isn't it?" she asked.

Luther raised his eyebrows and whistled. "Sure rattled me," he said.

She grasped his shoulders, pressing them back and down. "The key to horses - and maybe hestias, it seems - is leadership. You need to master your fear. You must let go of what happened in the past."

Luther's eyes were wide as he met her gaze, his mouth slack. "That's just life lessons, isn't it just?" His words growled through him, his voice vibrating through his shoulders and into her hands.

Mylah didn't respond. Didn't want to think about how hypocritical she would sound if she agreed with him. Could she really take her own advice and let go of what happened in her past?

"Head down," she instructed Luther, shaking off her thoughts and focusing on the task at hand. "Relax your stance but remain strong. Root yourself into the Tyrinth, keeping your energy down here in your legs and feet, and not up here in your chest and head."

Luther was a receptive learner, and once he'd mastered his energy, he approached the hestia with an all-new demeanor. Mylah also gave him a cookie. The hestia lipped the cookie into her mouth and crunched, not nuzzling into Luther, but allowing his touch as he stroked her neck. She tolerated his approach to her side and seemed to begrudgingly allow him to mount her.

Once they were all atop their hestias, Leviatha leaned forward and whispered to her horse, "Can you find the Uul River and take us there?" The hestia pinned its ears first, swiveled them forward, pawed once at the ground, and shot away in a streak of golden light.

Mylah looked over to Luther, who rolled his shoulders and neck. He inhaled and exhaled deeply, before requesting their destination.

Mylah thought to Aerys, *Do you think you can find the Tyrmini boy who is near the Uul River?* The hestia's eyes widened, head swiveling. He pawed the Tyrinth and then they flew.

Wind whipped through her hair, smothering her so she could barely breathe, as the world shot by. Streams of light and color flew past them in a blur. Mylah leaned down into the hestia's neck, hoping to reduce the wind resistance. From time to time she shielded her face and took a breath.

The creature's muscles undulated beneath her legs, wings pumping hard. Mylah braced herself as she rode the creature and knew tomorrow her inner and outer thighs would be a mass of solid ache. After what seemed like a short span of moments in which Mylah wondered exactly how fast they were going, they slowed. Mylah looked up, shocked to find instead of rolling hills and copses of autumn-gilded forests, she stared at wide open plains snaked through with creeks and occasionally dotted with willowy trees. The grasses here were a bluish green and the ground beneath the hestia's hooves squelched.

Amongst the fields, creeks, reeds, and short trees, a small cottage of cobblestones crouched on the crest of a grass-laden hill. The day here hung in gray silence, solid cloud cover pressing down on the lush green landscape. A light drizzle prickled Mylah's exposed skin. All around her the soft trickle of water echoed in varying pitches on the still air. Mylah saw no sign of Leviatha or Luther.

The hestia walked forward, eyes fixed on some distant point. They approached the house and slowed, the hestia bobbing its head in the house's direction. The front door hung open. Mylah peered in, growing unease hunching her shoulders. She could see nothing past the threshold, but there was a distinct smell in the air surrounding the place that Mylah couldn't name. The horse creature moved on before Mylah could dismount to investigate further.

The further they walked, the stronger the scent of water grew. The light drizzle turned to an enveloping blanket of moisture that clung to Mylah's skin, clothes, hair, and eyelashes. Her teeth clacked as they made their way toward a pond. The grasses marched right up to where the mud and water met. The hestia stopped, legs splayed out, head tossing over and over. Mylah slipped from the creature's back and landed with a squelch. She rounded the hestia and spoke into its mind.

Can you wait for me? The creature ignored her, wings spread and ready to launch, nostrils flared, eyes wide, mouth tense. *Danger*, the creature blared into her mind.

Go if you must, she told it. The hestia backed up, head still tossing, turned and trotted away, tail tight against its backside.

She supposed they couldn't all be brave.

Mylah shrugged it off, setting aside the problem of a return trip for later. She pulled her booted feet from the sinking mud and trudged ahead. She passed a pile of logs all jutting above the water's surface, the trickle sloping around the mound to continue on in much smaller fashion. A splash drew her attention with a snap. Ripples emanated from the pond's center. The hair on her neck sprang to attention. At the pond's opposite end the mound of tree limbs and logs made a makeshift dock of sorts and bared the weight of two lumpy piles of fabric.

She aimed for the wooden platform, casting a look about her, hoping to see her companions. Aerys dotted the distant horizon, a gold speck against the green and gray behind her, but she noted with some satisfaction that he'd stayed in proximity. Perhaps he was waiting after all. She turned to face the dock again and halted dead in her tracks. Something or someone crouched over the lumpy piles. The shape shifted. The Tyrmini boy she'd seen in the dragon's eye turned as he shoved at a large rock. Mylah ducked behind a nearby willow and watched. The boy grasped a nearby rope and a second something she couldn't quite make out. Mylah shifted closer, adjusting her gaze to make out the object. With dawning horror Mylah realized the thing the boy was tying up was a person's ankles.

Mylah didn't think; she ran. Ran toward the boy and the people he was tying up, instinct propelling her into action. The same old fear washed through her. The same crippling panic that she would reach out to protect someone and she would fail. That she would once again be too late, too weak, and too small.

"Hey!" she shouted. The boy shot up, rope and ankle falling with thuds from his hands, face filled with fear and horror.

"I didn't mean it," he said.

"Back away," she yelled. He didn't move. "I said move away."

"They - they held me down. They dragged me into the water. They -," the boy's voice cracked, tears streaming down his face, his body shaking, breath heaving. Mylah came to a halt in front of the boy bordering manhood. His blue eyes reflected red veins, pale skin ghostly white. He towered over Mylah by head and shoulders, and yet, he was so vulnerable. He wore a light long-sleeved tunic and despite the rain, his clothes remained dry. She could swear the moisture seemed to be repelled from the young man.

It was then that Mylah's gaze slid to the two people laid out on the makeshift dock in front of him. The ankles and feet the boy had been trying to tie to a boulder lie still, skin a sickly blue, wrinkled and puckered. Their chests and abdomen swelled past normality. Mylah tried to look away but failed as her eyes, as if of their own accord, roamed up the body to the face.

Froth spilled out of their mouths and nose, their eyes staring, as if shocked, into the gray sky. He'd already killed them, as the High King had indicated.

"I couldn't help it," he screamed, wringing his hands and sobbing. "They attacked me and tried to kill me. All I wanted was to live. So I fought and I didn't know. I didn't know it would hurt them. I just wanted them to stop. I couldn't breathe." He choked on a strangled sob, coughing, then launched in again. "I couldn't breathe and they still held me, held me under the water and laughed. They were killing me and they laughed. And I couldn't take it any longer. So I kicked and pulled and shoved and then, the water exploded around me. It exploded." He gestured with his arms and hands, his eyes wild, snot running down his upper lip, spit flying from his mouth.

"When I stood up from the water, I stood... I stood up, and..." his eye twitched, gaze shifting as he peered into the past before snapping back onto Mylah, as if remembering she was there. "That's when they appeared. I should never have talked to them. I should never have -. They wrapped them both up and squeezed." The boy gripped his hands into fists and pulled them away from each other, as if miming the pulling, squeezing action 'they' had done.

"Who? Who did this?" Mylah asked.

"The elementals. They pulled them down into the water and held them there, held them while they kicked and thrashed... and then... they went still." He held his hand to his heart, tears slipping down his face. He looked to the two other boys, both about his age. "And I didn't even think to tell them to stop. Because I didn't want them to stop. For years... years, they'd done stuff like this to me. Beat me. Shattered my nose," he pointed to his crooked nose, "broke my arm, my ribs, my fingers, blackened my eyes, yanked my hair out. And so when I saw them drowning. I let them," he said savagely, twisting a hand into a fist in front of him.

Mylah rocked back on her heels. A noise to her left caught

her attention and she turned in time to see a slender snaking tube of water race past her and toward the boy. He lazily waved it off. "I'm not going to be bullied anymore," he said, his voice skipping octaves. "They got what they deserved, even if I didn't have the guts to do it myself. That's why they did it for me. They knew me." Leviatha raced toward them, underneath her a solid sheet of water carried her forward faster than just her feet could manage.

Behind her, Luther levitated two chunks of fiery Tyrinth in the air and hurled it at the boy. The Tyrmini youth dodged the first, but that motion ran him into the second. He screamed as the rock found purchase and he hurled backward across the grassy marsh. The fire extinguished immediately, and the boy struggled through the pile of dirt heaped atop him. Heaving, he pulled his leg free and stood atop the mound. A drop of water in front of him expanded until a full wall of water shimmered and wavered. He gestured toward the wall and it flew toward the oncoming Leviatha. She received the water like it was meant to be a gift, opening her arms wide. She blew on the massive sphere in front of her as she elongated the liquid. Shards of ice blew away from her, as she shot them back at the boy.

He didn't have time to react. He turned as if to shield himself with his back. The first ice spike skewered him in the shoulder, causing his body to pivot, opening his torso toward Leviatha. The second spear hit him in the chest with a wet thud. The boy choked in surprise, mouth hanging open, bloodshot eyes wide. Blood spread across his simple beige tunic, the fabric hungrily lapping it up. He touched the spike, looked up at Leviatha, inhaled, as if he would say something. A ragged moan warbled out. He tipped to his knees then fell forward.

"It wasn't his fault," Mylah said, eyes filling with tears. "He was just defending himself."

"Yeah?" Luther asked. "Maybe you missed the four dead bodies back at the homestead. Or are you saying he needed to protect himself against his little three-year-old sister?" Luther shook, face a mask of anger.

Mylah inhaled sharply. "What?"

"He slaughtered his family. Drowned them in their beds. You might have compassion and a heart and love, but this power twists people, Mylah. That boy was about as twisted as they come."

"He said they bullied him, that they were trying to drown him," she said.

"That's probably why he snapped," Leviatha said. "But snap he did, and he killed six people because of it, including his younger siblings."

"He - ?" Mylah started, not finding any more words as horror filled her. "And this -," she gestured around her, "happens often?"

"More often than the alternative. You don't understand how rare you are, Mylah. Most of us can't handle the power's pressure surging inside us. It breaks us."

Mylah didn't remember how she got back on Aerys, nor the return trip, and certainly not the trip from the stables to her quarters. She had shucked her uniform, bathed, shimmied her way into her nightgown, crawled into bed, and wept. She wept for the boys who died that day, for the family who'd been slaughtered. She cried at the injustice of it all, and she cried because she had survived when the boy today had died. When her cousin had died.

She and Luther and Leviatha all had maintained their humanity after their power had manifested, after their tragedies, and had learned to wield them with control. Why did some break and not others? Why was it so polarizing? She could hear the dragon's voice in her mind, replaying from earlier that day: *A threat that would not be a threat if he had not enslaved us.*

Mylah wept until the tears ran out, her belly hard and sore from the effort, and then she slept. But not peacefully. Never again would she sleep peacefully.

CHAPTER SEVENTEEN

Mylah rose at the near dawn, moving through the dressing process unsure what she planned to do. She wrapped her arms in linen strips as was her peoples' custom, then fastened on leather bracers. The dull-white linen shone against her golden-brown skin. The black and gold officer's jacket hung in the wardrobe on one wall of the room. The leather breaches skimmed her legs with comfortable tightness, the shirt a simple sleeveless thing that left her arms bare where the linen wrappings ended just below her elbows.

Yesterday's encounter left a hollow mass in her core. She cast around her room at the walls closing her in. She must escape them.

She retrieved her boots and laced them up before pulling her leathers back down over them. She would head to the training grounds. She needed to move, to melt the emotion stuck in her veins, and breathe out the horror of yesterday.

She stalked to the door and pulled it open. Standing with a hand ready to knock was none other than her fellow and mentor Tyrmini. Luther stood in front of her. He was in uniform, his golden pin glinting against the black coat. Mylah cocked her head to one side. "What is it?" she asked.

"We've got another one," he said, dropping his fist to his side. His dark eyes roamed over her, assessing her in a dissecting way.

Mylah blinked. "Now? Today?" she asked. Her heart thudded to a stop.

Luther nodded and propped a fist onto his hip. "Sounds dire. The king sent a servant first thing to call on us."

Mylah slowly shook her head. She couldn't do it. She couldn't kill a child. "No," Mylah said simply, crossing her arms over her middle, her belly quaking. Where moments earlier she'd been a hollowed-out husk, her thoughts and feelings now boiled away inside her, rich and raw. She let them simmer, savoring the hurt.

Luther met her gaze unflinchingly. "May I come in?" he asked.

Mylah considered slamming the door in his face. But his warm comforting presence called to her. She moved aside, uncrossing her arms. Luther crossed the threshold, and Mylah closed the door behind him. He looked around the room, taking in the furniture, the closet, the large window looking out onto the gardens.

He perched on the unmade bed, one boot propped on the frame, the other on the wooden floor. Soft morning light filtered in from the window, keeping the shadowy corners wrapped in their dark secrets. She faced him, fists clenched at her sides.

He didn't speak.

Mylah wriggled under the silence until she couldn't take it any longer.

"You expect me to go cut down some other child hours after that boy yesterday was killed?" she snarled, lip curling in disgust. She flung her arm at the door, pointing. "You want me to go right into that cold, cruel husk of a human and do his bidding without question. How could you? How could you kill a young person so easily?"

Tears streamed down her face, her stomach all knots and hardness, chest a raging fire. Her breath rattled before she shouted, "That boy couldn't help it, and we offered him no help, no resources, no other way than to give into the power. Why did he deserve death? Who are we to dole that out?"

Luther simply listened, his brown eyes fixed on her, shoulders slumped.

"I'm not doing one more thing for him. Not one more! I can't. I can't do it. You have no idea. You have -," her words cut short in racking sobs. She heaved in a breath as she drowned on memories blurring together: the water Tyrmini boy's face, her cousin's face as lightning struck him, her aunt's howling screams of mourning.

Mylah fell to her knees, body shaking so hard she placed her hands against the cool wooden slats of her bedroom floor. Nausea and horror swept through her. How could she honor her cousin if she acted out the very things that had brought about his death?

Warm arms wrapped around her, pulled her. She let them as she was plunged into memory. Somewhere in an intangible reality, she sat in Luther's lap, her head resting on his chest, his chin pressing into the top of her head as she sobbed. Her body rattled as cold sweat drenched her body. He stroked her dark hair and rocked her as her emotions stormed through her.

Fire sprung up within her and she let it burn, hoping beyond hope it would devour her. Luther never stopped, he simply stroked her hair, rocked her and didn't speak. Mylah quaked and lost herself in the flames, and then to the rhythm of his rocking, in the hard muscle wrapping around her, pressing into her cheek. Flashes of lightning, flashes of the stranger's face, her uncle, her father, her cousin's last moments stampeded through her brain without her bidding.

Flame danced white hot, panic fueling it. Luther hushed and rocked her as she wept and burned.

Finally, the memories slowed, she breathed, and she came back.

She opened her eyes and saw nothing but flames dancing around her, shimmering in shades of blue and gold. She called the flames back into her, worried she had set her quarters on fire, but everything was intact. She turned to Luther. He must have held those flames, that fire of her own making at bay. They were nearly nose to nose, his dark eyes warm, tears tracking down his face.

Mylah reached a hand toward his cheeks and lightly wiped away the wetness. It was replaced by new tears.

"I'm sorry," she said.

"No need for apologies," he whispered, his voice that wonderful rumbling velvet that reverberated through her. "No one asked us before we got landed in this life. It ain't fair. Days like yesterday are rough. Today is different. Come with me, and I promise you'll get to see the brighter side of this whole thing."

Mylah wriggled a little and Luther eased open his arms, releasing her. She pulled away to look at him. "Why? Why are you so kind to me?"

Luther never broke her gaze. "Because I understand."

She ducked her head, sudden shame burned her throat. She looked around, not sure what to do next, how to extricate herself from the situation.

"Thank you," she said. She wanted to say more. Wanted to tell him how when she was with him, she felt safer and more accepted than at any time in her life. Wanted to say that he felt like home, like a ray of the Goddess reached out to her through him.

She rose, cool air replacing the warmth of his body next to hers. He pushed himself to his feet, dusting his hands. She wrapped an arm over her middle, grasping her other arm with her hand. She had no idea what to do with herself.

"I don't mean to rush you, doll..." he said apologetically, wrapping a hand over the back of his neck.

Mylah remembered why he came, why she'd had the outburst in the first place. "Oh," she said, grateful for a reason to end this awkward moment. "Yes. Let me grab my sand."

She crossed the room, his eyes on her back. She wanted to melt into the floor. In the end, there simply was no time to dwell on the embarrassing thing that had just happened between them. She grabbed the simple leather pouch, heavy with the sand's weight, and strapped it across her body, buckling it at her left shoulder, and followed Luther out of her room. She closed the door to her room and to all the emotion that had spilled out of her.

Mylah followed Luther through the winding halls of the castle, wondering if she would ever get used to all its sprawling, labyrinthine corridors. Two guards greeted them, flanking the antechamber door and watched them enter without a blink. In the antechamber, they waited, surrounded by tapestries covering every wall, telling the story of Achyla the First's conquest of the dangerous dragon. The final scene was stitched to portray a triumphant hero, sword lifted to the sky. Mylah sneered at it.

Another guard admitted them into the High King's private study, closing the door behind them. Today's weather boasted big, billowing white clouds that skidded over a dark, pre-dawn sky with purpose, as if they were in a hurry to get to their destination. The treetops visible through the bank of windows bent and swayed in the wind. Mylah reached for a leather strand she had wrapped around her wrist, just below the bracer, pulling her hair back and tying it in place.

The High King was in fine clothing today, his golden hair loose and hanging around his neck. He wore a black jacket with tails over a black vest embroidered in gold swirls. The dragon's eye sat perched on its wood base over the map of Landsend. The eye swiveled to Luther, mirroring his brown eyes, then shifting to Mylah and reflecting her golden gaze.

"You're here. Good," said the High King. "Mylah, join me." He looked up from the map and motioned to her with the wave of an elegant hand, bejeweled today with a large sapphire and silver ring and the usual black and silver bracelet.

Mylah did as she was told, grinding her teeth and growling mentally at the command. Once she stood beside the High King, he intoned, "Show us the Tyrmini with Tyrinth and water ability."

The eye shifted, reflecting more colors than Mylah could

name before it clouded over and a new image appeared on the glass's surface. The image of a young girl swam into view, almost seeming to look into the eye. Mylah guessed she was only ten or eleven - young for a Tyrmini. She had rich auburn hair and large emerald eyes. Freckles spread across her cheeks and nose and when she smiled a noticeable gap yawned between her two front teeth. Her heart-shaped face peered up at them, her head tilted to one side.

The girl's head jerked to one side, hair spilling over her shoulder, eyes widening. The view zoomed out enough to see an adult man's large hand grip the girl's arm and yank.

"Location!" the High King yelled. "We need the location, and quickly." The dragon's eye misted over and then their view was zoomed into the map, a pinpoint just south of Udari City. She was close. Mylah took a step back, her heart picking up speed. She would not be party to another young person dying, and this one even younger than the last. She opened her mouth to say so, but the High King turned to her and gripped her shoulders.

"You must bring her to us alive. Do not let any harm fall on her. Those people will set upon her their vendetta against Tyrmini and they will kill her," he said, and Mylah's emotions swirled to a halt. He wanted them to save her.

Luther walked toward her. Mylah looked deeply into the King's sapphire eyes, trying hard to find feeling reflecting the same compassionate urgency he emoted and only saw hunger. She nodded, confusion mashed up against relief.

Still gripping her arm, the High King reached his other hand to an object on the desk's littered surface. "Before you leave," he started. He dropped her arm and faced her. "I understand you handled yourself well yesterday. So, I bestow this upon you and make you an official Tyrmini Royal Guard."

The High King pinned something on her linen shirt. She looked down as he moved away and saw the pin representing the four elements, gold glinting brightly in the sun. She snuck a look at Luther, who didn't smile, but set his mouth in a stern line of acceptance.

She didn't want this. Didn't want the weight of the pin against her chest, over her heart, and filling her soul with that awful responsibility this proclamation came with. The blood that would stain her soul because of its presence. The High King released her, and Mylah and Luther sped from the room.

At the stables, Mylah sought out Aerys. He proudly approached the stable door, hanging his massive head over the gate. Mylah pulled an apple from her pocket and offered it to the creature. He turned his head away, looking down at Mylah from the side of his face. He shook his head. Mylah's eyebrows went up into her hairline. She pocketed the apple and instead pulled a shortbread biscuit from the other pocket. She offered the creature the baked treat, who lipped it up eagerly.

"Hm," Mylah said, "You and Sybille could be best of friends. I shall have to let her know of your love for confections." Mylah rubbed at the hestia's muscled neck, glancing over to the stall that had the day before housed the dam and her foal. Today, it stood empty.

Mylah wondered if the parent and baby had been relocated. She looked around but didn't see the pair.

Luther stood at the mare's stable.

"Where is Leviatha today?" Mylah asked.

Luther offered the mare a cookie - it seemed he'd learned quickly what the creatures liked. He looked at Mylah, his face turning grim as his eyes flicked to the empty stall next to Aerys. Mylah looked back at it then to Luther. He scratched at the hestia's neck, sorrow filling his dark eyes. "She's workin' on somethin' -," he paused for a moment, swallowed, then continued, "- special for his majesty."

"What does that mean?" Mylah asked.

"No time, darlin'. We gotta get."

Mylah frowned but set about opening Aerys's stall. Once they were on their mounts, Mylah asked the beast to take them to the Tyrmini girl just south of the city. Within moments, they arrived in an open terrain spotted with large trees. Mylah, who had grown up in the desert, didn't have names for these trees, but appreciated their towering height, massive trunks, and sprawling canopies which shone ocher, red, and gold under the autumn sun.

Dark fields stretched away from them, plants burgeoning with giant orange globes of vegetables, stalks of fully grown corn, stampeded into the distance in perfect rows. Mylah could smell the crops, rich, fibrous, sweet, pungent - all ripe for harvest. The morning air snapped cooly, and Mylah wished she'd grabbed her wool officer's coat. She drew on the elemental heat flowing through her body to warm herself and watched steam rise around her. Aerys shook his head.

Pink sunlight crested the eastern horizon to Mylah's left. Luther rode at Mylah's right. His face reflected that same stern, troubled expression as when they'd ventured out the day before. He looked at her, catching her gaze. "Ready yourself. This could get ugly," he said.

"Uglier than yesterday?" she asked, her voice a raw rasp. He frowned, reached out to her and touched her arm, gently. The warmth of his hand sent a shiver up her arm. He gave her an understanding squeeze.

"Let's hope not," he said. "It's unusual we have two so closely together. I've never had back-to-back days. Unusual indeed." He dropped his hand and Mylah wished he hadn't. She craved his touch, the reassurance she felt with his skin on hers. She shook herself from those dangerous, distracting thoughts and focused on the task at hand, searching for some sign of their quarry.

Further south, Mylah picked out a group of people gathered near one of the large trees. She pointed, whistling to get Luther's attention. He drew his gaze in her direction from where he'd been looking toward the west. They urged the hestias forward and found themselves skirting the throng before Mylah could register they'd moved. She slid from Aerys's back. As she landed onto firm Tyrinth, she called on the element to root her, even as she shook with nerves, some of her earlier panic rising again.

Women, men, and children gathered near the tree, its golden leaves shimmering in a mild breeze. The women wore similar cotton skirts of dark hues, their stays wrapped over simple blouses, aprons tied in place, and bonnets or hair coverings topping their pulled-back hair. The men wore either loose pantaloons or coveralls of thick canvas. Some carried implements of their trade. One man leaned into a metal rake. Another man hefted a hammer. One other held a length of thick rope.

The small children clung to older children or the women, faces still sleepy, as though they'd just woken. All in all, the crowd numbered approximately fifty, and they all faced the tree. Mylah's heart thundered away while her boots froze her in place. Maybe she'd grounded too much.

A woman screamed, someone up front, by the vicinity of the noise, and it broke Mylah's temporary paralysis. She moved as the rope and noose sailed over a giant limb. A young girl's cry ripped through the dawn, high and horrible.

Visions of her cousin tied to a striking rod flashed across her mind.

Mylah pushed through the gathered bodies, jostled and slowed as she frantically made her way forward. The young girl rose into her line of sight, over the heads of the gathered people.

"No," a woman yelled.

"Please, don't do this, Mather," a man said. "You don't know for sure she's Tyrmini."

Luther and Mylah burst through the crowd as the girl gripped at the rope tucked under chin. She stood on a worn wooden platform. Its specific reason so clearly the same as the striking pole her people had: to punish criminals. Yet, here a young girl stood, bent under the weight of the rope and noose.

Flame erupted within her at the sight, licking eagerly down Mylah's arms. She pulled the pouch she'd strapped to her torso.

Calm yourself, a voice spoke into Mylah's mind. She whirled, looking for Tijhi, her companion. And there they were, perched on the tree limb the girl was about to be hanged from. The little gold fox sat pristinely on the tree, tail twitching slowly.

Where did you come from? Mylah asked.

While it's true I've taken the form of a humble fox, I am Tijhi, an ancient elemental dragon deity, with a few more powers and abilities than are known to mere mortal kind. The Tijhi looked down their nose at their companion. *Now, focus. Get your head out of your heart and keep your wits about you.*

Mylah looked toward the man who held the other end of the rope. He was one of the largest humans she'd ever seen, with forearms that rippled from the tension of gripping the rope. His massive pectorals, covered in a plain cotton shirt and crossed by overalls bulged, his biceps threatening the integrity of the shirt's material. His soft brown eyes turned harsh by a sneer at the young girl.

"There is no doubt. She is Tyrmini," the man said.

"Don't do this, Daddy! I promise, I won't hurt anyone!" she said, her tiny voice strained.

"Silence!" the man shouted, tears welling in his eyes and spilling down his cheeks. "You'll ruin us. It's not your fault. I know it. But it can't be helped, Olivia." His voice cracked on her name, his body shaking as he held the rope meant to snap his little girl's neck with one quick, easy jerk.

Tijhi moved silently, without a soul watching except for Mylah. They picked their way across the tree limb, bent over the rope and touched their open mouth to the threads. Smoke bloomed out of the little fox's mouth and when they moved away, the rope glowed red for a moment before flame burst to life.

"You can't do this," a woman's shrill voice called out. She knelt in front of the platform, her hands pressed to the ground. "Please, please, don't kill my little girl." Mylah honed in on the flame and teased it to grow. Just a little nudge, which took strength of will to bank the vast power coiled inside her. The fire devoured the rope's dry twines.

The man ignored his wife's cries as his muscles bunched. Mylah thumbed the pouch's stopper. Sand hissed out of its container. Mylah gathered the material into a ball which she compressed through her link to the element. The man yanked. Mylah aimed and lobbed the sphere, now rock hard and hot. The rope lifted the girl, Olivia, from the platform for a mere moment before the final strands were consumed by Tijhi's fire. The rope snapped, the man caught off balance, Olivia fell to the platform, gasping.

Mylah's weapon thudded into the man's stomach. Air whooshed out of him in a surprised exhale, as he stumbled and fell from the platform. The rope dropped from the tree branch, fire licking at the fibers. Luther stepped up beside Mylah, inhaled and exhaled, gestured to the soft dew-drenched Tyrinth, and made a scooping motion. The ground shook and dislodged itself, plant life ripping through the air. The dirt pile hovered before it landed squarely on the burning rope.

Mylah called her sand back to her, separating the grains before guiding them back into their container strapped across her body. A breeze ruffled through the tree's leaves, calling the throng to quiet. Olivia pushed herself up from the platform, eyes bright with tears, shoulders quaking, cheeks red.

She looked at her father, who'd scrambled to his feet. She looked to her mother who climbed the platform steps. Her father clambered over the platform's edge and launched himself at his daughter, a knife drawn. Her mother would be on her in two strides, but her father was closer. He arced the knife up. Olivia looked up at her father, eyes wide with horror. Mylah drew on fire as she released the sand in her pouch a second time. This time she shaped the sand into an arrow and lit the whole thing on fire. She gestured to the father and the arrow sang through the air, pushed by a sudden breeze.

Before her arrow could meet its aim, the girl crouched next to the pile of dirt Luther had dumped on the stage. Vegetation burst to life, vibrant green leaves and vines groaning into existence with her simple gesture. Olivia's father slammed his hands down, aiming at his daughter, but instead met a coiled mass of vines. Mylah's molten glass arrow whizzed over their heads. Thorns the size of daggers jabbed into the man's arms, hands and stomach. He yowled in pain. Olivia covered her ears, folding into a tight ball, her smallness made even smaller.

"Olivia!" her father shouted. "Make this stop right now." Olivia only cringed more deeply into herself. Her father gasped and swore.

"She's a Tyrmini!" someone shouted. Her mother halted, and stepped back, shock stretching her eyes wide. To her right, the man that had been leaning into his rake, straightened, gripping the instrument and lifting it from the ground. To her left, a woman with three children gathered around her gasped, backing out of the throng. Someone jostled Mylah. Pushing through the gathered crowd to stand in front of her, a man in coveralls and a scythe stepped up to the platform.

Mylah righted herself and lunged forward, standing in front of the man with both hands splayed out. "That's enough," she shouted. The man looked down at her, another massive specimen - what did they feed them down here? The man moved forward.

Mylah called on the elements she'd joined into a glass arrow. It zoomed through the air toward her. She aimed it for the man, and before it skewered through his left eye, she halted its momentum. The man jolted back, hands rising, although not releasing his grip on the tool he carried.

Luther lunged for the platform, scrambling to the top, and faced the crowd.

"By the High King's order, this girl is under arrest for possessing Tyrmini powers. She is in our custody from this moment forth." An appreciative hush rippled through the crowd.

Olivia's father pulled himself from the thorned bushes, carefully extracting his body parts from where he'd been skewered. He grunted and growled, blood smearing on his simple shirt. The girl whimpered.

The mother had scampered off the platform and rounded it toward her husband. The woman grasped at her husband, looking from his wounds to her daughter to Luther standing authoritatively on the platform. Livvy still cowered under cover of vegetation that had only sprung to life to protect herself. Mylah wondered if Olivia's powers had been met with kindness and nurturing if the thorns would not have grown flowers in their stead.

"Thank the High King," the father said, relief relaxing his features the barest amount. The crowd shifted, the scythe-wielding man lowered his instrument-turned-weapon, as whispers of "he's always looking out for us" and "thank the Maker for his majesty" punctuating the near-death experience with a reverence that to Mylah felt all wrong. The girl would have died had it not been for their intervention.

Mylah climbed the platform and knelt beside Olivia. "Olivia?" she whispered. The girl peered up at her, dark lashes dotted with tears. She sniffed and rubbed an arm under her nose, then swiped at her face with her palms. Her breath hitched twice, a little sob escaping her mouth. She looked out at the gathered crowd, then over to her parents. Her father's face reflected stern disappointment. Her mother stared wide-eyed and open-mouthed, confusion and shock clear on her face.

"May I call you Olivia?" Mylah asked, hoping to draw the girl's attention. Olivia swiveled her head, eyes wide in terror.

"Y-you can call me, L-Livvy," she said, hiccupping her way through the introduction.

"Livvy," Mylah said softly. "I know this is really scary and difficult, but Luther and I are gonna take good care of you now, okay? Will you come with me?"

Livvy looked back to her parents, then back to Mylah. Mylah let her work through it, wondering if she would fight her, wondering if she would fall apart at the thought of leaving her parents with two total strangers. She imagined herself at this young age, and what she might have done.

Livvy looked back at Mylah, inhaled a long, rattling breath and blew it out in a great whoosh. She lowered her forehead to her crossed arms, propped on her knees, and mumbled, "I s'pose I better."

Mylah touched Livvy's shoulder, brushing away a long lock of auburn hair and rubbed at the girl's shoulder. "Okay, then, come with me."

Livvy scrambled out from her cocooning nest of vines and stood. She let Mylah take her hand. They walked off the platform and around the throng of people. The mother ran to Mylah, tears streaming down her face from the same emerald eyes as Livvy.

"You'll take care of my little girl?" she asked, gripping Mylah's arm with surprising strength. The woman sobbed as more tears ran down her freckled cheeks.

"Mama," Livvy said, tears starting again. She reached for her mother, but her mother shied away from her touch. Mylah saw Livvy's heart crack, a sudden wide-eyed shock stealing over her young face as she pulled her arm back into herself.

Mylah tucked Livvy in closer and pulled her arm from the woman's grip. Anger ignited that inner fire, all those years of her own people's rejection swelling within her. This woman, though, at least she wanted her daughter's safety. That was more than what she could say for her own people, who'd taunted and berated her for years. Livvy's mother might be afraid, but she also cared for her daughter.

"Please," the woman said, "I beg you. Look after her and keep her safe." She looked down at Livvy, tears still streaming. "I love you, my darling girl. Be good and serve our High King the best you can." She choked on the last words, sobs wrenching free. She looked back to Mylah, devotion and fear and love consuming her gaze.

Mylah tilted her chin up, looked the woman in the eyes, and promised, "Under the light of the Goddess, I swear to protect your daughter."

The father, Mather, sidled up to the mother and wrapped a strong hand around her upper arm, pulling her away from Mylah. "Come, Tessa," he said, "she will be in good hands."

Tessa sobbed and turned into her husband's waiting embrace. Mather looked over the top of his wife's head to Mylah. "You have our gratitude, and should you need anything at all that we can supply, it is yours." Mylah nodded once in confirmation and turned away.

With Livvy still firmly tucked under her arm, she led the girl through the throng to the waiting fields beyond. Someone mumbled something. Another person followed. A chant gained volume. Mylah exited the throng and turned back to the crowd as they all lifted left arms to the sky, repeating in unison, "Achyla saves! Achyla saves! Achyla saves!"

Mylah turned away, hiding a sneer. If they only knew. Her own people were clutched in his power. One wrong move and they would not survive Achyla's grasp. He saved, but only when it served him.

Before they reached the hestias, which had wandered up a hill and nipped away at golden grass, Livvy paused. She looked up at Mylah and asked, "May Critter come with us?"

"Who's Critter?" Mylah asked, wondering if this was a doll the girl had grown attached to.

Livvy looked past Mylah, cupped a hand around her mouth and whooped three times. From a far-off copse of trees, the loping form of some animal bounded toward them. Mylah couldn't make out what sort of animal it was. Perhaps a dog? But then the creature shimmered, disappeared, and re-appeared once again, much closer than it had been. It jumped through time and space and appeared out of nothing once more.

Mylah thought she shouldn't have been shocked, despite her surprise. Mylah had only heard stories about the creature on the road when she'd accompanied Maka to sell wares. Its golden black coat glinted bright then faded into shadow. It moved with ease and grace over land. An exuberant Tijhi joined the creature as it made its way across the fallow field. Critter, as Livvy had called it, hesitated for a moment, peering back over its shoulder at the appearance of the little fox, then tossed its head into the air and bounded forward again.

"Critter! Come, Critter!" Livvy shouted, smacking her palms against her knees, a smile breaking across her face like the goddess cresting the eastern horizon. Critter skidded up to Livvy and Mylah finally got a closer look. Across its face spread a row of six eyes, over a long slender snout tipped in a shiny wet nose that boasted long golden appendages which hung loosely on both sides of its mouth. Its mouth was lined with large flat teeth and its black tongue hung out of its mouth in joyous delight, its whole body wagging. A short stub of a tail flicked in excitement. Livvy reached for the creature's neck and stroked its long ears, scratching and smiling. "Good Critter."

Critter backed away, turned a circle on long legs ending in hooves, flashing in and out of existence as it did so. Livvy looked at Mylah. "His mother died. I had to hand-feed him when he was a baby. Can he come with us?"

"What does he eat?" Mylah asked.

"Mostly golden gas grass. It's okay. I can grow it wherever we go," she said, stroking the creature's neck and ear until it thumped its back leg and leaned into the touch.

"Is Critter an -," Mylah started.

"Air creature. I think they're called Muldonis? Muldanis -?"

"Muldonidei," Mylah said. "A close cousin to the antoli which are white and have no eyes. Yes, I thought so. Fascinating creatures, and very rare these days."

"So?" Livvy asked. "Can he come with us?"

"He most certainly can," Luther said. The muldonidei paused, fixing Luther with all of its six black eyes, a slow warbling growl issuing a warning. Hair rose on its spine, creating an impressive ridge that would no doubt scare its enemies by accentuating its size. Luther, however, seemed unimpressed. "Oh hey now, I'm on your side. Just you come along with us and you'll be fine."

Critter sniffed the air between them, golden whiskers reaching out, dancing as if on an unseen wind. It sneezed, loud and forcefully, and turned its attention back to Livvy.

"Critter is very good at finding things. I promise, he'll come in handy. At least, once you've made friends with him," she amended.

Tijhi sauntered up to Mylah and sat regally beside her, tail ticking from one side to the next. *You would be wise to befriend this particular elemental. There may be something very soon you need to find.*

Cryptic, Mylah answered the fire dragon.

An elemental deity has to maintain its mystery, my dear.

CHAPTER EIGHTEEN

With all the company they now had, Mylah and Livvy mounted Aerys and walked the company back to Udari City, traversing roads situated between harvest-ready crops. Light wind and occasional rain accompanied them while big clouds passed over them in the blue sky above. By the time they arrived back at the High King's keep, the sun had set and the three moons made their appearance.

After the hestias had been put away, and Tijhi had volunteered to watch after Critter for the night, Luther had gone his own way and Mylah escorted Livvy inside the castle to see about some living and sleeping arrangements for the girl. She had confirmed along the way that Livvy was twelve springs, and that her power had manifested as she'd played in the farms around her home, about a year ago.

She'd stumbled upon Critter shortly after, and they'd kept each other company. She'd told Mylah there had been a drought in the area last year, and to help, she'd used her ability to help grow her family's crops. They'd done well, despite the other farmers around them having struggled. That's when suspicions arose, but the family had shared their bounty with the other farmers, and so, no one had said anything. It was only today that her father had caught her tending seedlings in the wrong season, that things had gone badly. She had intended to only grow the plants a little, but the magic had gotten away with her in a way it hadn't before, and the fields where she'd nudged the seeds had exploded into a mass of twisting vines, fruits ripened and abundant.

Mylah wondered what they would do with the bounty that had sprung up overnight from barren fields. To use it would spark suspicion. Considering the fear in her parents' eyes, she counted on them burning the field and letting lay fallow for the season. All that waste, she thought. She looked at the girl walking beside her up the cobbled steps to the castle's entry, hands twisting in her apron, hair hanging in long loose curls around her face. She was barefoot and her dress was so plain and dirty. The castle loomed ahead, spires scraping the sky, its expanded buildings and wings stretching out and beyond sight with their close proximity to the monstrosity.

The familiar chill only the castle affected settled in Mylah's bones. She still hadn't grown accustomed to sleeping inside the large thick walls. She could only guess Livvy would feel the same way.

Sybille greeted them in the great foyer with a tray of food.

"Welcome," Sybille said to Livvy. She smiled at Livvy, even as Livvy looked around her at the foyer with wide eyes, her hands moving to her hair to twist and pull at the locks. She took in the large portraits of past High Kings, the giant crystal chandelier, the ornate furniture and pristinely clean oil lamps hissing as they imparted golden light into the spacious room.

"Have a piece of chocolate cake," Sybille said, craning her neck to catch Livvy's attention. Livvy looked back at her, eyeing her with flat distrust. Mylah sidled up to the tray, looked at Livvy and deliberately took a cake.

"Sybille is an excellent baker," Mylah said. She took a bite, to show Livvy it was safe. Mylah savored the deep richness of chocolate and smooth buttery caramel sauce. She purred. "That's your best batch yet, Sybille."

Sybille lit up, smile stretching wide as her cheeks glowed with color.

Livvy watched her with rapt fascination. Then, with shaking hands, she reached for a cake, and shoved a giant bite into her mouth.

Sybille set the platter on a nearby piece of furniture and returned, holding a napkin in her hand discreetly.

Livvy chewed, eyes watering, and grunted nonverbal approval, nodding and gesturing to the cake. She swallowed and it looked like it hurt. Mylah thought she was going to say something, but instead she shoved the whole cake into her mouth, dancing from foot to foot, caramel sauce smeared across one cheek.

Sybille grinned as she watched Livvy scarf the cake with gusto. Once Livvy had polished off the cake, she licked her fingers, purring her satisfaction. "I've never had anything like that," she said. Judging from her waifish form, Mylah would have been unsurprised if regular meals were a rarity.

Sybille handed the napkin to Livvy who took it but looked at it with curiosity shining in her eyes. Sybille said, "You've got a bit of cake on you." She pointed to Livvy's face. Livvy took the napkin and wiped her face.

"Did I get it?" Livvy asked. She had. Mostly. Sybille nodded, a grin quirked one side of her face, and mumbled an "Mhm."

"Would you like to see your room now?" Sybille asked.

"Room?" Livvy asked. "I thought it would be a cell."

"No cells," Sybille said, and there was a glint to her brown eyes, a harsh set to her eyebrows and mouth. "Come on, I'll take you there. Mylah, thank you for bringing Livvy to us. She's in good hands now." Sybille took Livvy's hand and led her away.

Taking that as a dismissal, Mylah nodded. Sybille led Livvy down one of the many corridors leading from the foyer, and Mylah stood there, unsure of what she wanted to do next. The thought of her room's walls around her, tight and cold, sent a shiver down her spine. Sighing, she turned back to the doors and exited the castle once again.

Outside, the air grew cool as night settled in. The sky stretched away above her, deep blue, stars winking against the darkness. Mylah bowed her head to the lights, honoring those lesser and unknown deities who were not her own Goddess. She honored them but she did not worship them.

The steps from the castle's main entrance swept wide. She descended the stairs until her boots crunched over the rock drive, and she wondered where her feet would take her. She let them lead the way, and found herself in the royal gardens, the rock and dirt path grown smaller the further in she went. The royal gardeners had been busy with the harvest of vegetables, beans, grains, herbs, and fruits - everything matured and plucked daily to be jarred and dried and stored for the upcoming winter.

To her right, bean vines climbed up wooden rods and expanded across rows of twine, their fruit hanging heavy. To her left, greenery crowded together, dead leaves mixing with surviving green. She walked along, taking in the woody scent of rosemary. She snapped off a tip, rolling it between her hands and inhaling deeply. The plant's medicine was strong, filling Mylah with a sense of growth and groundedness.

Further down, lavender filled the air with its comforting, floral odor. Mylah took several sprigs of the plant and added it to her sprig of rosemary. Thyme was up ahead on her left and she took a sprig of that as well. She twined it in, its strong peppery odor melding with rosemary and lavender. At the end of the aisle a cherry tree boasted limbs laden with ripe fruit. She tucked her bouquet into the linen wrappings around her left arm and launched herself up onto a tree limb.

She reveled in the feel of her muscles as she hauled her body into the tree. The crook of the tree welcomed her, curving just right to support her in a seated position. She let one leg dangle, swinging it slowly, the other leg pulled into her chest. She pulled the bouquet out of her linen wrapping and reached for a small twig covered in cherries. She plucked the fruit, tossing the overripe ones to the ground and popping a perfect berry into her mouth, pulling the stem free. She worked out the pit and spat it out.

Rocks crunched in a steady rhythm, growing in volume with proximity. She froze. By the sound of it, there were two sets of feet walking toward her. Not wanting confrontation, Mylah pulled her leg up, tucking herself into the tree's crook, hidden behind its boughs of leaves and fruit.

"...and the Baron's daughter is too young still. Just a toddler," a voice said.

"The throne is in a precarious situation. We have but myself with no heirs on the horizon. We must find a wife quickly. Who else do we have?" Mylah recognized that voice. She'd taken his orders two days in a row, one to kill and one to rescue. Her emotions still ranged wildly, mostly riddled with confusion.

"The barons and lords of Aelos this generation have produced few heirs, few of which are daughters. And those have each met a premature end to their life. There is but the one option, sire."

The High King growled. "I do not like this option. It is an ancient practice. One I thought we'd done away with centuries ago." Mylah had that feeling again that his words did not quite match the tone of his voice. Like when his seeming compassion had not reached his eyes. She remained still and quiet, listening intently, wondering what the one option was.

He means to marry his sister, Tijhi's voice caught her by surprise. Further surprising, the small fox phoenix appeared in front of her on the tree limb out of a puff of curling black shadow and sandy-colored fur. Mylah clapped a hand over her mouth to keep from shouting and gripped a nearby branch to root herself to her perch.

"What was that?" the king asked. His boots scuffed against the rocks until he stood directly under the tree. Mylah stopped

171

breathing. Tijhi picked their way down the limb toward Mylah, finally sitting down next to Mylah's legs so that their back was pressed against Mylah's shins. The fox shifted, fur undulating, paws turning to talons, feathered wings sprouting silently from their back, tail elongating. The creature stretched out its wings. The air shimmered around them, rippling and seeming to stretch and swirl until they were surrounded by a pearlescent sphere.

Everything outside the sphere turned to grays, whites and blacks, while everything within the sphere remained vivid. Mylah peered down at the king. To her horror, he looked up at her. Their eyes met, and just when she thought he would cry out, call her a spy and shout for guards to haul her to those deep dungeons in the castle's bowels, his blue eyes slid past her, past the bubble in which she and the Tijhi sat, and he moved on.

Once the scuff of his shoes halted, the other voice continued, "It's not ideal, but rest assured, the blood line has been invigorated by outside contributions for many generations now."

"Seven, in fact," the king said.

"Oh, you know then," the voice said.

"Certainly. Or don't you expect the High King to have a grasp on his own lineage?"

Mylah thought his tone rang with acidity, dangerous to this other voice.

"Certainly, your majesty," the voice intoned.

"Very well," the king said. "When do you recommend the union take place?"

"The princess is eighteen, which is the customary age. It is autumn. I recommend we do not delay but arrange for something in the next two weeks." the voice said.

The High King sighed, pausing before answering, "See to it, then."

Their footsteps echoed then faded away. Tijhi shifted, melting back into their fox form as the bubble around them dissipated.

Tijhi faced Mylah.

"We have to stop them," Mylah blurted, skipping the psychic means of conversing in favor of expressing her intense disgust and shock.

This must happen. The princess must bear the king a child.

"No!" Mylah said. "This will destroy Sybille!"

You do not give the girl enough credit.

"She's too young, too fragile, and too wonderful to suffer this."

The child must be born of this union. It's the only hope of freeing our world from Achyla's rule.

"We have to find another way. There are too many casualties, Tijhi. This is so much darkness to get to light," Mylah said, that companion fire rising within her. The water Tyrmini from the day before flashed through her mind. She closed her eyes against the horror.

Tears slipped down her cheeks. *I can't do this,* she said to the Tijhi. *I can't keep watching as young people are hurt, manipulated, killed, tortured.*

Then, please, Tijhi said. *Please help me end this. There is hope to reclaim our world, to right the imbalances, and to free Magloryn.*

Mylah jumped down from the tree, fury and sorrow and self-hatred filling her. She couldn't stand the little creature. Couldn't stand their demands and assertions. It was wrong. All wrong. Her legs pumped, arms swinging. Her jog turned into a sprint, and before long she found herself heading for the training grounds.

CHAPTER NINETEEN

Over the next week, Mylah lost herself in training. She woke early, arriving at the training pit before dawn to meditate, and then began the grueling exercises to engage her body and mind. She tapped into her powers more and more easily, tempering the fire with ever more ease.

Her soul suffered a gaping hole for the Tyrmini boy and his victims, so oppositely juxtaposed to Livvy's rescue. The persistent and invading thoughts of Sybille's fate also drove her to a focused frenzy. She rolled the experiences over and over in her mind as she ran the training property perimeter. This morning dark images dragged her screaming from sleep. The boys the Tyrmini had killed reanimated and stalked toward her, water pouring from their mouths, eyes bulging and bloodshot. When she ran from them she'd been confronted by the boy's family, a completely fabricated set of people since Mylah had never seen them. In last night's nightmare, one of the children had been a baby, the mother carrying a dead child, its eyes staring blankly, as she accused over and over, "Why, why, why?"

Mylah's stomach heaved. She halted mid-step, hunched over and vomited water, the only thing she'd consumed that morning. In fact, she'd started the practice of only drinking water in the morning and avoiding food.

She gripped her knees as the familiar wash of cold sweat stole over her, her hairline prickling, sweat gathering along her spine and the back of her neck. Her stomach cramped again around the sickness fighting to make its way out. She wretched, wishing the nightmares could be dispelled as easily as that morning's glass of water.

When her stomach was empty she stood, panting. Trees rose toward the sky, their solid massive presence blocked the rising sun, casting her in deep, cool shadows. It was oppressive. Mylah peered into the forest, unable to shake the feeling the trees hid something.

She was so tired. Tired of waking with a racing heart and a scream in her throat. Tired of the images lurching into her mind's eye with vivid clarity. Tired of the panic that accompanied her no matter how long she meditated, exercised, or practiced with her Tyrmini powers.

The dead stalked her.

They could not be denied or ignored. Exhausted from running, both literally and figuratively, Mylah gave up and entered the darkness. She dared the shadows, thinking she had nothing to lose. This new life would consume her.

Her boots crunched over empty acorn shells and twigs. The trees closed in around her, so still. Her body trembled, muscles sore and tired, and at the same time, her heart raced. She growled into the trees, "You think you can scare me?" She walked toward the center of the forest, toward its heart and its darkness. "I've lost everything. My people, my home, my whole family. What do you want from me? I have nothing. I am nothing. I can't change this. I can't bring them back."

Tears streamed down her face. She clenched her fists to her side and released them, let them hang loosely at her side. Mylah affected no change. She might have built practices to help her Tyrmini powers, but what good did it do when the magic in the world drove people crazy to the point of the death of others and the Tyrmini themselves?

She stomped ahead, looking into the high canopy, the sky

just a chink of gray through a frame of spearing treetops. "I'm no good, okay? I can't get anything right. Are you happy? You win." She sobbed, falling to her knees and reaching out to a log in front of her. Bark bit into her palms and the pain deepened her desperation. The trees didn't answer. They simply looked down, uncaring, nonpartisan witnesses to her struggles.

She folded her arms over the tree trunk, laid her head against her arms, closed her eyes and wept. She wept for the dead children, all of them, the Tyrmini boy and his victims, his siblings, and his parents. She wept for her family; she wept for her people. She cried until her face grew soggy and her guts and back ached from the effort.

Darkness wrapped around her, needling deeply into her soul, and she opened herself up to its demands.

A resounding crack echoed through the clearing. Mylah jerked up, jumping to her feet, and whirling. A bright pulse of pain throbbed in her neck and jaw. The world trembled through her gathered tears, eyes wide as she took in her surroundings. She unstoppered the leather pouch, sand hissing out and hovering in the air around her, ready to attack.

She peered through the trunks of the trees, expecting... she wasn't sure what she expected. An enemy? Here, in the High King's training grounds? The logic didn't check out and she knew it, but her being still vibrated with vigilance. There, against the dark solid trunks stared a stark, surprised face.

Mylah sheathed her sand, drawing it back into its pouch and replacing the cork stopper. Upon a rattling inhale her lungs ached against the pinch of anxiety.

"Mylah?" Sybille's voice trembled.

Mylah exhaled, gripping a hand to her chest, hoping the gesture would slow its race. Sybille walked over to her, picking her way over the forest floor litter, careful to keep her shiny boots clean. She gripped a handful of her sage green dress and beige, green, and purple plaid overdress. A giant bow hovered over her bustle in the back, bobbing with each step. Sybille's hair sat in meticulous curls that spilled over her shoulders, between her puffed sleeves and lacy collar.

"Are you okay?" she asked, her face a portrait of concern.

Mylah stopped breathing for a moment. No. No, she wasn't okay. Nothing about this was okay.

Tijhi picked their way through the tree trunks, their fox body shining like the goddess's light through the gloom. The squeeze on Mylah's heart eased the barest amount. The little dragon deity joined Sybille as they made their way toward Mylah, filling her space with warmth and love. Sybille wrapped her arms around Mylah's waist and pressed her head into her chest.

"It's the boy from Sylvanea isn't it?" she asked.

Tijhi trotted up to them both and sat on their haunches, looking up at Mylah with their deep golden eyes, framed in charcoal lines.

Mylah ran her hands down Sybille's silky hair, finding the gesture comforting. "Don't worry about me," she said. "I'll be okay."

Sybille pulled away and took Mylah's hands in hers. "You don't have to be, you know. I know I'm younger than you, but I'm a grown woman and I'm your friend."

Mylah considered this wonderful person she'd grown to love. Yes, Sybille was a friend, but she was also a person Mylah wanted to protect. "I miss my family. And doing this -," Mylah gestured to her training gear, to the pin weighing on her left breast "- gets to me. But I am grateful my people are safe."

"Why are you so positive?" Sybille asked.

"What are you doing out here anyway?" Mylah asked, shifting from the uncomfortable topic of herself.

"I have news," Sybille said. She adjusted her glasses as she stepped away, giving Mylah space. Mylah knew what news she had – or at least she guessed it – and she felt like a traitor for not telling

Sybille what she'd overheard.

"Oh?" Mylah asked, trying to sound curious and ignorant.

Sybille folded her hands in front of her. "I am to be married," she said. She tilted her chin up slightly before she continued, "to my brother, the High King." She squared her shoulders.

Mylah had mentally worked out how she would react to this news. "Wow," she started, and then the script she'd carefully crafted evaporated from her mind. "That's... uh, I mean, quite the news," Mylah said stupidly. "Is this a common custom among your people?" she asked, and as soon as the words were out she regretted them.

But Sybille spoke before she'd finished the upward intonation of her question. "I understand this is an ancient practice and I too thought we'd done away with it generations ago. Never would I have been prepared for this turn of events. I mean, it really makes everything so much easier," she said, and then she began to pace. "I'm not an insurrectionist; you might have noticed. I haven't a drop of rebellion in me. Mother always was very peaceful, and I suppose I've taken after her demeanor. But right is right," she said, and here she slammed a small fist into her other cupped hand.

"And my father might have believed he's had one over on the whole of Aelos, but he couldn't fool Bess, you know. She's too watchful, and too trustworthy, and loyal to the royal bloodline. Yes, I suppose it was really meant to be this way all along and it works out rather well for me -,"

Mylah snatched Sybille's shoulders and turned her so that they were face-to-face. "Sybille," she said. "Why are you okay with this?"

Sybille exhaled, as though in relief. "Because he's not truly my brother."

Mylah blinked, taking in what she'd just said. "What?"

"I don't suppose you've been exposed to many dignitaries. If you had, you'd know there's a nasty rumor about my late father and his inability to produce a male heir. In fact, there were two other wives before my mother, and between them and the mistresses, there are two handfuls of bastard or dead daughters and not one male."

"And in your customs, one must be male to rule?" Mylah asked, thinking how silly it was. Her people were egalitarian, and both women and men were looked to for wisdom and advice.

Sybille let out a huge sigh. "Not necessarily. It's only been the last nine generations that it's solely been a male heir to inherit the throne. The law doesn't state anything about the required gender. Something along the way shifted and it's been more of a custom rather than a law.

"So, anyway, no bouncing baby boys, so my father got creative. When any servant got pregnant my father would test the babe's sex with an ancient relic from Magys time. Until one day he got lucky enough to find a boy. So, he found a new wife (my mother) whom he could manipulate into going along with a ruse that she was pregnant, fostering the servant until she had her baby and then taking the child and raising it as their own."

Mylah stared, stunned. "And how do you know this? That seems like a secret that wouldn't be shared lightly."

"Not even my brother knows," Sybille whispered. "The servant who bore the babe was killed, and the only other person who knew of her existence was Bess. And Bess is loyal to the bloodline. My bloodline. Because unlike my brother, I am a rightful heir to the throne - except, I'm a woman."

"If your father was dead set on the lack of a girl's value, how did you survive?"

Sybille took a sweeping bow. "I am the younger, and so not a threat to the male heir. My mother convinced my father to allow me to live, and to consider my value as the royal uterus, of course. Kept for just this scenario when a suitable wife outside Udari City isn't found. The men must have their royal babies somehow." The biting sarcasm wasn't lost on Mylah.

"I'm so sorry, Sybille," Mylah said. It stuck Mylah that she and Sybille found themselves in similar circumstances. Both were tools being used to accomplish the High King's goals. The consequences of both were an end to their bloodline. In Mylah's case, it would be the massacre of her remaining people. In Sybille's case, the end to the royalty being passed back to the rightful heir.

Sybille stood and dusted herself, righting her glasses, and said, "Never be sorry for me. I'm about to get what I want. It's all working out." Although she held her mousy brown head high, her body quivered.

Chapter Twenty

Three months later, Mylah found herself in a vast and winding garden hidden in the cloaking trees of the castle's nearby forest. Livvy had been hard at work, and it showed. The High King had set her to grow a particular set of rare herbs. Livvy obsessed herself with every applicable condition needed to produce the plants, taking to the task with energy and fervor.

"I can finally do what I want," Livvy had told her one day, her green eyes glinting with excitement. Mylah was happy for her. At least one person in this whole situation could work at ease and comfort.

Mylah focused on the task at hand. She'd been asked to create a glass globe; one in which certain plants could be kept at a high temperature for peak growing performance, no matter the natural weather. Mylah had called the Tijhi for their help, knowing the fox's presence gave Mylah more control over her abilities. Luther also joined, helping to manipulate Tyrinth that had more water in it than Mylah could manage.

Sand had been transported by the cart-full to the area and Mylah and many Castle staff had succeeded in spreading it evenly in a circle. Mylah rubbed her hands together as she and Tijhi stepped up to the circle. The winter day offered cold and clear weather. She thanked the Goddess for her appearance to hone in on the fire element without the wet distraction of rain. She remembered the first time she'd created a glass globe and how it had not been on purpose. That had been three seasons ago and her abilities had come far since then.

With Tijhi at her side, Mylah found a spot near the perimeter and fully faced the Goddess. The energy coming off Tijhi was palpable - a warm ambient glow wrapped Mylah into a cocooning and familiar embrace. Luther stood opposite her, his face a still mask of concentration. Her energy reached out to his, caressed it, and drew back.

Luther shivered.

Mylah tucked away her smile.

Tijhi sneezed. *Focus,* was the dragon's only admonishment. Mylah grinned mentally anyway and began the mental and spiritual work of sending her energy into the Tyrinth, while opening her center to the Goddess. When she'd done this before, she'd done it unwittingly in an explosion of emotion. Her emotions were still there, but they demanded less attention. The power loomed big within her, but Mylah's control had grown bigger. She imagined herself as a giant and the power a force only she could allow to flow through her. With this sovereignty in place, the elements beckoned to her will without urgency or hesitancy. As if the fire eagerly obeyed her wishes.

The air around them warmed. Sweat slicked down her back. She had donned the clothing she'd come to Udari City in, knowing today's work would be hot. Her exposed arms and legs shone under the bright sun. Across from her, Luther glistened despite the cold weather, his hands stretched out to the circle then slowly pushing down, pushing away the moist Tyrinth that would distract Mylah from fire and sand. She pictured the dome in her mind's eye, large enough for the many varieties of plants Livvy would grow, its roof high enough for even Idalfyn's half-giant royalty to pass under.

The sand quaked, jumping and falling to the ground and leaping up again. Mylah reined in her thoughts, opening her mind to the outcome she wished. Fire washed through her veins, coalescing in her center. The sand rose and formed itself into her desired shape. She opened her mouth as heat built within her. She breathed it onto the sand dome. Where the fire touched, the sand glowed red hot, sparking and crackling. She walked the perimeter slowly, coaxing the flame through her and onto the dome, holding the sand element still and stable as fire consumed, melded and transformed the element.

It wasn't instantaneous and she meant it that way. She meant for the slow burn, the exercise of endurance and strength. Sweat slicked her entire body, hair dripping wet when the dome was at last complete.

She exhaled the last wisps of fire, letting its essence wane. When at last she stepped away from her creation she dropped the meditative state and commended her work. She'd done well.

Clapping filled the air behind her. She turned. Livvy, dressed in plain working pants, a tunic rolled to the elbows, and unbuttoned to the middle of her chest squealed and threw herself onto Mylah.

"That was amazing! Oh gross, you're so sweaty!" Livvy said and immediately pulled away from Mylah. Mylah laughed at her discomfort and disgust.

"Breathing fire tends to have that effect," Mylah said. Livvy wiped at herself where she'd met a very sweaty Mylah and walked away, surveying the dome. Mylah wiped sweat from her face using an undrenched section of her linen wrappings. Her eyes stung with salt.

Luther approached. He too glistened with sweat, and somewhere along the way he'd lost his shirt. She marveled at the rippling muscles. Not for the first time did Mylah take him in while another fire stoked within her. Luther caught her gaze and his eyebrows rose. Mylah matched his stare, daring him.

"Well done, darlin'," Luther said as he approached.

Mylah nodded. "You as well," she said.

He held his hands up in surrender. "The student has surpassed the teacher."

"Perhaps there are other things you could teach me," she said.

Tijhi sneezed. Mylah thought the dragon's presence inconvenient.

Luther took another step towards Mylah. "I think I'd rather be studious to learn your needs." His voice growled, warm and gravelly and it nearly undid Mylah. But the irritated chirp of a dragon masquerading as a fox brought their attention back to reality.

What is it? Mylah asked, annoyed.

I'm so sorry to interrupt this tender, albeit carnal moment, however, there are guards headed this way, and it seems to me you may want to clear your head before they approach.

Mylah grunted and turned toward the castle. Three guards marched toward them, making a beeline for Mylah and Luther. She sighed.

Luther looked past her, adjusting his focus to see what had caught her attention. "That can't be good," he said.

Mylah walked toward the guards. No sense in delaying, she thought. She called on the wind and a gust of air swirled around her, cooling her heated body. Luther, still in step with her, inhaled sharply at the sudden gust. "Mother of -," he swore. "Was that you, Mylah?"

"I'm hot," she said. "I figured a little breeze could help cool us off."

"You gotta warn a guy," he said. Mylah giggled, and called another breeze, this one blasting him full in the face. Luther gulped loudly on the sudden air and Mylah cackled. "That's about enough of that," he said, and Mylah found herself face down in the dirt, a bit of Tyrinth having jutted itself up to trip her.

She looked up to find Luther now jogging toward the guards. "Oh, you little coward," Mylah said, and pulling her sand pouch around she uncorked it and pulled on the dry element, sending a strand of it like a rope out in front of Luther. The sand hardened and clotheslined her fellow Tyrmini. His feet flew up into the air and he was knocked onto his back.

Mylah jogged up to him. "Got ya," she said. Luther groaned, then took a mighty breath.

"...knocked the wind outta me," he managed. Mylah extended a hand and yanked Luther to his feet, just as the guards approached.

Luther bent over, hands on knees. Mylah smiled smugly, arms crossed over her middle.

"Mylah of the Aestyrah?" one of the guards asked. The guard lacked the gold circular pin of a Tyrmini. His pale face and wide eyes made Mylah wonder if he was scared of her. She supposed he would be. Not that she minded overly much. Mylah propped a hand on her hip and gestured with the other hand on her chest to signal she was indeed the one he sought.

The other two guards, all dressed in the royal black and gold, wool black pants instead of the working leathers Mylah had become accustomed to. Their uniforms gleamed, clean and pressed, their skin glowing with health, figures fit and well-fed by the High King. "The High King requests your presence in the throne room immediately."

Mylah bowed to the speaker and moved past him, then noted the three guards followed her. Luther hung back, and she frowned as his figure grew small with separating distance.

Mylah steeled herself and picked up her pace, hoping to lose the guards behind her. As she crossed the open fields between the tree-enshrouded secret gardens and the castle, she caught the golden glint of Tijhi's fur and Critter's golden-black shine. Critter sat silently in front of Tijhi, his six eyes locked on the little fox, tongue lolling over his large flat teeth, golden mouth appendages swaying in the breeze. Tijhi stretched their nose toward Critter and Mylah thought the two to be locked in some silent conversation.

Before she could think further about it, the castle entrance came into view and cold stone swallowed her up.

CHAPTER TWENTY-ONE

Sybille sat propped in a lesser chair next to the High King's opulent throne. She looked awful, Mylah thought. Her skin paled lighter than normal, her lips colorless and cracking, and bags hung under her eyes. The High King paced instead of sitting, and he too looked unwell. In fact, it seemed to Mylah he'd aged since last she'd seen him - which had been only how long ago? Mylah calculated it had only been a little more than two months since the wedding.

Sybille was dressed in a beautiful sapphire dress with black trim, the bustle situated behind her forcing her to sit rod straight. The buttons in the front of the bodice marched from her belly to the middle of her neck, the collar tight around her throat and concealing half its length. Mylah thought Sybille looked so grown up, and she had a pang of worry about the princess - queen, she corrected herself.

Mylah stalked down the center of the throne room, its long open space lined on either side in alternating windows and fireplaces, all lit and crackling, dispelling the chill of the winter day outside. Mylah found it stifling after her work creating the glass dome.

The king saw Mylah and turned to her, scampering down the dais stairs to greet her. He took her arms in his two hands, fixing her with his blue eyes, which were crowned in crow's feet. Surely the man was no older than mid-twenties.

"Mylah, it is so good you came. I could not entrust another

soul. Do you -, Mylah, you smell awful," he said, dropping her arms and backing away, covering his offended nose.

"Your majesty," Mylah began, bowed, then continued, "please forgive me. I've been building the glass dome required to grow the herbs you need."

"You must take a bath as soon as possible. What I ask you to do now will require more delicacy than you may be accustomed to, given your rank with the guard."

More delicacy? Mylah crossed her arms, brows knitting together. "Shall I go now, your majesty, or would you like to give orders first?"

He waved a handkerchief. "No, no, please allow me to speak first, but do not approach your queen until you've bathed. You'll upset her... well..." he looked past Mylah. Two guards stood stationed at the entry. "You there, you're dismissed. Both of you." The guards shuffled out.

"What I'm about to tell you must stay in complete confidence," the king said.

"Of course, your majesty," she said, bowing slightly.

He looked deeply into her eyes for a long moment, as if to judge if she were capable of holding this secret. Deep in his gaze, Mylah thought she saw a predatory shadow pass through. Although his outward affect mimicked concerned, underneath, she sensed only cold calculation. Or maybe it was just Mylah's imagination. She couldn't say for sure.

"Your queen is with child," he said finally. Mylah dropped her arms to her sides and looked to Sybille. Achyla followed her gaze, smiling. Sybille, still looking sick, quirked a smile to Mylah. *Mission accomplished,* she thought she read in her expression.

"My congratulations to their royal majesties," Mylah intoned, but she didn't really feel excitement. Instead, a sense of utter danger settled within her.

"I need you to be my sis- my queen's personal guard. No harm should come to her as she grows and bears the heir to the throne." He gripped Mylah's shoulder, coming close to her despite his complaint of her smell. "Can you do this for me?"

"Is the queen in that much danger, your majesty?" Mylah asked.

"It is paramount we guard her with our lives," he said.

"But, what of my other duties?" she asked.

"Nothing is more important than this. Nothing. Guard her with your life. Failure to do so will result in swift and extreme consequences. We wouldn't want your people to come to harm, would we?" he said, and that glint of hard darkness shone brightly from his eyes.

Mylah's heart dropped into her stomach, a constricting hand wrapped around her throat, and her pulse quickened in her chest. She thought when she'd left the Aestyah, she'd left her people in safety. She thought by coming willingly to Udari City, she'd bound their fate to be left alone. She thought he'd never touch them again because she was here, serving him. But their lives still hung in the balance.

This realization nearly brought her to her knees right there in the throne room. And if it weren't for the detest she felt for the idea of bowing to the High King, her body might have given out at the threat. His eyes stayed clamped onto her own as he emphasized his point with a shake of her shoulder. The gesture stoked her inner fire.

A year ago, her power would have consumed him on the spot. Today, the fire within her sang at the ready, but waited for her command. She jutted her chin out. "I must do this task or you will slaughter my people. I've given up everything to serve you to keep my people safe, and you still use them to bend me."

He brought his face close to hers to whisper in her ear. "I will do anything - anything at all - to keep this child safe. Do not test me." The room darkened around her and the air grew chilly.

Shadows gathered in the corners. The fires in the hearths hissed as if water had been poured on them. Light leached away from the windows. Sybille sat up straighter, hands gripping the arm rests, eyes wide.

Under the king's hand where he touched her skin, a cold hot pain spread through Mylah's shoulder. She hissed. The king released her shoulder, and Mylah yanked away, grasping the spot he'd held.

"Go take a bath," the king snarled, disgust curling his upper lip. The shadows receded, fires breathing to life again. Sybille seemed to compose herself, folding her hands demurely in her lap, leaning back into the chair and arranging her features into one of calm regard. "Then, report to the queen's quarters. If I see you without her or her without you for the next seven months, your people will be wiped from the face of Tyrinth."

Mylah stepped back again, rage and fear building within her. The king turned away from her, stalking toward his throne. She looked down to her exposed shoulder; a dark handprint stained her skin in shades of night and shadow. What was she dealing with here?

She turned and stumbled out of the hall, head buzzing, heart thrumming, and the king's threat echoing through her. Whatever she'd been doing up until this point to protect her people, it hadn't worked. They were still in danger. She made her way to her living quarters on numb feet, her mind racing. Maybe she would spare them again by playing guard to the queen, but the time would come she was sure when she would step out of line in his eyes, and her people would suffer for her mistakes.

Mylah brewed her thoughts in silence even as she obeyed her enemy and bathed off the day's sweat and dirt. She contemplated the shadows that had sprung from the corners as she'd incited the king's anger. Perhaps those shadows had always been there and waiting. She needed to talk to the Tijhi. She needed the dragon's wisdom.

There was more to this than a king being protective of his offspring and Mylah would discover the truth.

CHAPTER TWENTY-TWO

Mylah called Tijhi as she made her way to the queen's quarters. She remained clothed in attire that would befit a guard, choosing her linen wraps and bracers with bare shoulders and upper arms, that spot on her shoulder aching like cold death.

The sand's weight hanging across her torso comforted her. Mylah wended through corridors as she contemplated shadows. The darkness had snared her. She saw it in her periphery before it flitted from her sight. Over and over, shadows seemed to gather and dissipate.

Tijhi, Mylah called again, flinging out her thoughts onto that etyric network they connected through. Mylah pushed through a door that took her outside, the sudden cold winter air slapping against her warm body. She stomped along the covered stone walkway, her thoughts churning, fire chewing at her gut, even as the cold reminded her...

Mylah reached for her shoulder, barely noticing the small courtyard of dead grass, an empty fountain quiet and still.

What happened? Tijhi asked. Mylah pulled herself from her thoughts, searching around to find the fox trotting beside her, seemingly from out of nowhere.

Where did you come from? Mylah asked.

A fox can come and go as they please, Tijhi said, nose held high in the air.

Mylah stopped in her tracks and turned to the Tijhi. *The High*

King, he...

Mylah trailed off and instead of thinking the words, she let the whole scenario play out to Tijhi, mind to mind. Tijhi turned their head as they listened into Mylah's thoughts.

When she was done, she asked, *Why would he threaten my people? Again?*

The child is that important to him, but I do not understand yet why.

And what were the shadows? Mylah asked. *What did he do to me, Tijhi?*

Tijhi put a paw up in the air and pulled it toward them, making a 'come here' motion. Mylah lowered herself to her knees, opening her arms to the Tijhi who leaped into them, placing their front paws onto Mylah's chest and leaning in to sniff at the cold, dead shoulder. They sneezed. Mylah opened her arms and Tijhi jumped back to the ground again.

That wound smells of Shadow, Tijhi said, seeming to capitalize the word as if it were a person or named object. They looked out into the afternoon, the sun skirting the horizon. They seemed to peer far past the azure sky into some other reality. *Perhaps that is why his presence is as faint as his twin's,* they said, almost as if to themself.

Shadow? Mylah asked. *As in the element?* She didn't have any knowledge of the element, although she knew it existed. Achyla the First had imprisoned Magloryn, the Dragon of Light, which had unhinged Magys elemental magic. But no one knew where the twin elemental dragon to light resided, if they even knew the dragon existed at all.

Tijhi turned to Mylah, as if seeing her for the first time. They blinked their golden eyes. *I must go,* the little fox announced and turned away. They trotted several feet before Mylah called out to them.

Wait, she said. Tijhi turned back to her, their eyes glinting in the late afternoon sun, golden fur shining, and Mylah thought she saw the faintest hint of wings stretching up and away from the creature's body. *What am I supposed to do?*

Keep the child safe. See what you can learn about the royal house, and any magic that may be mentioned. I will return soon, hopefully, with some answers.

Mylah watched Tijhi trot away, their steps light against the cold Tyrinth. They slipped around a garden wall and were gone. Mylah's emotions resonated with relief that the little fox seemed to be on the hunt for more information, simultaneously suffering great panic at her companion having left her alone. The responsibility of keeping an unborn child safe in the castle of a child-murdering monarch loomed ahead of her, and she wasn't sure if she was up for the task. She had failed so many times in the past. Could she succeed this time?

Mylah inhaled raggedly, realizing she'd been holding her breath. She exhaled in a whoosh, steeled herself, and marched back into the castle.

Two guards in standard black and gold uniforms, black wool pants and two swirls of gold over their jackets, stood positioned to either side of the Queen's suite door. Mylah nodded at each of the soldiers in turn before she pushed open the wooden door and passed over the threshold, noting immediately the chill in the air.

She'd never been to Sybille's rooms before, and inhaled in sharp surprise at the state of chaos.

"Don't you have servants to clean your room?" Mylah asked. She plucked at a towel slung over the back of a dining chair, surveying what looked to be an uneaten meal situated on the dining table, boasting a piece of toast with exactly one bite taken.

Sybille mumbled, "don't want anyone here." Mylah looked around. The four-poster bed was occupied by a twisted lump of sheets and blankets, the mattress stuffing sorely in need of turning. She raised an eyebrow as she turned to the queen.

Sybille sat in front of a dead fire, curled up under blankets in the corner of an overly large and cushioned chair. Coals gathered under the grate glowed and faded while Sybille stared and shivered. To the right and left of the fireplace, giant paintings of landscapes hung in golden frames. The painting on the left depicted a grotto with a fountain sculpted to portray a hero with a sword held to the sky. The one on the right was similar except it had no fountain.

"Are you unwell?" Mylah asked, looking around at the disarray. Mylah crossed the room from its entrance to stand over the queen with crossed arms. Sybille looked up at her, dark shadows staining the space between her eyes and cheeks. In the time Mylah had taken to wash and dress, the queen seemed to have faded all the more. Mylah wondered how much of that had to do with the shadows that had gathered in the throne room with them.

Sybille's breath sawed in and out of her mouth. Her face went from ashen to green, sweat beaded her forehead. She turned from Mylah, grabbed a small bucket that had been tucked somewhere in the folds of blankets and cushions, and vomited.

"That answers that question," Mylah noted, and turned to the dying fire. She tossed on another log and invited the flame to eat. Voracious, the element nibbled into the bark, finding purchase in the dry fibers before it bloomed into large flames. Mylah reveled in the heat, that cold, dead shoulder throbbing despite the warmth that blazed to life.

Sybille moaned. Mylah turned to her, brows nettled over her golden eyes. She had no idea what to do with sick people. "What is wrong with you?" she asked, her nose wrinkling at the smell of vomit.

"I'm pregnant," Sybille said, looking up at Mylah incredulously. "Haven't you ever been around a pregnant woman before?"

"I have never seen a woman vomit from pregnancy," Mylah said, thinking back to the women in her village who bore children.

THE DRAGON'S FIRE

Pregnant women didn't curl up in balls under covers in her village; they just continued. Even those women who mined the caverns didn't stop. She searched her memory, thinking back to those moments, witnessing mothers-to-be at work, and recalled something her mother had said when Mylah had been very young. A woman had been chewing a stick, and Mylah had asked her mother what she was chewing. Her mother's face had softened, her voice low as she told Mylah the woman was pregnant and the stick helped with upset stomach.

Mylah turned away from the queen, crossing back to the entrance. She pulled open the heavy door and addressed a guard. "You there," she said. The guard turned to her, a man of maybe twenty years. His face was soft, and he turned a wide-eyed blue stare. His brownish-blond hair was covered by a black officer's cap, the visor short, the crown close to the head, with no plumage. In short, he was new.

"What is your name," she asked.

"G-gavick, ma'am," the young man said.

"Well, G-gavick," she began, "Go see Bess in the kitchens and tell her to give you a few ginger roots. Tell her it's to lighten the scent in Sybille's room."

The guard turned to his senior, a middle-aged man whose stripes and plumage told Mylah he was likely in charge of a group of younger guards; not high-ranking, but not low on the totem pole. Fire licked up Mylah's spine as the older guard looked at Mylah, his dark eyes glittering in dislike, mouth a down-turned line. He turned back to the young man and jerked his chin down the barest amount to indicate his consent. Mylah wanted to set him on fire.

The guard turned back to her, bowed slightly, and said, "Yes, ma'am," before he turned and jogged down the cold, stone hall.

Mylah turned back to the older guard. He growled, "Don't tell my men what to do," he said. "I'll give the orders."

Mylah looked up and down the hall, making sure it was clear. The guard followed her suit, seeming to keep one eye on her as he did so. She came out of the room and approached the guard. She walked right up to him until they were toe-to-toe. She crossed her arms, peering into his brown eyes, his mustache scraggly over thin lips.

"Do you want to be here?" she asked.

"Excuse me?" he said. "That a threat?"

"Do you want to be here? Or are you here from some obligation? Perhaps, there are circumstances," she said the word slowly, "that have transpired to bring you to this position, but it's not actually what you want to be doing with your life?"

The man stared at her, his eyes hard, a sort of feral meanness dancing behind his flat stare. She had the sense he might lunge at her at any moment. And she was completely unafraid.

"That's none of your goddamn business," the man bit out.

Mylah stared at him. She was not a small woman, and he was not a large man, so they were eye level. Maybe in more ways than one. Mylah inhaled deeply and gambled on her next words.

"If I've learned anything about our mutual employer, it's that he is a collector of those whom he can easily control - usually by holding them hostage with some threat." That deep cold numbness in her shoulder throbbed.

She let the words sink in while the man turned his head the slightest distance away from Mylah.

"He has leverage over us," Mylah said, and she paused.

The man's shoulder barely rolled. Indication enough for Mylah.

"My leverage is my people. All of them." Her voice cracked on the statement, even as the picture of their annihilation sprang into her mind, their imagined screams of agony leading to the silence of their death, echoed in her mind's ears.

The man's face softened, a look of angry pain crossing his

features - and Mylah knew she'd been right. She took a step back, giving the man his space. He inhaled and exhaled quietly through his nose. That predator-backed-into-corner look in his eyes faded. "My wife," he said, his words grounding out of a mouth that didn't seem to want to say them. Mylah nodded, lowering her head in respect.

She looked back up at the man. "You and I," she said, gesturing to the air between them, "are not enemies." She extended her arm to the guard. "I am Mylah of the Aestyrah. What is your name, friend?"

He looked at her extended arm, eyeing it as if it were a creature that might bite. Then he turned his eyes to hers, one corner of his mouth quirking upward. It wasn't a smile, and his eyes still held a fierce mix of anger and sorrow, but it was better than that awful frown he'd worn. "Shilbin," he said, and extended his own arm. Mylah grasped its full length, the inside of their forearms pressed together, hands clasped around the arm near the elbow.

Mylah placed her other hand over her heart as she intoned, "The Goddess smiles upon our greeting, Shilbin."

His face slackened a little more. "Yeah, that sounds alright." His eyebrows rose as a true smile spread over his face. Mylah chuckled as she dropped her hands to her sides, gestured over her shoulder to the queen's waiting quarters. "I better get back on duty," she said.

Shilbin saluted with two fingers to the visor of his cap. Mylah escaped into the room, hoping the new bond would help her - or at least not hinder her - in what she had to do next.

Gavick returned with the ginger. Mylah pulled a blade from a sheath on her thigh and went to work cutting the root into the sticks she'd seen her village women chewing. Once she had produced several of them, she proffered one to the queen, who dozed in the over-sized chair. Sybille licked the stick experimentally, sniffed it, then put it wholly into her mouth.

"Take breaks with it," Mylah instructed. "It can be very spicy."

Sybille pulled the stick out of her mouth and set it daintily into a small dish on the side table next to her. "We need to talk," the queen said, color returning minutely to her face.

Mylah snatched a chair from the dining table situated under an expanse of windows and hefted it to the queen. She sat on the chair, legs wide, and leaned forward toward the queen, forearms resting on her thighs. She fixed Sybille with a serious gaze.

"You saw what I saw, then," Mylah said. She knew Sybille had, but would the queen admit it? Would she entertain discussion about the king and his strange ability to call shadow to him?

"And it's not the first time," Sybille said. "But it was not from my husband," she said.

CHAPTER TWENTY-THREE

Sybille piled dishes onto a platter and hefted it off the table. Mylah took the platter, balancing the piles of dishes to keep them from spilling. Sybille chewed a ginger stick as she turned away from Mylah, mumbling a quick thank you. Mylah carried the tray of dishes to the door, propping its weight on a side table, bumping a large oil lamp in the process, and pulled the door open.

Gavick rushed forward and took the tray from Mylah. "Thank you, Gavick," she said, sincerely.

"Do you or the queen need anything else?" Gavick asked. He shifted away and a teetering cup clattered to the tray. He adjusted his hold, his mouth forming an O, eyes peeling wide as a bowl and a plate slid, threatening to leap from the tray.

"No, I think we're good here," she said. He looked up, smiled lopsidedly, and hurried away from the door. Shilbin rolled his eyes, then smiled at Mylah. Mylah smiled back, saluted with two fingers, and retreated into the queen's quarters. She stopped by the fireplace, tossed in another log and teased the flames to life. When she backed away, she noticed the landscape portrait on the left was crooked. She adjusted it, taking in the picture, a fountain of a man with a sword held aloft, the bright sky and greenery surrounding the structure. A cool breeze caressed her arms. It was labeled, "Grotto". Mylah wondered exactly how long the painting had hung in that place.

At the table, Sybille rolled out parchment onto the now-empty dining table, placing a goblet on one corner, a random book on the other corner. Mylah approached, pulling an oil lamp from a nearby stand and placing it on one of the parchment's empty corners. She peered over Sybille's shoulder. "What is this?"

"I've been thinking," Sybille said, standing straight over the table, pressing a finger to her mouth, nudging her glasses with the back of her other hand, before placing it on her still-flat lower belly. "I don't believe there's any way this child will survive if it's a girl. We can't take any chances. So, this -," Sybille pointed to the parchment she'd rolled out, "is a map of the underground."

"The underground of what?" Mylah asked, taking in the sketches stretched across the parchment. Long corridors marched between circular and rectangular markings, offshoots spreading like the limbs of a tree. There were labels here and there. "Throne Room," "Grotto," "Study."

"This is the castle's underground," Sybille said with hushed awe. "And perhaps a place with information."

"Where did you get this?" Mylah asked.

Sybille leaned over the map, drawing a finger over its surface. "Mother gave it to me. Before she died," Sybille said, her face going flat. She pulled the chewed stick from her mouth and placed it on a tiny plate she'd taken the habit of using for the ginger.

"Why would she give this to you?"

Sybille looked around her, spotting a chair. She gripped the seat and pulled, scraping the feet across the stone floor and up to the table. She folded herself into the seat, crossing her legs and tucking them beneath her. "Mother never believed I was safe. She started sharing with me the castle's secrets at a very young age."

"Secrets?" Mylah asked.

Sybille nodded even as she looked intensely at the map. "It's ancient, and at least some of our ancestors were terribly paranoid. One seems to have taken issue with the original level of the castle and buried it, building the current structure atop it."

"All this," Mylah started, gesturing to the map, "is beneath the castle?"

Sybille nodded, then pointed. "This is where I think we should start," she said.

Mylah skirted the table, leaned over the map and read the label Sybille pointed to. "How are we to get to this underground library?" she asked.

Sybille leaned back and folded her arms, then nudged her glasses back up her nose before replacing her arms across her chest. "That's the problem," she said. "I don't see any entrances marked."

Mylah pored over the map, searching for some marking that would indicate an entrance. There were some symbols and glyphs that made intuitive sense, such as thick lines between halls and rooms to indicate doors, squiggly lines that denoted water, horizontal hashes that Mylah took to mean stairs. But there were others she couldn't decipher at all. In a circular room in the map's center, someone had penned a filled and irregular round shape, almost tear-shaped. In the map's upper-right corner, surrounded by empty parchment, sat a faded faintly bird-shaped icon.

"Are there other maps?" Mylah asked.

"What sort of other maps?"

"Well, since this map doesn't seem to note any passage between the level we're on now and the underground, perhaps what we need is a map of this level that indicates the underground entrances."

Sybille slowly nodded. "You might be on to something." She picked up the ginger stick and popped it into her mouth, having suddenly gone a shade grayer. "C'mon," she said, and rose from the chair. "We need to get to the map room."

CHAPTER TWENTY-FOUR

It had been several months. Sybille and Mylah had searched the map room, and the library, and found nothing that would either educate them on the nature of the king's magic, or entrances from the main castle to the mysterious underground outlined on Sybille's map.

Tijhi returned, giving cryptic answers that involved admonishing Mylah to have patience. The place on her arm the king had touched no longer showed the bruise of a hand, but an irregular splotch in the center remained black as a tattoo and dead to sensation. Mylah had built a habit these months of stroking the numbness. She wanted to remember the shadows, the threat, the darkness that had loomed in his eyes.

Spring was in full swing, and the castle bustled with the season's tasks. Sybille was showing, if you knew to look. No one in the castle besides Sybille, the king, and Mylah knew of Sybille's condition, but Mylah wondered if Bess was savvy. She'd caught the cook watching Sybille closely, and she recognized the truth flashing in her eyes, even if the woman had not confronted her ward. Perhaps she knew better.

Mylah now spent much of her time in the kitchens, because Sybille spent most days in the kitchen. Today, she'd settled into making a meat pie. Sybille rolled the dough, a light coating of flour dusting her apron. She nudged her glasses up with the back of her hand, succeeding in planting a white print onto her cheekbone.

Bess surveyed Sybille's work. "Very good, dear. This will be a treat. What sort of meats would you like in this one?" Bess was a plump woman who had probably been very pretty in her youth. Her hands were rough from years of work, her face rosy in the nose and cheeks, and her eyes sagged with age. Still a brightness shone in her brown eyes that spoke of mischief and a rebellious spirit. Mylah liked her.

Sybille huffed and wiped at her brow, smearing more flour onto her face. Bess took a tea towel and wiped it away. Sybille allowed it. "Have we any ham in the larder?" Sybille asked.

"We may," Bess said. "Mylah, you come with me. Our last ham was a beast and I may need your help to carry it."

Mylah looked at Tijhi, perched in an open window with the sun spilling over their gold fur.

Keep an eye on Sybille and let me know if you sense the High King coming, Mylah said.

You are awfully bossy to such as I.

Please? Mylah asked. *Oh, mighty dragon of fire and cuteness?* The little fox raised their head and fixed her with a golden stare, then lowered their head, pointing their gaze in Sybille's direction.

Very well, the dragon sighed. *But only because you said please.*

Mylah hopped off the counter where she'd been sitting and reading a book about the life of High King Achyla the First and his conquest over Tyrmini. Each tale painted Tyrmini as savage monsters and the king a glorious hero who saved his citizens' lives. But there was one description Mylah read that stood out: "Aelos's king confronted Serena of Landsend, and only after the town's devastation was the Tyrmini cut down. Our beloved monarch wielded his black sword, a weapon of his own crafting, made to conquer evil magic."

Bess walked past Mylah. "This way, dear," she said. Mylah followed along as they passed through a dark and small stone corridor. Rooms opened up to the left and right and ahead a large rounded wooden door ended the hallway.

"Where does that door go?" Mylah asked.

"That's where the deliveries of food come in. This'll be the castle's west side, accessible through the city's inner wall. To get to this door, you have to go through a castle gate that's guarded, dear."

Bess was chattier than normal today. Mylah leaned into it. "And are there any other entrances on this side of the castle?"

"Just this one. All of these storerooms are only accessible from this hall." At the hall's end, near the arched door, they took a sharp right into a tight descending stairwell.

"Where does this go?" Mylah asked.

"This is the cold storage, dear. You need a basement for cold storage. Ours is especially deep to prevent spoilage. It's also very dark down here. Do us a favor and conjure some light."

"That won't scare you?" Mylah asked.

"Been around far too long to be scared of a little fire. And Sybille says you've got more control than she's ever seen by a Tyrmini. Hurry up, dear, I can't see the tip of my own nose."

Mylah stilled and stoked the fire within her, drawing out just enough to bob merrily in the palm of her outstretched hand.

"That's much better," Bess said and continued the descent. "We'll light the lamps once we're down. Handy having you along. Most of the time I forget the matches and just stumble around until I land on what I need." She giggled like a young girl. "You get silly when you're old."

Mylah smiled but kept her silence. As they reached the last step and small landing, Bess pulled open a wooden door and entered a dark room. Mylah followed, grateful she was no taller than she was. She only had about a hand's width between her head and the ceiling. Bess waddled over with a large oil lamp in hand. She set the glass chimney on a nearby barrel and extended the wick. Mylah lowered her flame to the wick which flared to life. Bess set the lamp back on its barrel, and replaced the chimney, stepping away from the now-glowing corner.

Bess proffered another lamp which caught fire with a blaze before Bess lowered the wick to control the burn. The scent of kerosene wafted through the room. A third and fourth lamp were lit and placed throughout the room, and when that was done Bess seemed satisfied. "You can douse your flame now, dear."

Mylah obeyed the small woman.

"Now," Bess said with a business-like tone. "The reason I've brought you down here is not for ham."

Mylah straightened. "What is it I can do for you, Bess?"

"Oh, it's not what you're going to do for me," she said, and sat on a nearby stool. She pulled another in front of her and patted its seat. "Come and chat with me."

Nervous, Mylah joined the woman. She placed her hands on her thighs and faced Bess with honest curiosity.

"There isn't much that gets by a cook, you know," Bess said. "Might seem like a lowly station, but the better to slide right under the noses of those I serve." She made a sliding gesture with a shaking hand. "And I've been Cook here for a very long time."

"Indeed?" Mylah asked, as if her age were not apparent.

Bess turned her face, looked at Mylah and tutted. "Don't flatter me, young lady." Mylah inclined her head in defeat.

"I know things that would make your gold eyes turn black," Bess said.

A chill snaked down Mylah's spine.

"Such as?" Mylah asked, prompting the woman.

"I know you know that I know the High King is no heir to the throne. Sybille told me she told you. And do you know how I know he's no heir?"

Mylah shook her head.

"Because 'twas me who served the food to the pregnant girl and the queen. And drew their baths, turned their sheets, and lit their fires. I was the only soul who knew and was trusted to take care of 'em. The queen trusted me, but the king was a different story. We had to hide that I was involved. Couple of near misses," she said, pointing her finger into the air. "Almost caught a time or two. Very strange and stressful days. But the queen wanted me to know. She wanted one other soul to hold that secret. That one and many, many more.

"And I've been around enough pregnant women in this castle to know the signs. I raised Sybille, didn't I?" she said. "So, now, don't you go thinking you can have one over on me. Asking for ginger to 'freshen the room'." She rolled her eyes. "Ginger is an anti-nausea remedy. And then, recently, no more requests for ginger. She's past the illness portion. Sybille is with child and that child is the true heir to the throne. And you need me to know this. Do you know why?"

"Please tell me," Mylah said, not really fussed that Bess knew the truth.

"Because I know she'll be in danger soon, and I know how to keep her safe," she said.

"Why in danger?" Mylah asked.

"She's carrying a girl. I can tell it. The High King is desperate for a male heir to carry on some wicked, wicked practice I don't quite understand fully. And he will not allow Sybille to bear a female. If he gets a cut wife there's likely chance she'll bleed out and die. I've seen it through three generations," and here she held up three gnarled fingers. "And we can't let that happen because she is the last true heir. She or her child must take back the throne. This evil cycle must end."

She was breathing heavy. Mylah reeled. "What evil cycle?"

"Can't say for sure, but every time a new heir takes the throne, their personality shifts to that of their predecessor. There's a darkness, a shadow that clings, especially when he thinks no one is looking. And it perpetuates with each new king."

Mylah chewed on the woman's story, wondering. She certainly

had the shadow bit correct. "How is such a thing possible? Are you saying the king is somehow the heir and the predecessor?"

"You probably think I'm batty, but I've doted on each heir for the last three generations and I know their heart and soul. When they take the throne, the old king comes back!" she shout-whispered the last words, dark eyes wide.

Mylah wondered if the old woman really was batty.

"I didn't bring you down here to tell you just that. What I brought you down here for was to show you something. Something no one else in the castle knows."

"Why?" Mylah asked.

"Haven't you been listening? To save our girl, Sybille, and to save her babe." She stood from the stool, bones creaking and crackling. She hobbled to a nearby shelf, turned and waved Mylah over. Mylah followed. The old woman put a gnarled hand on the shelf and pressed down hard. There was a protesting groan and creak and then a passageway yawned before Mylah. A dank breeze wafted up to her. Mylah called fire back to her hand and peered into the tunnel. The flame bobbed, shadows dancing against the walls and shelves and foodstuffs.

"Where does it lead?"

"It leads deep into the castle's underground. I don't yet know a way out once you're down there, but it could save you if you need a place to hide."

Mylah's heart fluttered against her ribcage. The answer they'd been seeking all this time had been buried amid sausages and cheese. Mylah doused her flame and pulled the door shut. She turned to the woman. "Why do you trust me with this?" she asked.

Bess considered her for a long moment. "Something in you has shifted," she said slowly, as if she was sorting out in that moment what exactly it was she could see shifting. Mylah shuffled. Dirt scraped between her boots and the stone floor, filling a long silence.

"What do you mean, woman?" Mylah asked, cross at being dissected.

"I know you trained and grew, started taking on tasks the High King asked of you. But, that never changed why it was you were doing what it is you're doing."

"Which is?"

"Surviving," the old woman said, as if this were perfectly obvious. "Protecting your people in the only way you knew how. Don't look at me as if you're shocked. I told you. I know things. And I know the High King set you off. I don't know exactly why, but there's a new fire in your eyes I haven't seen in the last year since you came here.

"Something shifted," she finished.

Chapter Twenty-Five

Mylah's quarters had been moved to sleep in the collection of royal rooms held by the Queen. It had been an upgrade. She and Tijhi's room boasted a wall of windows that displayed a glittering night sky, the three moons in their varying phases pinned amongst the stars. Mylah stared out from the room's center; no lamps lit to disturb the night view. Her mind whirred, her body restless. Training had become less frequent since her assignment to Sybille, and with her growing belly, they'd become more and more secluded to these quarters.

She couldn't bear the hours spent surrounded by walls and windows. She needed to get out. The queen slept, her room guarded by Shilbin and his trustworthy guards whom she'd formed a sense of loyalty based on their shared experience with their employment to the High King. Mylah looked at her door, fingers flexing at her sides. The queen was safe. She could take a break from her duties, she told herself. But the gnawing fear that the king would catch her neglect made her hesitate.

Tijhi, perched on a pillow in the vast expanse of bay windows, lifted their head and opened one golden eye. *Go,* they said. *Get some fresh air and exercise. I will keep watch over the queen.*

The Tijhi uncurled themself from the window and arched their back in a mighty stretch. With that, the fox leaped from the window and pattered over to the door that linked this room to the queen's private bedroom.

With a sigh of relief and swelling excitement, Mylah charged for the windows. Carefully, she swung a large pane of glass open on its hinges. Cool night air, rich with the warm fragrance of summer, caressed her face. She stepped through the giant window's opening onto a stone balcony and felt herself come alive. She thanked the Goddess and all the lesser gods that shone in the night sky that the queen's quarters were just one floor up from the ground. She shimmied over the balcony railing and jumped. She called on Tyrinth to rise and meet her, shortening her fall. She jumped from the new mound of dirt and darted away from the castle walls.

Her body delighted in the physical exertion of running, and as she moved into the steady rhythm of a jog, joy filled her body and soul. She was made to move. Mylah exited the inner castle wall by vaulting herself over it and into the secondary corridor. The stone here was more pliable to her abilities. She jogged to the west end and skidded to a halt, facing the wall that stood between her and the training grounds.

Mylah grounded herself, reveling in the way her breath expanded and released, her heart thumping with the effort of her jog, muscles warm and alive. She widened her stance, slightly bending her knees. She let the moment's exhilaration fill her to the brim as she called on Tyrinth and fire together. She raised her hands, focused on the stone wall in front of her, and willed the elements to rearrange themselves.

Mylah kept the picture of what she wanted formed clearly in her mind. The stone groaned as it rolled in on itself. The wall formed a crease which dipped further and further, widening until at last a chink of open air and land appeared.

Mylah continued rolling the stone wall out until it was just wide enough for her to fit through. She walked through the small door she'd created, its walls still hot from the fire element she'd used to coax the stone into moving. She turned back, facing the rolls of stone on either side of her fabricated exit. She contemplated whether to keep it open, but in the end, decided to close it, just in case anyone happened to wander up to the wall.

She dusted her hands as she turned from her handiwork and set her sights to the training ground. Picking through the wild grasses and weeds, she made her way to the main path. She would love to spar with Luther under the stars and moons, but settled with a solitary run, looping the training grounds. Her boots crunched rocks and dirt, eating up distance in that starved way that lack of exercise spurred.

She'd run several miles, having settled into the steady meditative rhythm when she saw something coming toward her. She halted, fixed her vision, and realized it was not something but someone. She grinned.

Mylah picked up her jog, her heart singing in a way that was not all about the movement. When he saw her, he slowed, flashing her a surprised smile. She didn't slow. She ran toward him, realizing how much she'd missed him over the last several months.

She halted, breath heavy, body covered in sweat. A smile spread across her face as she took in his rich dark skin, his rich, brown eyes, and full mouth which seemed to mirror her own expression. That he seemed as glad to see her, made her even gladder.

"Couldn't sleep, doll?" he asked, and he reached a big hand to the back of his neck and rubbed it, peering at her through upturned eyelashes.

Mylah shook her head. "You?" she asked. He turned upward facing palms to the sky, eyes taking in the night around them.

"Seemed like an awful waste to sleep through a night like this," he said.

"Walk with me?" she asked.

"It would be my pleasure," he said. They set off at a leisurely pace, exiting the training loop and wandering into Livvy's gardens. Here and there, wooden signs jutted up from the ground.

"She's been busy," Mylah said, reading one such sign, which noted: Carnivorous. Do not approach.

Mylah sidled away from the sign and the surrounding white flowers that shone ghostly in the moonlight. Their scent made Mylah's mouth water. Several tree frogs crept toward the cluster of bone-white flowers, pausing as they looked up the black stems toward the open blooms.

One small frog leaped, shiny legs vaulting the critter into the flower. Green liquid splashed from its center as the outermost petals coiled around the frog. The flower shone brighter, as if a lamp lit from within it. A soft sizzle emanated from the flower. Frantic croaking accompanied the frog's shadow scrambling up the inside of the flower. The neon green liquid bubbled, little flecks spraying out of the flower's top. The frog's shadow stilled, the croaking abated. The remaining frogs gathered around the flowers croaked, turned, and fled.

"It's about all we do these days," Luther noted as he walked alongside Mylah. Something about his tone of voice made her turn. His eyebrows pinched over his eyes.

"You help?" she asked, hoping to coax more from him, eager to hear about his activities since she'd last seen him.

He nodded, worry pulling at his features.

"What is it?" she asked, and grasped Luther's arm to turn him toward her. His bicep was hard, and she suffered a small shiver at the contact.

He allowed her to control his movement, facing her. He looked up and down the garden trail, lips pursed tightly. Mylah followed suit, checking their surroundings and finding no one, not that she expected to see another soul out in the dead of night.

"Follow me," he whispered. He turned away from her and led the way down the path. They passed bushes with lurid pink berries, a sign stating: Poisonous. Do not eat. On the trail's opposite side, a constant hiss filled the air as tall dark reeds emitted plumes of yellow mist. The sign there read: Noxious Gas. Do not inhale. She clinched her hand over her nose and mouth as they passed.

Further along, the trail twisted left then right, then right again seeming to spiral in on itself. A copse of small evergreens tipped in a vivid orange and sticky looking substance also had a sign, and now Mylah was not surprised at the warning: Toxic. Do not touch.

Luther led the way down an ever-tightening circle until he took a sharp turn onto an obscure animal trail. "Um," Mylah said, feeling a bit panicked as she searched for more signs, "are we sure this is safe?"

Luther paid her no heed as he pushed through slender green trees, ringed in a pattern of brown and black. The vegetation gave way easily and sprang back to place, but Mylah found golden black fur clinging to it.

Luther slowed as the slender trees thinned. He made a clicking noise. "Critter," he whispered. Mylah saw and heard nothing. "Hey buddy, you home?"

The trees dropped away to an opening filled with golden gas grass, which occasionally puffed up small clouds of purple gas. Luther stepped into the clearing, alert, casting glances around them.

With just the stars and moons for light, Mylah made out indistinguishable shapes on a dark mound. As they drew closer, she saw the mound was comprised of a collection of disparate objects. There were shoes and random bits of clothing, a broken oil lamp, gardening tools, and laying atop it all was Critter. He perked his long ears as Luther and Mylah approached. His head rose, nose working, his six eyes reflecting an animalistic blue glow, golden mouth appendages floating toward them as he sensed them out. As he caught Luther's scent, the creature's short tail wagged as he rose and shambled over to greet Luther.

"Hey, there ya are," Luther said. Critter zapped out and into existence immediately in front of Luther, circling in front of him, disappearing and reappearing in his exuberance. Luther stroked the creature's long neck, scratching behind the muldonidei's long ears until his back hoof thumped in delight. Critter reached his long snout toward Luther's face, golden appendages caressing his chin.

Mylah stood by, watching the exchange and smiling to herself as Luther's demeanor shifted from worry to joy. At last, the greeting ended and Luther turned to Mylah. Critter fixed Mylah with his animal-blue gaze and turned stock still. Before Mylah could worry about the creature's shift in behavior, the elemental loped over to its mound of collected things, rooting around in the massive pile of stuff.

"What is it?" she asked Luther. "Why have you brought me here? And what is all this?" she gestured to the mound.

"Muldonidei are collectors. They're excellent finders of things. This is aided by the fact they can move through space and time and walls are really no obstacle to them," Luther said. "Critter is damn smart too."

"Looks like he's good at finding a bunch of junk," Mylah said. She approached the pile and toed a collection of candles. A deep rumble emanated from the creature. Mylah backed away from the collection as the muldonidei glared down at her, hackles high.

"The High King is looking a bit haggard these days, don't you think?" Luther asked.

Completely unsure where this conversation was going, Mylah paused. Then she thought back to the last time she'd seen the High King and how he'd seemed to have aged rapidly in just the months since she'd left the Aestyrah.

Luther crossed his arms. "And you suddenly getting assigned as a personal guard to the queen."

Mylah shifted, but said nothing.

"I've been here a bit longer than you and in my seven years,

I've seen some things," Luther said.

"Such as?" Mylah asked. The memory of shadows gathered in the throne room's corners as the High King threatened her people crowded her mind. She touched that still-dead spot on her arm. Luther's gaze shot to the gesture, but then he refocused on her face and Mylah thought she'd made up that flash of recognition.

He looked around them, licking his lips, eyes wide. "What I'm about to tell you, you can't ever, I mean never can you repeat this."

Fear squeezed Mylah's chest and gripped her throat.

"I was here when Achyla the Seventh reigned. He was the one who brought me here, just like number eight brought you here. I was here when the monarchy transferred to Eight." Luther's eyes were wide. He stepped in closer to Mylah, still looking around to ensure they were entirely alone.

Critter sniffed around the mound of collected things, stub of a tail wagging occasionally.

"I was on guard when the king and queen met their untimely demise. Me and only me, per the king's orders."

"Why not Leviatha, the Captain?" Mylah asked.

"Leverage," Luther said simply. "I've got more to lose. Leviatha? She's happy to be here. Happy to serve and live in luxury. Never a missed meal. Clean clothes. Roof over her head. Coming from where she came, this is a treat and she justifies her work saying she's keeping people safe."

Mylah heard the king's voice in her ears all over again. "Guard her with your life, or your people will be annihilated." She nodded, understanding. "Tell me what happened."

Luther kept his voice low, his head bent toward Mylah so the sound would carry only to her ears. Critter sifted through the objects on his nest. Muffled thumps, clangs, and clatters filled the quiet inner sanctuary. "King Seven was aging rapidly, just like Eight is doing now, but not as bad. Eight was barely sixteen. Sweet kid. He really cared about people, and would go into the city, visit schools, frequent merchants, talk to farmers." Mylah thought back to the day she'd entered Udari City, the way the barkeep had been so loyal and admiring of High King Achyla the Eighth. "He absolutely doted on his little sister. He was fascinated by Tyrmini and our powers, and incessantly asked questions. I thought he'd make a great king.

"Seven, on the other hand, was distant, cold, sometimes cruel, and explosive. Compared to his father, Eight was a shining star of hope and compassion." Luther paused, shook his head, and if Mylah weren't mistaken, heard a quiver of emotion in his voice.

"Seven says to me that day, 'Go get us a carriage. I want to take my family on an outing outside the city. Sybille's staying with Bess. You'll be our guard.' 'Just me?' I ask, and the king confirms, 'only you'. So, I do as I'm told. We get out to a lake outside the city and Seven tells me this is the spot, and he wants to set a picnic. I lay out the blanket, get the basket out, but there are some odd items in that basket."

The hair on Mylah's arms and neck sprang to attention, gooseflesh covering her skin. "What was it?"

"A book - very plain with a symbol embossed in the cover, a black crystal bowl, a few candles, and a vial of red liquid," Luther said. "By the time I get back to the carriage, the queen is dead, and Eight is knocked unconscious.

"The king tells me to drag them both to the picnic blanket, but now I know this is no picnic. He says to me, 'Luther, you are sworn to secrecy. I find out you've told a soul about what you're going to see, I will assure your family suffers unspeakable pain.' I know a lot of Tyrmini who end up here have zero family left they care about. They've been betrayed by their people, turned in by mothers and fathers, or like Livvy, rescued by the Tyrmini guard before they're hung by their neighbors and friends.

"Not me. My family protected me. Every last damn one of them tried to hide me. 'Course they didn't know about the Dragon's

Eye and that it was impossible to hide from the High King. They gave me space to flex the power, away from those who might harm me, and to keep me from accidentally harming others. They taught me mind practices to control my emotions. They loved me so much, they put me above their own safety. In my years here, hunting or recruiting, I haven't run across one other family with the same commitment and kindness to one such as we. 'Cept maybe yours."

Mylah hung her head, pressed her left fist to her heart, a gesture of respect and honor for her family.

"The king knows you and I are the most valuable people to keep around. He can boss us around no problem, because he's got our family in his grasp. One wrong turn, and our families suffer."

"Tell me what he did," Mylah insisted. "Tell me what happened next." Because she had a hunch. Bess's observations rang in her ears. The king before became the next and so on. Bess had seen it for three generations.

Luther took another step toward Mylah and there the space between them evaporated. His strong hands encircled her arms, pressing their bodies against each other, as if this would seal the secret between them.

His face grazed hers, his breath hot against her skin as he spoke, his words barely a whisper. "We laid out the queen and Eight. The king had me hold the book open to a page which seemed to give him instructions. He took a black dagger and made a slit down the queen's arm and let the blood spill into the black bowl. Then he drank it. Shadows sprang up around us, wrapping us completely in darkness, save for the candles he'd lit. He took the blood and dribbled it into the unconscious mouth of Eight. He chanted, and his voice seemed to take the rhythm of some other beat, drumming out of the shadows around us. He took the vial of red liquid, dabbed some of it on his finger, drew a symbol onto Eight's forehead as he chanted. He slipped off that silver and black bracelet he wears, knelt beside his son, and slipped the bracelet onto Eight's wrist, even as he held it tight in his hand. Then he took the knife and slit his own throat.

"The blood sprayed out onto his child. A child so unlike our previous High King. I thought I was staring at a family gone crazy. A case of homicide and suicide. The shadow still hovered above us like a dark cloud, so still and silent. I stood for a solid minute, not knowing what I'd do next, but then the young king stirred.

"Eight began to chant in that same language of his father. The same words repeating over and over. The Shadow started to stir, twisting, turning, and wouldn't you believe it seemed to fight, like it too was a prisoner trying to escape."

Mylah's breath sawed in and out of her, her heart leading the charge. Shadow. Luther too had seen this shadow.

"Slowly the shadow sank into the young king's body, entering through his eyes, nose and mouth. When every stitch of shadow was gone, the young king stood. He ambled over to me, big blue eyes wide, but no longer with that beautiful spark of curiosity and joy. He looked at me and said, 'Remember, you tell a soul about this and your family suffers in ways you can't imagine.'"

Mylah shivered.

"It was Seven!" He shook Mylah, hands gripping into her arms, desperate to have her believe him. "I swear, the man must have found a way to transfer his soul to that of his child. And you know what haunts me most?"

Mylah shook her head. There were too many things that haunted her about that tale. She couldn't pick one. The horror of it all shook her to her core.

"If the old king's soul is in our new young king, what happened to that sweet boy's spirit?" A tear traced his cheek, and then another.

Critter approached with soft footsteps, hooves thumping in the dirt. Luther reached out and took something from the creature's mouth. "Here," Luther said and handed Mylah a book.

Mylah took it and immediately regretted holding the object. A zing of recognition shot through her as she stared at the plain, leather-bound cover, a symbol etched in black, as though branded: one outer circle and two ellipses joined in the center, tracing an eternal loop, one ellipse filled in black and the other empty. It was the same symbol on the Tyrmini magic meter, except both semi-circles had been empty. She'd seen the book at her first meeting with the High King, now almost a year ago. "This is it?" she asked Luther, slowly opening the cover. The binding creaked, the pages hushing against each other. "This is the book he used to perform the magic?"

The front page was simply inscribed in handwritten ink, "Achyla"

"Best keep it someplace you think it won't be found. Glance in there for a deep look inside the High King. You'll see it doesn't matter which number he goes by. They're all the same."

CHAPTER TWENTY-SIX

I have harnessed the power of creation.

Mylah read the first line and shuddered.

I will make Magyskind obsolete. There will be no more bowing and scraping to lords of magic who all consider themselves above the regular person. They hold all the power, and I will wrest it from them. Those born without magic will praise me as their Savior and those with magic will rue their own birth. This revolution begins with me.

Mylah had ferreted her way down to the cold stores, ensuring she hadn't been followed, and that she was truly alone before she popped open the secret door. Sybille cooked in the kitchens, slaving over a new dessert recipe which involved cream, cheese, and fruit. Sybille had agreed to this plan. To busy herself in the kitchen so that Mylah could spirit the book to the underground.

Mylah had wandered a little way into the tunnels, afraid to lose her way in the unfamiliar dark, that secret map tucked under Sybille's bed. She'd brought an oil lamp with her, and it flickered from time to time in the random breezes that sprang up and died away.

She cast about her. She sat in a circular room with brick floors, a fountain in its center. The fountain hadn't felt the touch of water in what looked like decades, maybe centuries. Thick cobwebs and dust coated the statue depicting a man holding a sword aloft, face lifted to the ceiling. Stone benches perched beneath giant arched openings which were filled with dirt and stone. Mylah sat on one such bench after dusting off several layers of dirt, sending spiders and beetles skittering away.

Her lamp hissed, and aside from the occasional scratch of rodent toes against stone, it was the only sound to accompany her in this dark space.

Mylah looked back to the book and flipped past the first page. The material felt thick but fragile, and Mylah wondered exactly how old the book was. The first section was titled, The Nature of Light and Shadow.

Handwritten text scrawled across the pages, outlining the nature of Magloryn, and how he could oppositely apply the information to Shadow, in the lack of information he'd gleaned from the tome. The tome he'd obtained, Mylah realized, from her people's ancient library.

The next section seemed to be a dedicated journal, with long entries of text carefully written in quilled ink. Partially through the book the pages started taking on a different format.

At first, Mylah thought she read one of Sybille's recipes. But the ingredients were odd things, such as amatsu fur, dirt from a newly dug grave, berubula saliva, a drop of blood. The titles were equally disturbing: Speaking with the Dead; Night's Cold Breath; Plague; Soul Despair; Lingering Sleep; Revival.

Mylah turned the pages with growing unease, perusing notes that read things like, "I used this on the Inilu Chancelor with great success. One less enemy to oppose me." Another page read, "The Magys Counsel gathers upon the full moons. I will make the most of this luck at having them all together." This one was under the title, Noxious Fog.

As she flipped further and further into the book, the more manic the writing became, some with splotches of ink and unidentifiable stains. Others folded with bits of feather or plant between the pages. The pages boasted about the deaths of

Magyses in power, of conquests over royalty, and the gruesome dismemberment of elementals in search of one ingredient that would be used in the next spell.

In one section, the king described the nature of magic. She read through outlines and sketches of portals, their anatomy deconstructed to understand the elements involved and how they worked in unison to transport users from one location to another. Despite all his study, the king expressed his extreme frustration that he could not make the portals work for him.

Near the book's last pages Mylah stumbled on a dark bookmark. The pages here slid softly under her fingers, as if worn from use. Mylah pulled the black bit of material from where it had been wedged between the two pages. Mylah held the material, thumb stroking the velvety irregular shape as she read the title: Soul Transference. A cold hand stroked her spine and the hair rose, skin prickling.

The elixir used in the ritual called for fierystwhiel essence, a creature Mylah had never heard of. The essence was apparently extremely difficult for the High King to obtain, a point which angered him immensely. In the end, he'd been triumphant. There were no details on how he'd been successful, but the notes on his other creature parts procurement were enough to inform her whatever method had been used was not pleasant.

Mylah stroked the bookmark in her left hand and turned the page with her right. Crudely illustrated on the next page was a dragon. Mylah assumed this was not the Tijhi, because she'd seen the Tijhi's dragon form, and this did not match. Neither did it seem to be Magloryn, because the wings looked bat-like rather than bird-like. The sketch was filled in with black ink, so the details were difficult to make out. Under the sketch, Achyla had made a note.

Mylah folded the bookmark over in her hand absently as she read, "I have called and captured the great dragon of Shadow.

Between these pages is a momento of its body." Mylah's heart sped. She looked at the thing she held in her hand. Horror filled her. This was a piece of elemental dragon. Shivers racked her body as she carefully placed the dragon part back between the pages, scalp tingling. Widdawah, dragon of Shadow, was often associated with evil. Maka had educated Mylah that Widdawah was a pure source of creation, and yes, sometimes creation also meant chaos, but that was not the same as evil.

What the High King had done... that was evil.

The Tyrinth had lost its dragons and perhaps it had all started when the High King had lured and imprisoned the spirit of Widdawah. She read on, "I have obtained a knowledge tucked away in the ancient tomes kept by the Aestyrians. And with that knowledge, I captured the dragon.

"Imagine my surprise when once I called Shadow, Light also arrived, though I could not contain the dragon.

"I have since learned the form of containment must be imbued with the dark dragon's essence, as well as fierystwhiel essence. I laid the trap after much toil to create the appropriate chains. And I have done it! I have captured Magloryn, twin to Widdawah, and she is mine to wield.

"Since their capture, magic as we have known it has transformed. Elemental power is now more polarized, less nuanced, and most importantly explosive and dangerous. I am using this to launch my campaign to rule Aelos. I will hunt down and capture those with what I'm calling Tyrmini abilities, but only after this chaos causes enough damage to stir fear in the hearts of our unmagical citizens."

Mylah!

Mylah yanked her eyes from the pages, her heart still galloping with discovery. Tijhi's voice stirred new anxiety. She shot up from her perch on the stone bench and snapped the book shut. She searched around her, jogged to the fountain, and placed the book into its dry pool.

What? Mylah asked Tijhi.

It's Sybille.

Mylah ran before Tijhi could continue speaking. She made it to the secret opening in moments, climbed through the hole and shoved the door closed behind her. She cast about and grabbed a wheel of cheese. With her decoy in hand she launched through the store door, took the stairs two at a time, and dashed down the hall, the oil lamp clanging, light bouncing against the darkness as she went.

She skidded into the kitchen, breath heaving. Tijhi stood near Sybille, teeth bared as they looked up at a man Mylah had only seen once in her time at the castle. The adviser was an elderly man with a U-shaped swatch of cropped gray hair surrounding a gleaming bald spot on the top of his head. The advisor pulled a gold pocket watch from his black vest pocket, snapped it shut and stowed it away. He held his hands up in a pleading gesture to the queen. "Please, your majesty, the king is not a man who waits patiently."

"I am busy," Sybille said. She faced away from the adviser, rolling out pie dough, as though his presence was nothing more than an annoyance. "And I will not be going anywhere without my guard."

Mylah cleared her throat, mastering her breath as though she had not just sprinted from the underground. "Here is the cheese you requested, my Queen." She set the wheel and the lamp on the counter, turning the wick down to douse the flame.

Sybille looked over her spectacles at Mylah, and relief shone on her face, breaking through the facade of calm irritation. She winked at Mylah, a smirk tilting her mouth.

"Ah," Sybille said. "Here she is. Thank you for fetching that critical ingredient for me. The stores are such a dark and gloomy place." She dusted her flour-covered hands, untied her apron, and pulled it over her head. The dress she wore, a deep, dusty blue, draped over her very pregnant belly and in no way hid her condition. The secret of her pregnancy was only maintained by keeping her from sight. Mylah had arranged an escort with Shilbin, Gavick and herself, providing a concealing wall to block the queen's appearance from view.

Sybille turned to the adviser. "Very well, I am ready now." Tijhi backed away from the adviser, sitting on their haunches in satisfaction.

The adviser sighed in relief. "Let us go then and make haste."

Shilbin and Gavick, who had remained at the dining tables on the far end of the room jumped to attention at their queen's and Mylah's approach. Mylah fell into step in front of the queen, while Shilbin and Gavick took up either side. The adviser led the way, boots clicking out a hurried pace over the stone floors.

Mylah's mind whirred, thoughts alight with her new understanding of this ancient man ruling the continent of Aelos. Her hands felt haunted by the velvety touch of Widdawah's wing, her eyes still saw the collection of spells, smudged in stains, her ears rang with the words littered on centuries' old pages. Achyla was a monster of his own making. She could not underestimate a being of such clever cunning, to have devised his own magic system to overthrow the whole of an original and inherently natural magic across the continent.

Mylah understood the state of the world to be out of balance, and appreciated some wickedness ruled through the High King, but she'd been unprepared for the depth of darkness stretching across generations.

Tijhi, what is this about? Mylah asked.

This one, Tijhi said, looking up at the adviser, *said something about a ritual.* Mylah's mind went to the tome of rituals, experiments, and journal entries she'd just been sifting through and alarm bells rang in her mind.

What sort of ritual? She asked, panic building.

I believe the dark one means to determine the babe's sex.

Can it really be that time already? Mylah counted the months in her mind, stunned to find Sybille was likely nearing her child's birth, and Mylah had developed a plan no more effective than heading into a kitchen larder's secret tunnel. Her heart thumped, sending pressure into her neck and head. She played out the ritual in her mind. Would the king truly call a cut wife if the child were indeed a girl, as Bess believed?

The adviser led them to the High King's private study, Shilbin and Gavick remaining in the hall outside the antechamber. Mylah caught the old guard's eye before she ducked into the small space and saw worry pinch his expression. When she and Sybille emerged from the antechamber into the sun-drenched study, Mylah's mouth went dry, body trembling in the presence of ancient evil.

"So good of you to finally arrive," the High King bit out the words. His face had gathered more wrinkles, his skin a bit grayer than last Mylah had seen him.

"Husband," Sybille said, and she curtsied. "To what do we owe this pleasure?"

He looked to the adviser, "You may go."

The adviser bowed, turned, and exited through the antechamber door.

Mylah and Sybille faced Achyla. A perfect summer day reflected through the bank of windows. The king wore a loose silk blouse, the neckline ruched with strings that would allow tying to close the v-neck draped open to reveal the king's sternum and the hint of ribs. He was skinnier than Mylah had seen him, with shadows dusting under his eyes and cheekbones prominent over sunken flesh.

He rounded the desk and approached Mylah and Sybille. He smiled at Sybille. "How are you feeling? Is your condition treating you well?"

He reached a hand and placed it against her belly. Sybille twitched, as if she would recoil from the king's touch, but controlled the motion. Achyla sucked in a breath of surprise and pulled his hand away as if burned. He laughed. "I've just been kicked." He laughed again as if in surprise and delight. But Mylah could only think about the spirit residing in the body, and how all it wanted was a new body to replace the one disintegrating before their very eyes.

"This one seems to have spirit," the High King said without inflection. "Surely a boy, then," he said. Mylah bit back a growl. Were boys the only sex blessed with exuberant energy? She'd like to show him her 'spirit'.

Mylah's mind painted creature after creature sacrificed in experiments to gather pieces and parts to build the monstrosity of a generations'-old spirit sustained through murder and manufactured magic.

"Let us see for certain, shall we?" he said, his eyebrows rising. "Are you excited, sister?"

"Wife," Sybille corrected, with some fire Mylah was unaccustomed to seeing in her kind and scatter-brained friend. "Or Queen, if you prefer," she said. The king rocked back on his heels and back to his toes, jaw grinding to one side.

He shifted his glance to Mylah, anger dancing behind his brilliant blue eyes. Mylah noted how his platinum hair had thinned and lacked the same golden luster it had had when she'd first met him. Mylah intervened.

"A mother in the making can be a volatile creature," Mylah said. "It is only the energies at work to make a life."

"Yes, I forget how delicate women with child are," Achyla said quietly, as if to himself, looking down at his toes as he rocked back on his heels once more, hands clasped behind his back. Sybille sneered and opened her mouth to speak, but Mylah cut her off before she could cause herself real danger.

"Indeed, we must take special care of our mother of kings and allow her these little outbursts from time to time," Mylah said, placing a firm but gentle hand on Sybille's arm. Sybille swung her head to Mylah, rage flashing. But Mylah winked while the king turned his gaze to the summer day caught in a prison of glass, and Sybille's face slackened to confusion, then calmed to understanding.

We are playing a game here, Sybille, Mylah thought. *And it is a dangerous one. Tread carefully.*

"Let us proceed, then," Achyla said.

"What will you do if it's a girl," Sybille blurted.

"Dear sister," the king said, and Mylah felt sure he used the word to instigate Sybille's continued irritation and anger. To show her he had the power to call her whatever he wished. "I am not our father." He walked back to his desk and beckoned them forward, gesturing to a chaise between the desk and the windows. "I'll not stain my hands with the blood of our child. Not if it can be helped. No, we'll simply appoint a wet nurse and try again as soon as possible. One girl is hardly a reason to give up hope. Best to know now so that we may procure someone for the babe immediately after birth."

Sybille seemed relieved as she allowed Mylah to ease her onto the chaise. The king picked up an item from his desk. Mylah positioned herself between her queen and the bank of windows.

"Now, this device is very clever. I saw father use it with our mother." He smiled as he unfolded a square of silk from a small device that almost looked like a large metallic insect. A dome shape affixed to six bent legs, each of its small foot segments covered in soft padding. At the top, two pieces covered each hemisphere of the dome. Protruding from the mechanism's front two spindly black appendages hung forward, each length segmented many times.

As the king approached, an odd and erratic clicking echoed

across the room. Sybille drew back as the king stood above her, the mechanism coming alive. The device whirred as the king bent and carefully placed it onto the queen's blue-swathed swollen belly. The child inside the womb kicked. The antennae-like appendages stirred, flexed, and erupted into a collection of wispy black strands.

Before Mylah could shout in surprise, the wisps swept back into the antennae. The antennae then disappeared into the dome. The semicircular pieces atop the dome clicked open to reveal the shiny black surface beneath. What seemed like a singular black needle shot from the dome's top. A deep rhythmic hum gathered speed, the semicircular shapes glowing. As the rhythm steadied its pace, the needle atop the mechanism disappeared into the dome, and it was only when Sybille shouted in alarm that Mylah realized the needle had not gone into the dome, but through it and into Sybille's belly.

Mylah shouted, "It's hurting her!"

"Nonsense," the king said. "She is perfectly safe. Do not interfere, Tyrmini."

"What is it doing?" Sybille screamed.

"It's simply taking fluid from inside the womb. This is how it determines the child's sex."

"It's going to stab my baby!"

"Calm yourself. It will do no such thing."

The black dome's inner segments contracted and swelled, then the needle pulled back into the dome. A mechanical grinding emanated, as if gears inside the dome churned against each other. The appendages slowly grew back to hang from the mechanism's front, the grinding slowed, and the semicircles closed. The wing-shaped pieces' silver sheen shifted from silver to black to red.

"A girl is indicated by red while a boy is indicated by green," said the High King.

The three watched, barely breathing. The wings cooled from red to blue to green, then from green to blue to red, and back again.

"Is it broken?" Mylah asked, as she watched the thing shifting from one color to the other.

"Curious," the king said, and swiped the mechanism from Sybille's belly, turning it over and tapping at its domed surface. It resolutely flashed in regular intervals between the three colors. "It seems we shall have to wait until the babe is born. Now, on to the second test."

"Second test?" Mylah and Sybille asked in unison.

The king pulled another object from his desk and this one Mylah recognized immediately. A chill swept over her, goosebumps rising over her arms.

Achyla stomped toward the two, unwrapping the device with nonchalance and before either had another moment to process what was happening, the king placed the magic meter onto Sybille's belly, silver and black bracelet rolling out of his shirt sleeve and tinkling against the device.

The center two pools forming a never-ending loop sprang to life, the bottom filling with deep black while light reflected in the upper portion. The monarch removed his hand and both sides of the infinity loop quickly faded back to an empty silver. Mylah didn't dare look at the High King, though she could feel his eyes on him.

The device quieted. Sybille's breathing caused it to rise and fall on the apex of her belly. At last, it stirred. The intricately engraved hands whirred over the circle's four quadrants, pulsing to life with color. Mylah held her breath as the hands snapped home.

Click.

Click.

Click.

Click.

CHAPTER TWENTY-SEVEN

"Incredible," Achyla said.

Mylah couldn't breathe. The meter gleamed in multicolored splendor, reflecting not just two or even three elements, but all four. The two inner circles remained empty silver. This child would be a very powerful Tyrmini, which could ultimately curse them. She was afraid to speak. Only Achyla controlled the child's fate.

"What does it mean?" Sybille asked.

Achyla sighed, deep and long, closing his eyes. He ground his jaw in real frustration. In the corners of the room, shadows flickered. A stone dropped into Mylah's gut.

"I'm so sorry, my dear," Achyla started. "There can be no Tyrmini heirs to the throne."

"This means the child is a Tyrmini? But you are the only one who could save them," Sybille said, rising a little from the chaise. She reached for the device, but Achyla moved faster and swiped it away.

"Tyrmini are outlawed, dear queen," he said.

"And yet, one stands in our midst," Sybille said, pushing herself awkwardly from the chaise to stand next to Mylah, righting her long dress.

"Mylah is here because I allow it. There is no room in the royal line for heretic magic wielders. Everything our house is built on is in opposition to the volatility of Tyrmini magic. We bring order to the chaos."

"Please," Sybille said. "Put the child in your employ. No one will know it's your child. Mylah can raise them," she said, her brown eyes wide and wild, a protective hand clasped over her swollen belly.

Achyla ground his teeth once more, eyes squinting closed, he gripped his forehead with his free hand, as if Sybille's words caused him pain, and shouted. The shadows gathering deepened and spread. Mylah clapped a hand to the black mark on her shoulder. "Silence, woman!"

Sybille jerked back, but her face reflected only grim determination.

Mylah widened her stance and inched closer to her charge. The tingle of her power summoned to just the edge of her access. She fingered the cork on her pouch of sand.

Achyla turned from them, stalking toward the desk. He teetered and placed a hand against the solid surface, the meter spilling out of it. He fell into the chair in a heap, eyes still shut. "Mylah," he started. "Please escort my sister to her chambers where you will await the arrival of someone who will deal with this abomination of a child. I will request their haste, and they should arrive by dawn tomorrow."

Sybille inhaled sharply, and said, "But -"

Achyla flicked his eyes open and fixed Sybille with a stern, icy blue gaze. "I do not want to hear another word on the matter." A deep roiling sound echoed through the room. The oil lamps flickered, and the room dimmed. Mylah searched for the source of shadow, which seemed to be everywhere. Sybille gasped and leaned into Mylah. Mylah tucked her charge behind her, prepared for the threat closing in on them.

Achyla took a rattling, long breath and exhaled just as slowly. When he was done, the room lightened, sunshine seeped back into the circular space with cheer and life. "When you come to your senses, you'll understand," he said. He stood from his desk and

240

stalked toward them. He took Sybille's hands in his and fixed her with what might have been an understanding gaze. Sybille leaned imperceptibly away from him as he said, "Do not worry, sister. We can try again." He smiled at her. Mylah shivered at the expression.

Sybille said nothing. Her body shook as she pulled her hands from his grasp and backed away. Mylah took Sybille by the arm and towed her from the room, feeling the High King's gaze on their backs as they headed for the door.

"Mylah," the king said. Mylah halted, a hare caught in a snare. She turned when everything in her wanted to run from the room. She faced the High King, who stood with his back to the expanse of windows. The light washed away the details of his face. "I have another task for you."

"Yes, your majesty?" she asked, her voice harsh.

"The young Tyrmini building gardens and growing herbs?" Achyla said. He walked toward her, his face coming into view from the blinding light of day.

"Livvy, your majesty?" Mylah asked.

"She and her pet are no longer necessary. Please execute them."

Mylah couldn't have heard him correctly. "What about the tinctures she's made for you?"

"I find they are inadequate. Not that I need to answer to you," he said with a warning in his voice. He turned from her and headed toward his desk, lowering himself into his chair again. He pulled a pile of papers toward him and pored them over as if she were no longer in the room.

Mylah wanted to argue. She wanted to advocate for the girl and her creature companion. She wanted to fight him on it. To scream she had made a vow to the girl's parents and there was no way she was breaking it. But then she thought of the tunnels in the castle's depths and that map stowed under Sybille's bed.

"I want it done by sunset. And Mylah?" the king looked up

from his papers and fixed her with his sapphire gaze, the wrinkles gathered around them seeming to deepen by each passing moment. His eyelids drooped a little more.

"Yes, your majesty?" she asked, her heart pounding even as she formulated how exactly she would disobey, worrying about the consequences if she was caught.

"That elemental familiar. I believe it's taken something from me."

"Taken?" she asked. She knew exactly what the creature had taken. Shadows gathered, faint tendrils snaking toward her.

"It is a muldonidei, is it not?" he asked, really looking at her with a level of icy dissection that made her squirm.

"Yes, your majesty," she answered.

"I thought so. Muldonidei are very rare these days. Most were wiped out with the cleansing of elementals by my-," he paused for a breath, long enough that Mylah caught the space. Then he continued, "grandfather." As if he were counting the generations. As if he'd lost track. "I did not know the creature was here on the property until recently. Whatever possessed you to allow such an abomination onto my grounds?"

"Elemental familiars, as you call them, seem to both strengthen and calm our abilities."

A flash of anger passed over the king's expression before he smoothed them once again. "Muldonidei are finders and collectors. This creature has spirited away some very valuable old tomes. Works of fiction by an ancestor who fancied himself an inventor of sorts." He waved a hand in front of him in a gesture to suggest how silly it was, and yet there was a tone of pride in his words.

Mylah nearly choked on the description. Inventor indeed. The "ancestor" who had written the tome Mylah was currently keeping tucked in the corner of an ancient and forgotten fountain had invented horrific ways to torment elementals, harvesting them to use in his own form of magic.

242

"My ancestor was admittedly a little... eccentric. It's best you return the tome to me before anyone reads it. It would be bad for our family name to let that little secret out of the bag." He stared at her, expression flat. Mylah felt like an insect pinned to a piece of paper under a microscope. Could he see the secrets she kept?

Mylah did her best to act normally, despite her raging panic. She bowed to the High King. "Of course, your majesty," she intoned. "I will look for the tome," she lied.

"Very well," he said, his eyes still on her. "Return with the tome when the task is complete. And when you bury the creature, do so in the girl's gardens, in a marked grave."

Mylah stared at him, unable to speak, to ask the question, "What for?"

He seemed to read her, in that way that unnerved her, and said, "In honor of Livvy's service to us."

Mylah's stomach rolled as she mentally perused the High King's book of shadow, wondering what spell required muldonidei organs.

She stilled herself from fear that would cause her voice to quake, and carefully spoke. "Of course," Mylah said, and turned slowly away. She placed a hand on the small of Sybille's back and together they exited, the High King's shadow lurking behind them.

Chapter Twenty-Eight

S ybille paced her expansive room, a hand pressed into the back of her hip, skirts rustling. Castle maps littered the dining table. Some laid open, layered atop each other. Others skirted the edge of the table, rolled up or slightly unfurled, while others hid tucked away in their leather tubes. Mylah and Sybille had searched and searched and had found no other entrances to the underground.

Sunlight spilled into the room, catching dust motes in their soft descent. Mylah watched Sybille, wondering exactly what they would do, and knowing the king and time gave them little choice.

It was late morning already. She strode to Sybille, caught her arm and swung her gently. She held Sybille's other arm. "Stay here and wait for me. Do not let anyone into this room, do you understand?"

Sybille nodded, tears springing up in her dark eyes and streaming down her cheeks.

"We're going to get through this. I promise I will not let anyone harm your child."

Sybille nodded again, gently removing herself from Mylah's grasp to wipe away the tears, bumping her glasses out of place. Mylah reached up and adjusted them for her, stroking a stray strand of mousy brown hair behind Sybille's ear, then holding either side of her face. "I promise," she said again. "Be prepared to go when I return," she said.

Sybille inhaled and exhaled raggedly. "I will," she said.

Mylah gave her a gentle shake and a smile, then turned to go.

She exited the Queen's room. Shilbin and Gavick jerked their heads toward her where they'd been seemingly in conversation.

"What's all this about?" Shilbin asked.

Mylah straightened her spine. "The king has requested I complete a task. You are to guard Sybille's quarters, ensure no one is admitted. No one. Until I return."

"Very well," Shilbin said, eyes squinted as if trying to see what Mylah wasn't saying.

"No matter who approaches this door, do not allow them in." she asked.

"I understand," Shilbin confirmed.

"Do I have your word you'll guard her with your life? Do you swear fealty to the queen?"

Shilbin fixed his dark eyes on Mylah's and Mylah only hoped he could see the dire need for the queen's safety reflecting in her gaze. He slowly nodded. "On my wife's grave," he said, "I shall protect the Queen from any and all who mean to harm her." Mylah bowed her head as understanding passed between them. He'd lost his wife in some way to the High King. His oath meant only loyalty to the queen.

She grasped the man's arm. "I hope we'll meet again," she said.

Shilbin nodded gravely. "May your Goddess keep you safe."

Mylah smiled at that, warmth flooding her. She nodded, released the soldier, and turned down the hall.

She made sure other guards saw her on her way out to the gardens. She nodded to the gate guards, greeted the guards in the inner-city wall, and also the outer-city wall guards. She walked into the king's acres of land on the west and north side of the castle.

As she moved, she planned. She planned what she would say to Livvy, she planned her conversation with Luther, she planned how she would stage the girl's execution, and how she would get her "body" to the kitchens. There were a few details left to be decided, but all in all as she laid out the plan in her mind, she grew more confident. She could do this.

Tijhi, she called to the elemental dragon of fire as she gained proximity to the gardens. *I need you,* she said.

The little fox phoenix didn't answer.

Mylah continued through the yellow field. The Goddess looked down on her as grass hushed against her leather pants. Mylah touched the sand pouch strapped across her body, reassuring herself of its presence. Stillness stretched across the late morning air and set Mylah's nerves on edge.

When she made it to the gardens, she cast about the maze of foliage, unsure where to look to find the Tyrmini and her companion. She strode past section after section of herbs, flowers, plants, and fruits, listening, looking for any sign of Livvy and Critter.

Giving up on finding Livvy tending her garden, she went in search of the secret inner grove the girl had made for Critter. Finding the path Luther had led her down, she arrived quickly at the creature's nest. She stepped out of the tree line and into the gas grass.

"Stop right there."

Luther's voice found her before she saw him. She turned in his direction, shocked to find him squaring her off, a look of deadly determination in his eyes. "What -?" was all the intelligible response she could manage.

Luther held a blade in his hand, stance ready. The blade danced with blue fire and steam rose from his body. Tucked behind Luther, Livvy poked her head around the man. He waved her back behind him without breaking eye contact with Mylah.

"I heard about the king's orders," he said.

Mylah could feel the pouch of sand slung across her body, but it was achingly far away from her fingers. Unstoppering it to unleash her weapon would be impossible. Luther was fast.

"What do you intend on doing about those orders," she asked.

"Keeping you from fulfilling them," he growled, his voice a deadly calm.

She raised her hands even while she cast about for a source of Tyrinth dry enough for her to work with. "And what if I told you we are of the same mind?"

"I don't think anything would keep you from protecting your people," he said.

Mylah understood and felt another dagger to the heart. She played a risky game. If she were successful, if she were able to save Livvy and Critter, and the king uncovered what she'd done, her people would be slaughtered. No matter what she did, someone's blood would be on her hands.

"I want my people to be safe," she said, emotion roughening her voice. She remembered the ultimatum the king had given her, and how shadows had danced in the room, how he'd scarred her with his touch. Just one touch.

If Luther and Bess's accounts could be trusted, if their understanding of reality were true, if her interpretation of the Tome of Shadows was accurate, Achyla had been ruling and ruining Aelos for five centuries. He was the reason Tyrmini powers were so volatile. He was the reason elementals were scarce. He was the reason for the chaos. And he'd done it all for one reason: to assert and maintain control over the lives and fates of Aelosians for centuries.

Mylah had blood on her hands, but Achyla's hands were drenched and the ancient beast that he was, he had no intention of changing. He believed his actions to not only be justified, but to be the best action for the continent, and for its people. He could never admit that his motivation had anything to do with his own feelings of powerlessness, having been born completely ordinary in a world where those with power were those with Magys abilities.

It had been unfair; it seemed to Mylah. She could feel young Achyla's anguish at being shunned and rejected for his normalcy, and there was something in him that twisted when that happened. He had turned all his rage and powerlessness into motivation to create his own magic - no matter the cost.

And cost it had. The elemental twin dragons of light and shadow had been imprisoned and tortured, twisted to his will. With that imprisoning, Magys magic had been set off kilter, turning them to the newly dubbed, "Tyrmini", with explosive and dangerous power that made them enemy number one. Achyla had pulled the strings in the background to make this happen and then swept in to save the world from Tyrmini and the dangerous elementals that gave them power.

The truth was, Mylah felt sure of it, elementals helped balance Tyrmini. When Achyla had discovered this, he'd done everything in his power to eliminate the threat to the story that Tyrmini were dangerous. He'd spun tales around the reality to make it look like elementals made Tyrmini more powerful and more volatile. He then offered the solution himself: kill elementals.

Mylah could see history stretch back from where she stood in this moment and knew the Tijhi was right: this was bigger than her and it was bigger than just her people.

She took a shaky breath, fixing Luther with her golden gaze. "It turns out, 'my people' are not just those who live in the Aestyrah. The Goddess warms us all," Mylah said.

Tijhi took that moment to appear at her side, their dainty steps barely moving the gas grass before they sat serenely at Mylah's side.

Well said, Tijhi said, that mischievous smile plastered across their small snout.

Luther relaxed the smallest amount. "You mean to tell me, darlin', that you're not planning on executing this young girl?"

One side of Mylah's mouth quirked in a half smile. "No," she said sadly. "I plan to rescue her. Now, will you help me, or am I going to have to eliminate you?" She'd managed to get a thumb and forefinger on her pouch and uncorked it now. In one swift gesture, a dozen sand arrows hovered in front of her, flaming to life. They snapped and sparked as they began to transform into glass.

"I cannot continue to save the few and sacrifice the many. Something must change," Mylah said.

Luther dropped his knife and held his hands out in front of him in surrender. "We want the same thing, we want the same thing," he said. "I will aid you, Mylah, Master of Glass. But, how on Tyrinth do you plan on sneakin' around the Dragon's Eye?"

Mylah inhaled and exhaled, snuffing the fire and calling the sand back into the pouch. The bits of arrows that had already turned to glass fell to the ground. "You said it yourself," she said as she stoppered the pouch. "The eye doesn't work on the castle premises; too many Tyrmini to track."

"But..." Luther said, fixing her with a look of pure confusion.

Mylah smiled at him and got busy filling them both in on what she had planned.

CHAPTER TWENTY-NINE

Luther hefted the wheelbarrow, pushing it with ease. His regular training prepared him for manual effort, and he only showed signs of fatigue when they neared the city's inner wall that guarded the castle itself. Mylah stood before the stone wall and peered up at the sky. The sun was heading toward the horizon. They had little time left.

She squared herself off and got to work on rolling the elements back and open, creating a space for their party to pass through. Tijhi accompanied them, and as always with their presence, Mylah experienced a surge of calm control over the elements.

Once inside, Mylah turned back to the wall and resealed it. Only she knew the wall would not maintain its same integrity now that she had manipulated it, not once but twice. If ever the city was under attack, a clever person with some experience with stonework could identify the weakness.

Mylah led the way to the entrance Bess had pointed out, where food supplies were received into the castle's extensive cold storage. As they continued down the rounding corridor of stone, the castle looming over their right shoulders, the sun sinking to their left, Mylah hoped beyond hope Bess would be in the kitchens, would let them in, and play along with their ruse.

Two guards appeared from around the bend, stationed at a set of wide and high double doors that led to their destination.

Luther's muscles gleamed with effort, the cart clattering over the cobblestone path in an inconsistent rhythm which Mylah could only assume rattled Luther's bones. Seeing the guards, Luther immediately halted and called them over.

"You two," Luther commanded.

Mylah's eyes bulged as she stared at him with a *what-are-you-doing!* look.

"Get over here and help us out," Luther said. "These melons weigh a ton."

The guards looked sharp, their young faces flushed. They hustled over, black and gold uniforms seeming entirely too thick for the warm summer day. "Yes, sir," one said and immediately attempted to lift the wheel barrel by himself. Luther looked at Mylah and grinned.

The young guard failed to lift the barrel, and the second guard hurried to help. Together the two hoisted and rolled the thing to its final destination where they quickly collapsed against it, heaving. Mylah thought Luther looked smug about his ability compared to the young guards. She rolled her eyes.

Mylah approached the guards. "Go get Bess," she told them.

"I don't think we're supposed to -," a guard began. Mylah opened the doors to her power and let fire leap from within. It bathed her in flames. She had simply to jerk in their direction before they skittered away, into the doors, and up the hall.

Luther crossed his arms and frowned at her.

"What?" she asked.

"You really had to resort to using magic?"

"Oh, I suppose you believe that's worse than throwing your weight around?"

"I most certainly -," Luther began.

"Do you think you could get a move on? These melons are heavy, and Critter is getting restless." Livvy's muffled voice murmured up through a cover of fruit. A low growl that turned into a whine issued from under the vegetation.

Mylah and Luther quickly got to work, pulling melons from the cover until at last the girl and her companion were free. Mylah ducked a head into the hallway. The guards were nowhere in sight. She turned to Livvy. "Come, come, come," she said, waving them forward.

Livvy and Critter slipped through the doors and headed down the stairwell. Mylah turned to Luther, the goodbye suddenly stuck in her throat.

"I want you to take care of yourself," he said. He closed the space between them, grasping her hands in his. She reveled in the warmth, the slight scratch of callouses against her fingers.

"Come with us," she said, wanting to throw their plan away in attempt to keep this man who'd become a friend - more in her secret heart - close to her. She could feel her own selfishness in her words. But, for him to stay... it would be awful for him.

"You and I both know having someone on the inside is invaluable to the cause."

Her stomach tightened. Her heart broke thinking of what he would have to do in the High King's employ while in his heart he was a rebel. Would he be forced to kill more Tyrmini children and elementals?

She closed the space between them and wrapped her arms around him, the press of his muscle against the length of her body warming her. He followed suit, his strong arms encircling her in the last bit of safety she was sure she'd feel for a while.

"We'll meet again, sweetheart. Don't you worry." He stroked her hair. Mylah nearly purred at the touch.

"But when?" she asked.

"We'll find a way. Love always does."

Mylah pulled away from the comfortable hollow of his shoulder and neck, meeting him eye-to-eye. "Are you saying you love me?" her tone suggested she was teasing, not wanting to hope for him to be serious.

He didn't return her slight smile. He reached a hand up, tucking her hair behind an ear and his thumb stroking along her jawline. He tilted her head. His breath increased, his heart beating against hers, as he leaned down and kissed her. His lips were supple and firm, warm and soft.

Fire washed over her and inside her, consuming her and bringing her life, threatening to bring her to her knees and simultaneously soar. He moved his hands, one finding the small of her back and the other wrapping around her neck and pulled her in even closer.

Mylah kissed him back, wanting him to know how much he meant to her, wanting him to feel her adoration of him. She threw an arm onto his shoulder and caressed the back of his neck with a delicate touch. He growled into her mouth and she swept her fingers over his ear, pulling slightly at his lobe. She wanted more of him, wanted the touch and taste and feel to go on and on. But, a soft chirp behind her brought her back to reality. She closed the kiss, one last tender press of lips to seal the experience.

"I'll take that as a yes," Mylah said.

"Now," Luther started, "I'm not saying goodbye to you. I'm saying farewell for now."

Mylah bit back tears, swallowing hard to keep them down. Her heart cracked as she squeezed his hands, looking deeply into his eyes one more time before she turned away.

Tijhi led the way through the open double doors. The castle's dark interior consumed Mylah. She did not look back.

Mylah and Tijhi scurried down the stairs, deeper into darkness, waiting at the stairs' landing. Livvy bounced from foot to foot. She looked at Mylah as if to say, *where were you?*

"Apologies," Mylah said, the word barely made it past the lump in her throat. She approached the cold storage door, swinging it open and was greeted by the warm glow of a lantern.

Hissing, "Get back!" she tucked two creatures and two Tyrmini behind the open door, shoved up against the staircase landing's end. Her body crushed into Livvy and Critter, and she had no clue where Tijhi stood. She carefully peered around the door and watched as a boy in a plain, food-stained tunic exited the larder. He was so close she could touch his shoulder with barely a move.

The boy wobbled up the stairs, laden with onions, sausages, and cheeses. Mylah, Tijhi, Livvy, and Critter held their breath. Voices echoed overhead, Luther's among them. Mylah caught snatches about fruit and Livvy's garden, and even heard a squeal of delight from Bess, all while the boy ambled up the single flight of stairs, lantern jangling in his overburdened grip. Mylah prayed to the Goddess Bess wouldn't start directing any of her kitchen minions to move the melons into the cold storage when the boy finally rounded the top landing. Mylah pushed the door closed and opened it again for her and her three companions to enter the larder in blessed darkness.

Mylah stoked a flame to life in the palm of her hand and cast about to ensure they were indeed alone. When she confirmed the coast was clear, she hurried to the secret entrance and shoved the shelf down until it popped open with a groan. Waving away a cloud of dust she ushered her friends inside, snatched an oil lamp and oil from the supply, grabbed a bag full of jerked meat, cheese, bread, and apples before following them through the passage.

When the door finally closed behind her, she breathed a sigh of relief. They were safe.

"Did you really think the High King wouldn't know about this place?"

Mylah froze, back facing the new voice, a muffled scream accompanied by scuffling and grunts.

"Shit," she said before turning to meet their captor.

CHAPTER THIRTY

"If you care about your master, you'll stay exactly where you are," said Leviatha to Critter. A wild noise ripped from the creature's throat, wet and deep and savage. Its eyes glinted with green light in the darkness, its body crouched, head forward, body vibrating, snout appendages waving in the air as it sensed everything around it.

Livvy wriggled in Leviatha's arms, but the woman held her like life itself depended on it.

"You don't know what you're doing," Mylah told the captain. "There's more at stake here. If you would just stop to think about it."

"What's at stake is my reputation and you're dangerously in the way," she said.

"Is that what matters most to you?" Mylah asked. "You'd really kill this girl and her companion even though she's posed no threat?"

"All I want to do is grow things," Livvy whimpered.

"Silence!" Leviatha shouted, and yanked at her choke hold on Livvy. This caused Critter to snarl again, exposing his wide teeth and stamping at the ground with solid hooves.

"Where is the Tome?" Leviatha asked Livvy. She had a knife angled at the girl's throat. Livvy's green eyes were lamps in the near darkness, the only light a smudge of dancing orange flame from Mylah's cupped hand.

"I don't know what you're talking about," Livvy said, and whimpered. "What's a tome?"

Mylah lowered the supplies to the floor. She was aware of Tijhi's presence, but didn't see her companion. She inhaled slowly through her nose and exhaled through her mouth. She took a step towards Leviatha and Livvy.

How had he known this was her plan? Had he guessed? Had she somehow given it away?

She cursed herself. Achyla was centuries old. Of course he would know about these tunnels. He'd been alive when they'd sunk or been covered. Maybe he'd even been the one who orchestrated the concealment.

He'd somehow known Mylah never intended to obey him and he'd sent Leviatha. If that were true, would he also know her intentions to spirit Sybille from the castle to save their child and heir to the throne? A pang of terror zipped through her. She had to get to Sybille. Unless it was too late. She nearly choked on the rising panic.

"Tell the creature to find the tome," Leviatha said. A strangled cry ratcheted out of Livvy. Leviatha yanked a fist full of Livvy's hair and exposed more of her neck. The blade sliced Livvy's fair skin and a strand of darkness stretched and smeared down her throat.

"I don't know what you're talking about," Livvy cried. "Please don't kill me. I didn't do anything!"

"It doesn't matter. Tome or no, this has to be done," Leviatha said. She took a breath, the muscles on her forearm tensed as she made to pull the knife.

To Mylah's left, fire erupted from the darkness and the underground space filled with light and heat. More than that, the presence of Tijhi, who'd masqueraded as a small fox for over a year, exploded into the room as a fully formed dragon.

They stretched their massive leathery wings, rich red and lined with blue flame. Tijhi roared, their voice huge. The Tyrinth around them trembled. Leviatha screamed, her knife slackening. Mylah didn't wait. She unstoppered her pouch and pulled on the sand within. She'd shot her glass arrow before she could comprehend the full process of its making.

The weapon sunk home. It caught the captain's shoulder and shoved her back. Critter lurched forward, gone in a wisp of dust and air and there in front of Leviatha. He charged, head-butting into her stomach and sending her crashing against the far wall.

Tijhi took one giant step toward the captain, their mouth opening wide as they inhaled.

"Stop!" Mylah shouted. Tijhi turned flaming eyes toward her. "No more death. Not if we can help it. She's not going anywhere."

She's too dangerous, Tijhi said.

"No more death of Tyrmini," Mylah said, her own fire burning hot within her, deep in her belly. "She's incapacitated. Leave her."

Tijhi stared at Mylah and Mylah wondered if the dragon would obey. They were an immortal elemental deity. They didn't have to heed Mylah's request.

"Please," she added. "We have to try to do this the right way."

Tijhi blinked, then turned back to Leviatha.

"You've been spared this day. Do not forget it," Tijhi spoke. Mylah was unnerved by hearing the dragon's voice out loud. Their communication had been solely telepathic, and the dragon's voice rang deeper, layered, as if many voices spoke at once.

Leviatha looked up at the dragon, panting and wheezing. "You know what your problem is, Mylah," Leviatha said, and she coughed, sending blood flying from her mouth. It spilled onto her lips and chin, painting them red. "You don't know a good thing when you have it. If you would just serve, your life would be so much easier."

Mylah walked over the stone-covered ground and leaned over the injured Tyrmini guard captain. She opened her hand and called on the sand in her pouch. She shaped and hardened it, forming a handle and head. "Just because I don't want to kill you doesn't mean you need to keep talking."

She pulled back the weapon and hit the captain squarely in the jaw. The captain grunted and then was out.

Mylah looked up to Tijhi and smiled. "Thank you," she told the dragon. They blinked, and Mylah watched as the dragon dissipated in a cloud of sparks and smoke and was a small fox once again.

They stretched their limbs, then trotted to Mylah, sitting pristinely by her side. They peered into the darkened tunnels connected to the room they were in and said, *I hope we do not regret your compassion.*

Mylah approached Livvy, who trembled. She bent down, pulling a handkerchief from her pocket. "Are you okay?" she asked and dabbed at the cut on Livvy's neck, relieved to see it was merely a scratch.

Livvy nodded mutely. Critter appeared behind the girl and leaned against her, his head wrapping around to sniff at the girl's neck. Critter crooned and Livvy buried her face into the creature's neck, both hands tangling into his fur.

"That was scary," she finally said.

"Yes, it was," Mylah agreed. "And you were so brave. Do you think you can stay brave a little longer?"

Livvy nodded. "As long as I have Critter."

"Livvy, I need to leave for a little bit and find another friend," Mylah said.

Livvy looked over at Leviatha, eyes wide.

That won't be necessary, Tijhi said.

What do you mean? Mylah asked. Tijhi trotted toward an adjacent corridor. As they reached the opening, a form appeared from the darkness.

"Mylah?"

CHAPTER THIRTY-ONE

"Sybille?" Mylah asked.

Sybille appeared from the tunnel, Tijhi at her side.

"I figured it out," Sybille said.

The tension in Mylah's chest eased as she wrapped Sybille in a grateful embrace. "Thank the Goddess you're safe!" she said. "How did you make it down here?" she asked.

"There's a passage from my quarters," she said, a crooked smile on her face. "It was right under our noses the whole time."

Mylah stared at her. "You're kidding," she said. She scoured the room mentally, wondering where it was hidden. And then she remembered the painting, hanging to the left of the fireplace, depicting a fountain atop which a man held a dark sword aloft, and the fountain where she'd tucked the tome. "Oh," she said. There had been a label on the map, reading, "Grotto." And there on the painting had been...

"The Grotto," Sybille and Mylah said together.

Sybille nodded, smiling. "Yes," she said. "And -," she started and pulled herself out of Mylah's arms. She pulled a leather bag from her back to her front and lifted the cover to reveal a collection of leather tubes.

"The maps," Mylah said.

"I brought the underground map," she said, and tapped the roll. "I know we haven't figured it all out yet. But it's something."

"You are wonderful," Mylah said, relief washing over her. She looked around at the little group. "Stay here. I'll be right back."

Mylah retraced her steps earlier in the day. Had it only been that morning when she'd cracked open the Tome of Shadows? She was sure the time the king had given her had expired and he would be looking for them. They had little time to escape.

Mylah's people's lives hung in the balance now and she wondered if there was a way to save them. She set aside her anxiety over the matter as she climbed through the broken stone doors and entered the underground courtyard. She quickly retrieved the tome from where it was tucked away in the fountain and returned to the group.

"Now then. Let's look at this map and find a way out," Mylah said. "Here, let me take that." She took the bag Sybille carried, slinging it over her shoulder and making space to put the tome inside. Her fingers prickled at its touch.

There is one other thing we must find before we leave these tunnels, Tijhi said.

Mylah looked at the little fox, waiting for them to expound.

"What is it?" Sybille asked.

"Tijhi says there's something we need to find," Mylah translated.

"What?" Livvy asked, still stroking Critter's neck.

The little fox looked from Mylah, to Sybille, to Livvy, and back to Mylah.

I would have thought it obvious.

Humor us, Mylah said, annoyance seeping into her words.

We need to locate Magloryn, Tijhi said.

"They say we need to locate the dragon of light," Mylah said.

Sybille wandered toward the supplies, crouched with great difficulty, and retrieved the oil lamp, turning the brass knob to expose more wick. She waddled back to Mylah, removing the chimney and extending the lamp toward her. "Some flame, please?"

Once the lamp was lit, Sybille knelt and unrolled the ancient map. She adjusted her glasses and bent over the parchment, placing a hand on her belly. "This is much more difficult pregnant," she noted, trying unsuccessfully to lean further over the map.

Sybille traced the map with one finger, then pointed. "We're here," she said. "There's a glyph up here that looks like a dragon. Maybe?"

Mylah had seen the glyph before and had assumed it was a bird.

Tijhi trotted over, sitting next to Sybille and staring at the map. *That could represent Magloryn.*

"Tijhi says that could be it," Mylah said.

"The only problem is, there doesn't seem to be a path to the dragon. Look," Sybille said, and motioned Mylah over without looking up.

Mylah crouched and looked at the map, its drawings fine and faded. Now that they'd pointed it out, Mylah could see the dragonish shape but with what Mylah associated with bird-like feathers. Surrounding the glyph was a patch of nothing. Just a glyph floating in empty space. "The tunnels leading up to the glyph all fade away," she said. She traced one such tunnel back through a labyrinth of tunnels, through rooms, and back to where Sybille had pointed out as their current location. She looked at the other options. "This seems to be the most direct path, which looks to start with that tunnel." She extended an arm and pointed toward the left-most tunnel.

"If it isn't, we may be wandering these tunnels for days," Sybille pointed out.

"Or weeks," Mylah agreed. "But I'm not sure there's a better way."

"Critter can help," Livvy said. She looked up at her companion. "Couldn't you?"

Critter bowed his head to the girl and rumbled what Mylah

read as agreement, its short tail wagging, six eyes blinking out of unison.

"Oh," Mylah said. "How does it work, Livvy?"

"Critter is very smart. You just have to say what you're looking for."

This is how the creature found the tome, Tijhi said. *He simply needs the intention of what you seek.*

Did you set Critter to find the tome?

Tijhi sniffed, head held high. *I most certainly did.*

Mylah nodded, but shivered thinking of the book and its various spells. She turned to Livvy, trying to dispel the words she'd read. "Can you tell Critter we're looking for the dragon of light?" Mylah asked.

"Sure." Livvy spoke to the creature, eye to eye, while she stroked the creature's dark, golden fur. "Critter, who's a good boy? Yes, you are!"

Critter's body wagged in delight.

"Can you help us find the dragon of light? But we need to go with you, okay? We need you to help us get there. You can't bring a dragon back with you, right? Do you think you can do that?"

Critter's stub of a tail swished excitedly. He dipped his head and turned. He sniffed the open area, his nose appendages reaching out to each tunnel, sensing. His eyes shifted from their golden hue to silvery white, each blinking in turn. He disappeared and appeared within the center tunnel and turned back to them, as if waiting.

Mylah looked at the map. "I don't know. If we go that way, the trail twists and turns."

"You asked Critter to show you the way. Trust him," Livvy said, crossing her arms over her dirt-stained apron.

Mylah chewed her lip as she thought. What if Critter could easily make the way but the group could not. She weighed the options, unsure what was the best decision.

Trust the muldonidei, Tijhi said.

Mylah sighed deeply, worry sinking into her shoulders. She breathed, "Very well. Let us move forward then. I don't think we'll be safe here for long." She looked at the unconscious captain.

The group stood, gathered their supplies, and set off into the center tunnel, its cool dirt walls closing in around them. Mylah had a sense of belonging, her years of mining springing to memory. Critter took the lead, Mylah next, then Sybille, who carried the map. Livvy followed Sybille and Tijhi brought up the rear.

The tunnel stretched away from them, dipping and rising, but Mylah had the distinct sensation they were heading deeper into the Tyrinth, deeper into an extensive and unknown territory. She soldiered forward, but not without a wish for Luther's strong and patient presence.

They wandered the path, Critter stopping to sense the energy around them before moving on. Sybille occasionally gave verbal confirmation that their surroundings lined up with the map.

They'd traveled for what seemed like hours when their steps turned from dusty to muddy to watery. At the tunnel's end the hallway yawned to an underground lake. Mylah swore. This is what she'd been afraid of. That there would be no way the muldonidei could sense such an obstacle.

Critter halted at the water's edge and whined. Mylah wanted to whine too. She pulled a bit of sand from her pouch, fashioning it into a hollow sphere with an open lattice pattern. She hardened the shape to glass with fire. She set a living flame lovingly inside the sphere and cast the light out into the underground opening. She reached out to the flame as the ceiling stretched higher and higher. Sybille approached, map in hand.

"What do you suppose this icon could be?" she asked.

Mylah concentrated on moving her light globe around the room. She hoped to see bats flapping in the upper reaches, or rats skittering along the lake's edge. All she could see were the irregular shapes of stalactites hanging from the ceiling, dripping slowly into the still pool of water beneath them. The drip, drip, drip was the only sound besides her companions' collective breathing.

"Hm?" Mylah asked, the sphere still roaming through the cavernous space, darkness escaping and closing back in at the light's retreat.

"This icon," Sybille said. "I can't quite make out the shape of it. It looks like there may be something here."

Mylah continued her search. "I'm not sure," she said, half listening.

"Let me see," Livvy offered. Paper rustled, then a deep grown rumbled through the cavern.

Mylah froze, the glass sphere floating just above the lake's placid surface. Critter backed away, whining insistently. The shoreline shifted, lapping at Mylah's boots, then splashing up and over her toes. Livvy pushed the map down from where Sybille had raised it for her view. They each cast a wide-eyed gaze over the map, then looked at the lake ahead.

Tijhi circled, then sat pristinely a little way from the lake's edge. They let out a shrill yip, yip, which turned into a keening bird-like cry. Flames enveloped the dragon as they shifted once again to reveal their fox phoenix form. The bird and mammal creature launched themselves into the air, flapping over the shore, flame rising and spilling onto the wet Tyrinth.

A low clicking growl rolled over and over in a steady rhythm, first in fast succession, then slowing.

Back away from the water, Mylah, Tijhi said. *Unless you want to be elvathan food.*

Mylah searched her memory banks for any creatures called elvathans and came up short. Trusting her companion, she backed away from the water, arms stretched out in front of Livvy, Critter, and Sybille to keep them securely behind her.

She will not trust you. Do not approach.

You don't have to tell me twice, Mylah asserted. She doused the flame from the sphere, pulling it back with her and placing herself and her companions into the hall's near darkness. She turned down the oil lamp Livvy held, tucking it behind them.

"Either of you heard of an elvathan?" Mylah asked Livvy and Sybille.

"So that's what that icon is," Sybille said, nudging her glasses up her nose. She stretched the map out in front of Mylah and nodded in the icon's general direction. The drawing occupied the space indicating the lake, its shape depicted a roundish creature boasting long teeth, bulging eyes and two long appendages which drooped over the creature's eyes.

"I hope that map isn't to scale," Mylah whispered, leaning around it to look toward the pool of water. The still surface gave way to a roaring, bubbling bulge of water, that expanded, then rushed forward until at last the giant beast appeared.

Water sluiced off the creature in gallons, falling back into the lake. It was waist deep, if the creature's middle could be considered a waist. Massive rolls of flesh stacked atop each other. Its pink white skin shone faintly in the darkness.

The creature slowly blinked two bulging black eyes, as if the light from the fox phoenix was too bright. Even as Mylah thought it, the elvathan inhaled slowly, then snorted, blowing out buckets of water which doused the elemental dragon and completely extinguished their flame.

A deep growl echoed through the cave.

Mylah thought it was the elvathan until the giant creature ducked its head and whimpered. Tijhi inhaled and burst into flame again, flapping to maintain their height. Some private conversation seemed to transpire between the fire deity and the creature. The elvathan occasionally mewled as the Tijhi chirped and purred.

Eventually, the giant creature nodded, grumbled long and low as it lowered itself into the lake once more. Mylah noted the creature was not completely submerged. Tijhi returned to the lakeshore, extinguishing their flame and turning back into a small golden fox, large ears swiveling toward the lake creature. They trotted toward the group.

"We have permission to pass," they said, and again Mylah fought the discomfort of hearing the dragon's voice aloud, that strange layered composition, as though they spoke with several voices all at once. She shook herself.

"How are we meant to pass over the lake?" Livvy squeaked, but Mylah knew, and she thought Livvy knew and didn't want the answer.

"Elvathan has agreed we may use her body as a bridge," Tijhi said.

"Ohh... I was afraid you were going to say that," Livvy whined. Critter whined too. Mylah wanted to, but held it in. Barely.

Sybille moved confidently ahead. "This is such an adventure," she said, smiling. She approached the lake's edge, drawing close to the creature. Mylah hurried to catch up. She lent an arm to the queen, who took it gratefully. Sybille moved with sure feet despite the awkwardness pregnancy caused. Behind her, Livvy clutched Critter's side. Critter backed away from the lake's edge, his face turning away from the monstrosity filling the lake.

Mylah focused on Sybille and her own feet. The creature's surface was so wide the walkway of its back was straight and even, save for mounds of flesh which formed creases every few feet. Mylah's boots sank into the beast's flesh, giving her a sense of stability despite the wet surface.

Sybille paused midway down the creature. "Do you think I could just -," she started. She pulled her arm from Mylah's hand and placed her own hand in Mylah's. She then reached down and stroked the creature's skin. "It's so smooth. Almost velvety," she reported.

Mylah had no such need to satisfy her curiosity and wanted

nothing more than to be done and across the large body of water and its inhabitant monstrosity. "Hm," she stated in what she hoped was agreeable interest.

Sybille stood again.

"Let us move on, my queen," Mylah said.

Sybille's hand was still firmly in Mylah's, the other hand pressed into her lower back. She looked squarely into Mylah's gaze. "You're afraid," she said.

Mylah's temper flared. "I am standing on a giant creature that without the intervention of an ancient dragon deity might have eaten us, crossing a large body of water where I am completely helpless to protect my charges should a powerful water Tyrmini - say, Leviatha - come upon us and attack. We are running for our lives from your very twisted ancestor, who turns out to have employed a dark magic to supplant his essence or soul or consciousness from one body to the next. That same ancestor imprisoned twin dragon deities, Shadow and Light, and we are on a reckless journey, not knowing our way to find one of them, in hopes they will have the means to help us escape an underground labyrinth that looks to have been covered up, for what reason we do not know. I would appreciate it if we could get across this giant elemental's back and move on to our destination."

Sybille's eyebrows rose over the rims of her glasses, but then her expression smoothed. She rubbed Mylah's arm and smiled gently. "I'm scared too," she said. "I'm sorry I was insensitive. I just believe this is all going to turn out. You are Mylah the Mighty. We're in good hands. And we have the help of a dragon deity on our side," she said and looked over her shoulder to where Tijhi stood next to Livvy, looking up at the girl as she stood on the bank still, Critter nervously surveying the creature ahead.

Mylah exhaled a breath she'd been holding for far too long. "I appreciate your faith, your majesty," Mylah said. "May we please move along now?"

Sybille nodded. "Certainly."

Behind them, Mylah heard Livvy say, "Critter, we have to go this way."

Mylah and Sybille turned toward their companions.

Critter backed up again, mouth falling open to release a lolling tongue.

"Critter," Mylah tried. "Come. We must go this way to find the dragon."

Critter whined. And then, something seemed to catch the creature's eyes. He peered to the far bank, head ducking as his whiskery gold appendages waggled toward the opposite side of the lake. Critter circled once, leaned into Livvy who took hold of his fur and in a blink they disappeared.

Mylah sucked in a sharp breath of surprise.

"Where did they go?" Sybille asked.

Mylah clutched her charge, feet wobbling on the creature's squishy surface as they surveyed the bank where Livvy and Critter had just been.

A giggle echoed across the cavern. Mylah and Sybille whipped around to find Livvy and Critter on the opposite side.

"I didn't know you could do that," Livvy said. "Good Critter." In the darkness, Mylah could barely make out Livvy wrapping her arms around the muldonidei's neck and pressing her cheek into his fur.

"You could have offered escort to your whole party," Mylah groused.

Critter lowered his haunches to the stone ground, eyes blinking one by one, tongue lolling out of his mouth. He nudged Livvy, as if to say he'd taken exactly who he'd wanted to take.

Mylah huffed, but carried on. They made their way across the elvathan, and she breathed a sigh of relief. A low rumble echoed through the cave. Mylah turned as the lake bubbled and boiled, the elvathan lowering itself back to its depths, the water concealing it once again.

Mylah shook herself and looked ahead. Past the lake's shore, the cave was narrow but open above and below. She sighed. The Goddess must be testing her. She inched forward and peered down. Nothing but darkness met her gaze. She thought about sending the light globe into its depths, then thought better of it. The path ahead continued with a collection of rickety boards. Ropes on either side of the path were strewn with some sort of algae or moss Mylah had no name for.

Mylah groaned as her heart leaped into her throat, hammering away in her jaw as if it would make its way out and fling itself into the depths below. She inhaled and exhaled, pulling on her experience deep in the mines. She'd done this daily for years. She could do this again. Her palms grew sweaty as her vision narrowed. She breathed again as she stepped tentatively onto the first step. It held with partial weight so she put all her weight into it. It held. So did her panic.

"We should move forward cautiously," she told the group and backed off the bridge, not ready for the trek across. Sybille had unrolled the map again, her face close to it. Mylah leaned over her shoulder and held one side. "Where are we now?" she asked.

Sybille pointed to a place on the map past the elvathan icon. "Here's the bridge," she said. "Looks like it goes on for quite some time. After that the path squeezes back down to a tunnel again with all these rooms splitting off of it. After that we meet the empty space and the dragon.

"One bridge, a tunnel, then the dragon," Mylah simplified. "We can do this."

"Wait," Sybille said. "What's this icon?"

"I don't like when you ask that question," Livvy said from behind them. Mylah peered at the map to where Sybille pointed to a room off the tunnel after the bridge. The room was clearly marked, unlike others along the same path. It was larger and in its circular center was a small and irregular filled circle, almost tear shaped. Mylah recalled seeing the symbol when they first looked at the map.

"It's just a smudge or an ink drip," Mylah said, ignoring a nagging worry scratching at the back of her mind.

"I don't think that mark is accidental," Sybille said. She looked up at Mylah.

Mylah shrugged. "There's no way to know its meaning until we arrive," she said.

Sybille inhaled and exhaled. "Well, then. Shall we carry on?"

Mylah looked ahead toward the rickety ancient bridge then back to Critter. "Livvy, do you think Critter can get us across?" Livvy looked at Critter, rubbing a forearm across her nose.

"What do you think, boy?" Livvy asked. Critter clopped over to the edge of the bridge and peered across the dark ravine. Its opposite end was lost to shadow. Mylah couldn't see just how far the gap was and nerves danced in her stomach at the thought of traversing into the darkness, destination unknown.

Critter whined, circling back to Livvy, bumping his head up under her arm. Mylah's hopes rose. He was collecting Livvy to transport her. Relief gathered in her shoulders. Critter took a step and didn't disappear.

Mylah's kindling hope died as Critter led Livvy to the bridge and placed a steady hoof onto the first plank.

"One bridge, a tunnel, then the dragon," she muttered. She grabbed onto the rope handle and looped an arm through Sybille's. Arm-in-arm, opposite hands securely gripping the handle, the two set off across the bridge. Tijhi leaped into the air in their fox-phoenix form, blue, orange, and gold flame blazing around them, lighting their way through the darkness.

The bridge protested with each step, the structure swaying through open air. Mylah's body clenched, legs wobbling, and her grip on the queen tightened all the more. She searched ahead for solid ground and at last Tijhi's blazing body illuminated the far end of the bridge. As soon as the light touched the stone landing, Livvy and Critter snapped out and into existence, Livvy's giggle echoing around the cave.

The bridge shifted, swaying to and fro in the utter darkness, boards and rope wailing with the movement. Mylah's heart thumped wildly in her chest as her legs wobbled like jelly.

"Uh oh," Sybille said as the bridge's whine reached a crescendo with resounding snap. "Run," she instructed Mylah, but Mylah froze, legs shaking so hard movement was beyond her. Sybille yanked on Mylah's solid arm, which did nothing.

"Go, your highness," Mylah managed. She couldn't move and there was no sense in them both dying on this bridge.

"Don't be silly," Sybille said. Another stretching creak ended in a succession of pops. The bridge gave, lunging toward the darkness below before slowing to a bouncing halt. Mylah's side of the bridge sagged, knocking them off-kilter. Sybille crashed into her. Mylah grasped for the queen, barely capturing her arm before Sybille slid through a gap in the rope handle and into the abyss.

Sybille cried out, throwing her other hand up and onto Mylah's arm as ancient dirt sifted down onto the queen. She coughed, head jerking to the side and sending her swinging.

"Hold on," Mylah yelled, fear rippling up her core, nerves on fire. Gripping the rope with one hand, she pulled Sybille toward her, biceps screaming with the effort. She bellowed against the limits of her muscles, forcing them to give her more power.

Overhead Tijhi circled lower. Fiery light danced over the two dangling women, and still darkness loomed beyond Sybille's dangling feet. Sybille blinked away grit, glasses askew over her freckled nose.

Mylah ground her teeth as she heaved the pregnant woman up to the rope dangling freely over her torso. "Grab it," she yelled. Sybille released her grip from Mylah's arm and reached for the frayed rope, missing it by finger's width. She swung away from Mylah, her other hand slipping from Mylah's arm. Mylah flexed, squeezing the queen's hand in a grip between her biceps and inner forearm. It wasn't enough. Mylah screamed as Sybille's hand slipped further.

Sybille inhaled, one arm dangling beside her, the other creeping out of Mylah's grasp.

"Hold on," Mylah urged her. "Can you swing your hand back up to me?"

"Can't," she said, "I'll lose my grip." Sybille's eyes gleamed wet and bright through her dust-smudged spectacles. She screamed as her hand slipped again, a gut-wrenching sob erupting from the depths of her soul. Tears washed tracks into her dust-covered face. "My baby," she sobbed.

Mylah's heart wrenched, her right hand burning as the thick heavy rope bit into her palm. "You and your baby are going to be just fine. I will not let go," she said, meaning every word.

But, as the queen's hand slipped one final time, Mylah knew the bitterness of that broken promise.

CHAPTER THIRTY-TWO

Mylah screamed as Sybille's body dropped away from her. Darkness swallowed Sybille, the glint of her glasses catching Tijhi's light and throwing the blue twinkle back to Mylah. Red and gold streaked past Mylah, air rushing into her, sending the breaking bridge swaying again. Mylah watched awestruck as Tijhi in their dragon form raced after their falling companion.

Sybille's echoing scream halted with a whoosh and an "oof." Out of the darkness the mighty flap of wings echoed through the cavern, preceding the red and gold dragon's ascent, Sybille gripping Tijhi's neck.

Mylah hauled herself up, clutching tightly to the rope as she made her way over the tilted, damaged bridge. Her feet touched blessed stone and she lurched toward Sybille. Sybille slid from Tijhi's neck and Mylah wrapped her up, arms vice-like around her waist and shoulders.

"My goddess, I thought I lost you," Mylah said into her ear.

Sybille's body shook as she said, "Me too."

Tijhi exhaled. Mylah's hair rushed away from her. She released the queen and looked into Tijhi's golden gaze. "Thank you," she said.

Tijhi lowered their head, lids lowering. Golden light sparkled around them and the dragon disappeared, leaving the tiny desert fox. Tijhi trotted up to Sybille, looking up at the queen, the mother-to-be. Sybille crouched, the movement awkward and slow.

She stroked a hand over the fox's head and down their back. Tijhi's lids lowered, a smile spreading across their black and golden snout. "Thank you," she said to the dragon. "You saved both our lives."

If only I could keep that true, Tijhi said.

Mylah's stomach squeezed. *What do you mean?*

But the dragon didn't reply. They turned from the four companions and trotted toward the waiting corridor. Mylah offered an arm to Sybille, who took it gratefully, pulling herself to stand once again. She wobbled upright, then lurched forward, hand gripping her belly, eyes squeezed shut, face pinched in pain. Mylah suffered that same near-falling sensation again as she observed the queen and prayed. Prayed it wasn't time yet.

As quickly as the pain seemed to have gripped Sybille, it passed. Sybille's brown eyes opened, breath evening out, expression clearing. "Perhaps a little too much excitement back there." Mylah stared at the woman, the very young woman, caught up in a swirl of darkness through absolutely no fault of her own.

Mylah regarded her fellow rebel and marveled at her courage and strength. Sybille, the Queen of the Kitchens, Principal of Pies, Overlord of the Ovens. With her kind and encouraging words, and grounded listening ear. Sybille thought of herself as no warrior, but here she was, in the bowels of a secret underground, running from a monarch with hope held tightly in her womb.

She was so much more than a simple baker. Mylah looked at the swollen roundness of her pregnant belly, carrying a chance... carrying hope... and Mylah prayed for her queen. Prayed for her sweet presence, her strength, and authenticity to remain with them for long, long into the future.

"Shall we carry on?" the queen asked Mylah.

Mylah nodded, stowing away her thoughts and prayers. Livvy and Critter approached as Mylah pulled the map from the satchel slung over her shoulder.

"Any more surprises ahead?" Livvy asked, voice high and shaky, one hand clutched into the fur around Critter's neck.

Mylah found their location and followed the path ahead of them. "Looks like a straightforward path," Mylah noted.

Livvy's hunched shoulders relaxed. "Good," she said, hand still gripped into the muldonidei's fur.

Mylah rolled up the map and handed it to Sybille. She called fire into her palm and cast about her. The dust here was dry. Rather than use the sand in her pouch, Mylah called on the element, gathering it to her with a simple intention. She formed the same glass orb she'd created before, teasing out further artistic lines and dimples to reflect the fire she set inside it.

She cast the globe into the waiting darkness and the four moved forward into the stone corridor, cautious and alert, Tijhi leading the way.

What seemed like an hour passed as they placed step after careful step, occasionally pausing to peer at the map, for what, Mylah didn't know. There was nothing between them and the ink smudge that might be an icon. The five companions padded down the dirt-strewn stone halls, darkness gathered around them, save for the bouncing glass orb of fire that Mylah sent ahead to light their way.

"We're coming up on the marked room, ahead and to the left," Sybille noted.

Critter stopped and stood stock-still. Mylah peered down the darkened hallway where shadow swallowed the light of her bouncing glass light. Critter whined and crouched, hair springing up to form a mohawk of fur down his spine. Mylah pulled the fire orb back to her and doused its flame.

She turned and waved to the girls behind her in a frantic gesture to gather close. They obeyed, Tijhi trotting past them to stand next to Critter. Since Sybille had joined them, something had bothered Mylah. Now watching Tijhi's silent approach toward the marked room, her quiet suspicions snapped into place - and far too late.

"Sybille?" Mylah asked. "You said you got here through a secret passage in your quarters, right? Through a door marked with a painting. A painting depicting a hero with a sword lifted to the sky."

"Yes," Sybille answered, her voice quavering with worry. "Why?"

Be on alert, Tijhi said. *Something or someone is in that room.*

Tijhi crawled forward, body low to the ground, their padded paws making no noise. Critter took one step forward, his hooves clomping on the dirt-strewn stone floor before Tijhi turned, fixing the creature with a fierce golden gaze, ears flicked back. Critter paused, lowered himself to the ground, and stayed.

Tijhi swiveled back toward the looming darkness and stalked forward.

"That scene," Mylah whispered. "The posing hero with a black sword..." As she said it, she recalled the antechamber to the king's private study, lined with illustrative depictions of centuries' old wars and battles.

"What about it?" Sybille said.

Tijhi crept along the corridor, completely silent.

"There's another depiction like it," Mylah whispered.

"There are a number, actually," Sybille said, her voice an octave-breaking pitch.

Mylah swallowed panic. "Goddess," she intoned, beseeching her deity for support, but the Goddess was so far away from this secret and forsaken underground.

Mylah made her way to the front, bringing up Tijhi's rear. Behind her, Livvy made her silent way to Critter and wrapped a hand into the creature's fur. Sybille rolled up the map and wrapped an arm around Livvy's shoulders. Mylah motioned them to stay. Sybille nodded.

THE DRAGON'S FIRE

As she turned to face the upcoming room, a warm red glow burned to life, spilling into the hallway ahead.

"Don't be coy, Mylah of the Aestyrah. Join me."

CHAPTER THIRTY-THREE

Mylah and Tijhi were a toe's space from the circle of red light when shadowy tendrils shot out of the room, wrapping around their legs. The tentacle-like appendages pulled. Mylah's body slammed to the floor as she was yanked off her feet. She lurched forward, dirt and rocks scraping against her back. The bag slung over her shoulder pulled along behind her, its strap slipping from her shoulders to her neck and choking her. She whipped around a corner, her ribs slamming into the doorframe and grating down the side of her body.

Her involuntary movement halted next to Tijhi, who whimpered as thick shadow wrapped resolutely around the little fox's legs.

Mylah fought against the dark bonds, pulling herself into a kneeling position, ribs throbbing in pain. The room around them was a dark twin to the king's private study, except there was no bank of windows. Books lined shelves that covered the circular walls, but on other shelves sat sinister jars filled with cloudy liquids and bobbing bits. Some items were indistinguishable, and others were gruesomely identifiable.

In the room's center, a pool of utter darkness swirled and shifted, as if something within swam just under the surface.

Past the pool stood a worktable of sorts. Scattered across its surface were writing implements, a large mortar and pestle, vials of vividly colored liquids, and items Mylah could only venture a guess at. Mylah's stomach lurched as she recognized a soft, downy golden wing, so small. The hestia foal that had been there one day and gone the next.

Horror layered on top of horror as she took in the collection of parts. Next to the foal's wing, she was sure she spotted a detached clawed foot. A giant white-silver feather caught her eye. It seemed to glow with its own light. To one side of the table perched the dragon's eye on its stand. To the other side sat an empty book stand.

Achyla stood from the chair situated behind the desk and sauntered to its side. He still wore the same white tunic and leather pants and boots as he'd worn earlier that day. At least, Mylah assumed it was now the same day. She had lost track of time in the deep cavernous underground. Black bags hung beneath his eyes, which glittered brilliant blue and against reddened whites.

He chuckled. "It took you less time than I expected. How did you get past the elvathan?"

Tijhi barked in response, their ears swiveling back. The king turned to the fox, fixing them with a flat gaze.

"There's no need for that disguise," the High King said. He waved a hand toward Mylah's companion. Inky blankness burst from the dark pool. A groan filled the air. The hair on Mylah's arms and neck sprang to life. The shadow's voice echoed through the room, riddled with deep sorrow, anger, and longing. Darkness flowed up before washing toward Tijhi in a wave. The little fox braced themselves as the shadow overtook them. They were lost in a dark cloud before it whipped away, flowing back into the pool.

Tijhi stood from their crouched position, padded feet turned to talons, tail stretching away, longer than in their fox form, and wings and feathers adorning their body.

"That's better," Achyla noted. "And so, my dear Mylah, it feels as though we're meeting for the first time, since you now know my little secret." He reached for something on his desk as he walked toward her and twirled a silver dagger in his hand. He paused, clicking his booted heels together, crossing his left arm over his middle and touching the dagger's tip to his lips. He tapped it to his mouth, as if considering.

Mylah froze, imprisoned by the cold shadow. She cast about her, searching for a way out.

"I could use your essence, maybe. You are youthful, powerful. Perhaps your blood in a new spell to help -," he cut himself off. He smiled in that way Mylah thought ended at his lips, never lighting his eyes. "Never mind that."

"Or," he continued, "perhaps I could use my sweet sister's babe." He laughed as he gestured toward the door with his left arm, that black and silver bracelet catching the light. Shadow burst forward between Mylah and Tijhi and through the door. Thumps and shrill yelps filled the air and then Sybille, Livvy, and Critter were dragged into the room. The shadows squeezed around them.

"Let them go," Mylah said, squirming against her bonds. In her mind's eye she was eight summers old again. Her cousin cried for help. She fought as fiercely as a small child could, but she was powerless to protect him.

You must come to me. The voice was light and warm, and it filled Mylah with a sense of calm. Tijhi looked around as if they too had heard the voice.

"Yes, I think that's just what I'll try," Achyla said. He approached Sybille and ran the dagger tip along the swell of her stomach. She writhed against the shadow, brown eyes ablaze with fear and anger.

"Leave my child alone," Sybille screamed, desperation coating her words.

"Oh, but this is my child too," Achyla said, grasping Sybille's face in his hands. "And a Tyrmini. Such a thing cannot be allowed, sister."

"You are not my sibling," Sybille spat.

"So you know?" Achyla said. He chuckled and shook his head. "That was one of my better secrets. I hadn't thought there was anyone left who knew it. Tell me, how did you discover the truth?" There was a deadly note in his voice.

Sybille jutted out her chin and said nothing. With one swift movement Achyla swiped at Sybille's belly. A red line soaked through her delicate peach skirts. She gasped, her face a mask of terror.

"Answer me, and I'll make the extraction of our heir painless. Press me and I'll make you wish you'd never been born into this royal blood line."

"No," Sybille said, sobbing, tears streaming down her face. "You mustn't. Please."

Mylah wriggled against the shadow snaking around her body and limbs, searching for a foothold against the disembodied power which held her so tightly. She looked at Tijhi, who had bowed their head, eyes closed.

Achyla slashed another line into Sybille's bulging belly. Sybille screamed in pain, but more in fear as her blood stained her skirts in an opposing red line to the first.

"This is nothing, nothing of what I can do to you." Achyla gestured with his right hand and the shadow lifted Sybille into the air. Sybille yelped, blood dripped from the wounds on her stomach as she was hoisted, turned horizontal, and then slammed flat onto the worktable.

"Please, please, please," Sybille murmured as tears streamed down her face.

"My darling sister, I told you, all you have to do is give up the name of who told you about my current host's humble roots, and then I shall make the pain go away."

Sybille turned to Mylah, her eyes pleading. Panic nearly drowned all of Mylah's thought and reason. She would have to watch again as someone dear to her was tortured and killed.

Achyla shook back his faded golden hair, his sapphire eyes fixed on Sybille. He moved away from the worktable to the expanse of shelves. "You could have had a cut wife. Now, you'll have me as your surgeon. If you had just waited. We mustn't waste your body though. You will be useless dead. I do still need an heir." He wiggled elegant fingers in front of a vast collection of jars as he walked past them. "No, no, no... ah. Here we are."

Achyla snatched jars from their dusty shelves, pieces and parts bobbing in ambient liquids. He returned to the worktable and unburdened his load. He took one jar and displayed it to Sybille. "This one will keep you conscious through whatever horrors I inflict." He set it down and lifted another jar. "If I combined it with this, you'll go silent and still and yet will feel everything." He held a third jar up. "And this one intensifies sensation. I've had centuries to trial and practice, dear sister. Your torture will be my intense pleasure."

Achyla unscrewed the first jar's lid and moved on to the second. Mylah was trapped. The snaking darkness around her squeezed tighter, leaving dead marks wherever it touched. The death of sensation spread, and it wasn't just coming from the imprisoned dragon deity. It was coming from inside her.

Mylah couldn't breathe against her truth: she was powerless.

The only one who can make you powerless is you, the voice in her mind was rough and stern. But Mylah was already sinking into the abyss of her soul, that quiet place she kept to escape into.

Mylah, you are powerful. And you have a choice in how you use that power. Right now, you are choosing to allow what's happening in front of you. But there is another choice.

Numbness blanketed her senses and it was blissful, yet a part of her still couldn't bear to watch was about to happen.

Do you know what your greatest strength is? The voice asked her.

Mylah wasn't sure she had any strengths.

It is not your ability to wield the elements.

Mylah didn't think she could even do that very well.

It is not the power of your muscles, or your quick wit.

Then what was it, she wondered. She inventoried herself as she watched the High King extract a dripping tentacle from a jar of cloudy fluid. The king set the object onto the worktable near Sybille's head. He took the dagger and began to cut.

The voice in her mind quieted, as if waiting.

What? What is my strength? I have nothing to give, nothing that will change this reality. I'm going to watch my friend and her unborn child be tortured. This horror... what can I possibly do to stop it? His power is so much greater than mine. Look. He's imprisoned the dragon of creation. Creation! I can do nothing against that.

Help me, the voice was so faint Mylah believed she could have imagined it.

The dragon of creation, their essence, desires freedom, Mylah. The High King may be forcing their obedience, but he cannot fully understand the power he's imprisoned. What he underestimates is exactly what you have to offer.

I still don't understand, Mylah said.

Achyla had opened the second jar, and leaned over Sybille's shadow-wrapped body, speaking to her face-to-face with a sneer. Sybille shook her head, tears sliding down her face.

Achyla has been wronged. Long, long ago, people in power shunned and rejected his wild ideals. All he ever wanted was what we all ever want: a place to belong, a job, a means of contributing. And they took that one very human element and used it against him and told him he had no power. He was broken from the experience.

Mylah had felt sorry for the young being who had been Achyla but watching him as he traced a line over the top curve of Sybille's belly with his glinting dagger, she couldn't remember why.

But he was not powerless. That was a lie. He took what power he had and exercised it. He had no love and all ambition, and with his power he created his own world in which he could be king.

How am I supposed to stand up to that kind of power? Mylah asked.

The High King was motivated to create a world he could control. Everything he does is through the lens of needing to maintain control because it was once stripped from him.

I still don't understand how I'm any better off. How I have any more power.

Please. The third foreign voice bounced around in her head. She latched onto it, curious, wondering who it was. As she explored with tentative mental fingers, the answer came rising to greet her. Twisted in those dark shadows was the truth of its identity. It did not want to hurt her. It wanted more than anything to build, to produce, to create. It was not destruction. Its nature had been perverted by the one who held them bound.

Because it's not about control. It's not about force. You are more powerful because of your motivation.

My motivation? Mylah asked incredulously.

What do you want right now? Magloryn asked.

Mylah thought long and hard about this. *Life is sacred and shouldn't be used to fuel power. I can't stand by and watch others suffer. All this suffering in the world has been caused by one man. We have to try and make the world a better place where our people aren't threatened and our powers used to manipulate the world into the making of Achyla's choosing. What I want is for us to be free.*

I want the world to be free, she realized. It all boiled down to that.

We want to be free, her mind rattled with the intensity of the third voice.

Why? People will assuredly mess it up.

Achyla moved to Sybille's feet, gathering the three open jars in front of him. He pointed to each of the jars, his other hand gripping his chin.

We have to be allowed to try. The way it is right now, the only person choosing is Achyla, at the sacrifice of so many lives, Tyrminis, creatures, and elemental deities. It's all to serve him. He cares nothing for life outside of what it does for him.

So, what will you do? Magloryn asked.

Fight. I will fight.

We will help you, the third voice said. *We cannot do much, but we will try. But, please. You must find a way to free us.* The darkness that swirled around Mylah and her companions turned from sinister to mesmerizing. It was as if stars twinkled in their depth, as if eternity stretched away in the confines of collected shadows. Yes, the High King underestimated the power he'd imprisoned. He misunderstood its very nature.

Mylah lifted a hand full of the shadow and warmth instead of chill caressed her skin.

I am creation, the shadow spoke. *I am weakened, but I am still here.*

The shadow filling Mylah's hand grew heavy.

What if I fail? She asked the voice in her head.

Then at least you will fail having put a thorn in the side of a tyrant, it answered.

The High King turned from the table, walked toward the shelves lined with bottles and boxes, and beakers. He looked over his collection, his concentration fixed.

Fight, Mylah. Fight for Sybille and her child. Fight for Livvy and Critter. Fight for your people. Fight for Tyrmini. Fight for Aelos!

The silken darkness expanded away from Mylah, and Mylah took that opportunity, that one moment of freedom to act.

CHAPTER THIRTY-FOUR

White-hot fire coursed through her veins. Mylah unleashed it with precise accuracy as she pulled on the essence of creation, its presence around her somehow taming and expanding her ability. She instilled the elements with her intention and shot a wave of liquid glass toward the High King.

The shadow previously pinning each of her companions in place spread out like fog. Its darkness still twinkling with far-away lights.

I cannot hold this for long, the shadow spoke to Mylah. *You must act quickly.*

Tijhi lunged for Livvy and Critter, now free from their dark bindings. Together they rushed for the door and escaped into the hall beyond.

Achyla turned away from his horrific collection to Mylah, shock covering his aging face. He dropped the jar he'd just unscrewed even as Mylah's liquid glass encased him from head to toe. He screamed in agony, the smell of charring flesh and hair filling the room.

He writhed within the glass and then was still. Mylah ran for Sybille.

The silver feather, the shadow spoke. *Take it. It may help if I lose control.* Mylah scooped up her friend, searching the worktable for the feather she'd seen earlier. She snatched the feather up as she hauled Sybille to her feet. Mylah forced them into a run, even as a roiling, muffled growl built behind them. Mylah shoved the feather into her linen bindings as she guided a limping, sobbing Sybille toward the exit.

Snapping and cracking glass preceded a spray of exploding shards. Mylah covered Sybille's back and head, exposing her own back to the flying shrapnel. Glass bit into her flesh and she yelped in pain.

The force of the explosion threw them to the ground, Mylah turning Sybille's body to protect the child within. Her knees barked in pain as she landed hard on the stone floor. She didn't pause. She looped her hands under Sybille's arms and hauled her to her feet. Sybille pushed herself at the same time and with a grunt they launched toward the door again.

Wait, the Shadow spoke. Mylah turned back to the shadow roiling and shifting behind them.

What is it? Mylah asked, panic rising as the king pushed himself up from the stone floor.

Inky black tendrils shot out of the fog toward Sybille.

A gift, the voice said. *A gift that will empower the one you carry.*

"The shadow wants to bless your child, so that it might be strong," Mylah translated to Sybille. Sybille shook, gripping her bleeding belly protectively.

So that one day your child will overcome our captor.

"They say it will help the child conquer Achyla," Mylah told her.

Sybille nodded frantically. "Yes," she said. "Yes, help the child be strong."

Achyla groaned, body writhing and smoking. The tendrils of shadow rushed forward, sinking into Sybille's womb. Sybille arched back, a scream ratcheting out of her throat. Before Mylah could call out to the shadow, tell it to stop, the tendrils backed away and Sybille slumped into Mylah's arms. Mylah held her upright, her full weight slipping into her embrace. Mylah pulled her away, slipping on blood pooled at their feet. Fear sluiced down her spine at the amount of blood staining the stone.

"Can you make it out?" Mylah asked Sybille. Sybille wept, her brown eyes full of emotion, but she nodded, slipping her arm from Mylah's shoulders. Sybille fled, falling to a knee before she made it to the door. She gripped the threshold, leaned hard, then lunged through, disappearing into the darkened hallway. A bloody handprint smeared over the wooden frame.

Mylah turned back to the High King. Achyla's body smoked as he shook violently, whether from pain or anger, Mylah couldn't tell. His shirt was burned away, revealing blackened skin, oozing muscle fibers and exposed ribs and collarbone in places. His hair was gone, save for one tuft which smoked. He staggered forward, a cry of rage and pain rupturing from lips that were partially consumed from the liquid glass.

The High King gestured around him but the shadow swirled at their feet, unresponsive to his call. Mylah stood straight, despite the fear threatening to send her back into that quiet place of blissful anesthesia. She grounded herself, righting her energy as she faced the High King.

Achyla looked around him, gesturing once again, his eyes widening when nothing happened. Mylah drew on the elements at her disposal. There was a little sand left in her pouch, and an endless supply of roaring fire in her veins. She stoked the fire and called on the sand, creating small bullets of glass that she shot at the High King.

Holes punctured his smoking, ravaged body and he stumbled back. Mylah thought he would go down. She would run. She would catch up to her friends, they would find the dragon of light, and they would make their escape. But Achyla touched the holes, looked up at Mylah and snarled like a caged beast.

This time when he gestured, the shadow obeyed. Mylah

instinctively folded herself into an encasing tomb of flame before the shadow enveloped her. Where the shadow touched the flame gave way and that cool numbing darkness wrapped around her once again. It shoved her back and down, her head smacking the floor with a sickening crack. She saw stars and blinding white as the shadow encircled around her neck.

Mylah's body hoisted into the air by her neck. She choked, air rapidly evacuating her lungs, neck bones cracking, ligaments ripping. Panic consumed her as she fought for breath and failed.

"You utter idiot," Achyla said. "You think you could possibly stand up to me?"

Mylah gagged, clawing at the shadow.

I'm sorry, the shadow spoke.

Achyla swirled his fingers, and the shadow snaked down both of her arms and pulled. The opposing pressure tensed the joints of her shoulders. One shoulder popped. Mylah screamed. The other shoulder mirrored the first. Hot ripping sensations spread from her armpits, shoulders, back, down the backs of her arms. She would be torn apart.

She could scarcely see as she peered down at the High King, who grinned, one side of his mouth gaping where flesh had burned away, revealing white molars. His eyes, usually the richest sapphire blue were now darkest night.

"After I rip your arms free from your body, I'll take the rest of you apart bit by bit," Achyla said. "But first, I have a child to kill."

Mylah dangled in midair, the insistent stretch on her body pulling her slowly apart. She watched as the High King exited the room. She screamed in agony, and in fear as he went after Sybille.

She writhed once, pain splintered though her body, and then she stilled. She sobbed, hanging powerlessly. The muscles on her chest tore and she screamed again. Her wrists snapped next, then her forearm muscles. She vomited.

She only hoped as the shadow tore at her that her friends

would make it. More tendons and muscles gave way and darkness consumed her.

She woke on the floor, the giant white feather peeking out from beneath her linen wrappings. Her body was a prison of pain. Tears sprang to her eyes.

Mylah swallowed a note of agony. She had to get up. She rolled to one side, the action pushing her over an edge of torment the likes of which she'd never experienced. Her left arm hung limply at her side and despite her best efforts, she couldn't make it move.

Mylah unwrapped a portion of her linen wrappings, squelching her screams as the movement ripped on raw nerves. She wrapped the linen around her neck, circling behind her back and over her mangled arm, tying it in place. She grunted as she pushed herself to her feet, sweat sliding down her face and neck.

She stumbled out, past that blood-stained door frame, and lurched down the hallway. She gulped down air, fighting against pain that threatened to steal away her consciousness once again. Mylah could smell charred flesh and knew Achyla had gone this direction. As she reached the hall's end one torturous step at a time, the scent vanished. The hall opened to vast nothingness. That familiar squeezing fear stole over her, panic rising at the sight of great heights. She steeled herself before shuffling to the edge to peer into darkness below.

Mylah whirled, looking back down the hall, then back into the open abyss of darkness. Tijhi, Critter, Sybille, and Livvy were nowhere in sight. Neither was there a giant light dragon of myth and legend. Mylah's heart sank. Her friends were likely caught by the High King, and she shivered to think what he was doing to them.

Mylah stood suspended in indecision for one short breath, when a noise behind her made her jerk in that direction.

Standing directly behind her was the High King.

He smiled in that dead way, made gruesome with exposed muscle and teeth. "Your friends have gone this way," he said, and before Mylah could react, he shoved. Her boots scraped against the stone floor, then kicked up into the open air. Gravity claimed her, sending her stomach lurching into her throat. Her body stretched out in front of her, good arm flailing while the dead one pulled loose of its makeshift binding.

Every fiber of her being screamed in terror as the intense phobia realized itself upon her. Mylah fought the open space, the fall, the whooshing air, the High King's fading laughter. The feather tucked into her wrappings yanked loose by tearing wind, pulling away from Mylah like it was escaping that fate waiting for her at the bottom of the abyss. In the end, she could do nothing.

So Mylah swallowed her fear, let go and fell.

CHAPTER THIRTY-FIVE

As Mylah fell, she hoped. She hoped her cousin would forgive her. She hoped her friends were safe. She hoped Luther would make it out of this awful service to the High King. That somehow, he would find a way to free himself. She wondered what her cousin would have been like if he'd survived. And what he would have said when he found out she was the Aestyrah's Tyrmini champion. She hoped he would have been proud of her. Proud of her for fighting. Proud of her for trying to save people from the whims of an ancient evil. For doing something.

Tears slipped from her eyes as she considered her parents, that while they might not have ever been proud of her, perhaps her cousin would have been. Perhaps, in another existence, he would even forgive her for the awful terrible act she'd committed: believing a stranger would celebrate her cousin's elemental magic ability. And all that while, when she'd been celebrating her cousin, when her cousin had suffered so harshly in her stead, it had been her. It had been Mylah who had this wonderful terrible burden on her shoulders. If only she'd known. She would have gladly suffered his fate to save him.

Mylah reached out through etyr, if such a thing were even possible. She reached for her cousin, and she begged.

"Please," she said, as her dark hair flew around her, and tears ripped from her eyes into the air above. She sobbed. "I hope," she said. "I hope you'll forgive me."

From what?

The voice that answered back. It couldn't have been. It couldn't have been him. But if it was...

"I told the stranger," she said. "And he..."

You celebrated me!

"I got you killed," she screamed, wind snatching away her words. "It was my fault. He came after you, he strapped you to that pole and you died. Your father and my parents died." Years of welling pain burst from her lips. The guilt and shame boiled out of her, and into that dark nothing wrapping around her as she free-fell, as she plummeted to her death and gave voice to her darkest moments.

And you had to watch, he said. *You lost your parents. Your cousin. Your uncle.* Mylah sobbed, her stomach clenching, head throbbing, arm a tangle of twisted muscle, broken bones, and mangled nerves.

"I tried," she wept. "I tried, and all along it was my fault. All along it was me. You died for no reason. It should have been me. I'm so sorry. I wish I could change it. I wish I could be the one tied to that pole."

Cousin, he said. His voice held that familiar you're-being-silly note. *Did you ever think I felt the same way?*

Mylah hiccupped into the dark wind swirling around her. "What?"

I'm glad he killed me and not you. Just think of what would have happened if he'd had it right. If he'd understood those elementals had gathered for you and not me.

Shock stole through her senses.

You needed to live, he said.

"That doesn't mean you had to die!"

But, I did. And your guilt won't bring me back. I'm sorry, but it's true. You can't shame yourself into me living again.

Mylah fell, tears streaming, as truth dawned on her.

You can't change what happened. Everything. EVERYTHING that happened to me was his fault. If you take any blame at all, you take away his guilt. I'm done letting you let him get away with that. So, I'm begging you. Let go of that guilt and shame. It's not yours to carry.

Mylah opened her mouth, ready to ask more questions, when the screaming air and sense of free-fall vanished. Pressure and fur appeared beneath her good arm. A pocket of still air and silence expanded around her, and then the world came back into focus.

Mylah's backside slammed into the hard ground sending a jolt up her spine. She groaned, releasing the grip on the muldonidei. Tears poured down her face, pain searing her body and soul.

Critter sat before her, tongue lolling to one side. Her breath rattled on a sharp inhale as she replayed her cousin's words. The room glowed in a low blue light.

Mylah blinked, waiting for her eyesight to adjust. As the darkness took on shape, Mylah's head tilted back, then way back, at the imposing presence of a giant white dragon.

The dragon sat on its haunches, looking down on Mylah with one multicolored eye. On the opposite side of her face darkness gaped where an eye should be, the surrounding skin sagging around the socket. The deity seemed to shine with an innate inner light, the air glittering around her. White feathers covered the dragon's body, interspersed with opalescent scales and jutting above her eyes two swirling horns rose into the darkness. Around the dragon's neck wove ropes of dark chains. The dragon shook herself. Deep clanging echoed through the darkness and white down sifted to the ground.

Magloryn lowered herself onto her forelegs, putting her face closer to Mylah's level.

"Just when he thinks he's done his worst, he's pushed the odds into our favor," mused the dragon, looking up. Her sonorous voice filled not just the space around them but Mylah's mind as well. It touched a deep part of Mylah's aching heart in a way she couldn't fathom. The Dragon of Light, crossed her forelegs and looked back at Mylah.

Mylah rubbed her limp arm. "He's done so much damage, though," she said.

The dragon inclined her head. "We will make more from the pain he's inflicted than he can ever imagine is possible." The dragon exhaled slowly through her nose. Shimmering air whooshed over Mylah's broken body, swirling around her in a twisting cloud of light and silver.

Mylah threw back her head and screamed as torn muscles and broken bones stitched themselves back together. She crumpled to the ground, tears streaming, agony blinding her vision. Then the pain stopped as quickly as it began.

She inhaled experimentally, testing for torture. She stretched her broken and dead arm out before her. Muscles flexed, joints bent in the right directions, fingers wiggling. She touched the ribs on her chest, her shoulders, her neck. She was healed. Save for that still-bleeding wound in her heart. She thought even with her cousin's words ringing in her ears, she would take a while to really heed his advice.

Magloryn swung her head around to the rest of Mylah's companions. Livvy was perched next to Sybille who sat propped against a rocky wall, breathing rapidly. Mylah lunged into action. She darted across the cave, skidded to a halt and knelt next to her queen.

Livvy looked at her. "I think she's having her baby," she said.

Sybille grunted. Her gray face glistened with a sheen of sweat.

Mylah looked up at the dragon. "Is there anything you can do?"

The dragon peered down on them. "I can save the child."

"Yes," Sybille said through a grunt of pain. "Please save them. No matter what happens, this child has to be saved. Must be protected. Has to grow up and take over their father's place on the throne."

"The child will do this and more," Magloryn said, voice a rumbling marvel. "Once I grant this last blessing, I will be depleted of magic. At least temporarily. Achyla is on his way. You must find the portal near this room."

Magloryn looked at Critter. Critter approached the dragon and whined sadly. The dragon leaned into the creature, who bowed his head. Magloryn's snout touched Critter's head and light burst into the room.

The dragon turned toward Sybille again. "Every one of you will be immune from the king's use of my eye. Every one of you will be bestowed with a piece of my Light. But, none more than this child. She will bear this as a gift and a burden. To carry this, she must be stripped of all other elemental magic."

"She?" Sybille asked, panting.

"The choice is hers still, but I believe that is where she's settled."

Mylah couldn't help herself. "My people," she said.

Magloryn looked at Tijhi. "You are ready now," she said.

Mylah looked at the little fox phoenix. Tijhi bowed at Magloryn's feet and without warning vanished from their presence.

"Where did they go?" Mylah asked, looking at the dragon of light.

"To protect their people," Magloryn said. "They had to regain their power after their rebirth, but now they are strong enough to carry out the task."

"Will they be back?" Mylah asked, a sudden void of her companion's presence yawned around her.

"When they can," Magloryn said.

"And they'll be okay?"

"Do not worry. The Tijhi is powerful and clever. They can do much to outsmart such as the High King."

Mylah nodded. "Thank you," she said.

"I have one other task for you, Mylah of the Aestyrah."

Mylah looked up at the dragon. "Anything," she said sincerely.

The dragon shifted her body, revealing a pile of glittering white-silver scales and feathers. "Any who carry this in their possession will be protected from the sight of my eye. You must seek out Tyrmini and provide them with a talisman for their safety. You must help them control their magic until this child grows into her power and the magic on Tyrinth can be balanced again. I must rely on you. There is so little I can do, imprisoned this way. The tide is shifting. After so long, I can finally feel the tide is shifting."

Mylah bowed her head, accepting the responsibility and went to retrieve the scales and feathers. She dumped all the scrolls from the bag Sybille had given her and left nothing but the tome of shadow, somehow unwilling to part with it, feeling the need to whisk it away. She piled the scales and feathers into the bag atop the book. There were dozens and dozens and she hoped it was enough.

Once every talisman was piled into the bag, she hefted it back to the dragon. "Must it be the whole talisman?"

"A small portion is sufficient," the dragon replied.

"What will I do if I run out?"

"You must hope that will not happen before the child comes of age. When the child comes of age, you must return to her and help her with the next steps."

"How will I know what the next steps will be?"

"I thought it would be obvious," Magloryn said.

Mylah looked at her, nonplused.

"You must help her overthrow her father's reign."

Magloryn turned from Mylah and fixed Sybille with a knowing gaze. "A mother gives so much," she said. "Let us give this gift together."

Sybille nodded. "Yes," she said.

THE DRAGON'S FIRE

The dragon closed her eye, tilting her head up. She seemed to be caught up in a trance as light gathered and grew, first slowly, and then gaining luminescence. Mylah had to look away as the dragon grew radiant enough to challenge the Goddess's own strength.

Where do you suppose your Goddess gets her light? The dragon said into her mind.

Intense love swelled in the room, expanding Mylah's soul. She knelt to the ground as tears streamed down her face. In the presence of this love, she could see the nature of existence, everything with life interconnected, the balance of opposites, of what people called bad and good. She felt all people cherished in the most precious way possible. There was no judgment, there was nothing but love. It was intense and purposeful, and trumped every other mortal emotion.

She floated on the high of care, lost in the ocean of understanding, caught up by compassion. And as the light faded again, Mylah knew she would be forever changed by the Light's touch.

She opened her eyes, her cheeks wet with tears. She wanted nothing less than each and every person on Tyrinth to experience this, to know how much they meant to the world, to each other, to themselves. She wanted them to feel their own worth, and to know how loved they were.

On the heels of this glorious revelation was the understanding that one man kept this reality to himself. He was not even a gatekeeper; he was a prison guard.

Magloryn slumped as light faded away from her. Sybille's belly glowed brightly, then faded as well.

"You must find the portal," the dragon said.

"Is there no way we can free you?" Mylah asked. "Is there nothing we can do for you?"

"You've done it, dear one. The light now living with Sybille's child has freed me. So, go, and take care of her and all my children.

Help Aelos overthrow Achyla. And bring balance to Tyrinth."

Mylah leaned over the dragon's snout, stroking the soft downy feathers along her cheek. She didn't want to leave the dragon.

A rumbling growl echoed around them.

"Achyla," Sybille said, her face pale, black bags gathered beneath her eyes. "He's coming. Please. Help me." She reached a hand toward Mylah. Mylah gathered Sybille to her feet. Critter circled, bouncing in and out of existence.

"Livvy first," Mylah said to the creature, and he was gone in a flash, Livvy with him. He returned, staring at Mylah. Mylah draped one side of Sybille over Critter's shoulders.

Critter whined as darkness closed in. *Let's go*, he seemed to say.

Sybille groaned as a new contraction stole over her. There was no time left. Mylah barely placed her hand on Critter when the world swirled away in a blast of air and darkness.

In the last moment before they descended into nothing, the High King's livid, burned visage swarmed into view.

CHAPTER THIRTY-SIX

Her boots slammed into stone, and she buckled to her knees. Mylah's hands bit into stone floor. She blinked in the darkness surrounding them. "Sybille?" she asked.

Sybille panted nearby. "Mylah," her voice came out through gritted teeth, urgency pitching it higher.

Mylah scrabbled along the floor, reaching for her friend, her searching hand finally tangling and closing around Sybille's. "It's okay, I'm here," she said.

Sybille growled out a moan as a contraction clenched down on her.

"Breathe, breathe," Mylah instructed. Sybille took a shaking breath then panted as the contraction abated. "Good."

Mylah stood, cupped her hand around a flame, marveling at the ease with which the element sprang to life, the quality of its presence somehow an easier companion after Magloryn's blessing. Livvy and Critter padded toward the room's center, stepping over the deep grooves that formed an intricate pattern carved into the stone floor. As they stepped onto the ancient carvings, light filled the grooves. As Mylah approached, watching her own steps radiate in color and light, a spherical gem floating above the carving's center sparked and flared to life, casting the room in an ethereal glow. Mylah doused her flame.

On the far wall, covered in ivy, a trickle of water meandered through the vegetation, creating a soft patter as drops fell into a small puddle. The loam of earth filled her scent, but Mylah also caught the hint of fresh air stirring the stillness. Likely, where the ivy grew a hole must be open to the outside world. Because no light came from that corner, Mylah guessed it was night.

The carving in the stone floor was something she recognized from the Tome of Shadows. Something Achyla had spent quite a lot of time pondering over: the seven elements symbol. Its greater outer circle represented etyr. The gem nearest her feet, at what she would call the circle's base, was a vibrant green gem with veins of brown. To her left was a blue gem with waves of aqua; to her right a red gem with swirls of yellow and orange, and in the top corner a light-yellow with streaks of pink. Where the funnel dropped into the floor, its depths twinkled without color.

Mylah marveled at what she knew must be the portal. They were meant to use it, to take themselves to a place of safety. She combed through her memory of what the book had said.

"What do we do now?" Livvy asked, her eyes still locked onto the gem floating in midair.

"Achyla could never use this portal. As much as he knew where it was, and how it worked."

"Why?" Livvy aked, finally breaking her gaze on the beautiful crystal and looking at Mylah.

"He couldn't use the portal alone, and he had no friends. He also didn't possess any light element. Sometimes those two things feel like one and the same, don't you think?"

Livvy draped an arm over Critter, her face a mask of sad concentration. "It's dark when you're lonely," she confirmed.

Mylah nodded. The absence of her companion, Tijhi, filled her with an aching emptiness. But she was lucky. She had Livvy and Critter and Sybille. And Tijhi would be back.

Mylah adjusted the shoulder bag. Magloryn's talismans clanked against one another, the noise a promise of the community she would help grow. She was raised in a tight community, and she would have given anything to gain their respect. It was only when she'd been forced out of her bubble of safety that she'd built new connections. She thought about her responsibility to them and her newfound loyalty to ensure this new community's safety.

Mylah pointed to the gem at her feet. "Livvy, I think it'd be best if you stand here. This represents Tyrinth." Livvy nodded and placed herself on the gem. "Critter, you'll need to stand there. That represents air." Critter sniffed in her direction, nose appendages waving in the air toward her, before he too took up the place Mylah instructed.

She carefully hoisted Sybille up. Sybille groaned. She was sweaty and shaky, but Mylah knew having babies was no easy feat. She would be present for her friend when the babe was born. Mylah gently set her friend on the ground on the gem that represented the water element.

Mylah took her position on the fire element. She looked around at her friends, felt the welling love that had been imbued into her very soul, and took her first step of many in rebelling against the reign of shadow.